# THE GOVERNESS CLUB: LOUISA

**By Ellie Macdonald**

# THE GOVERNESS CLUB: LOUISA

## ELLIE MACDONALD

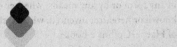

AVONIMPULSE
An Imprint of HarperCollinsPublishers

Excerpt from *The Governess Club: Claire*. Copyright © 2013 by Heather Johnson.

Excerpt from *The Governess Club: Bonnie*. Copyright © 2013 by Heather Johnson.

Excerpt from *The Governess Club: Sara*. Copyright © 2014 by Heather Johnson.

Excerpt from *Beauty and the Brit* copyright © 2014 by Lizbeth Selvig.

Excerpt from *Caught in the Act* copyright © 2014 by Sara Jane Stone.

Excerpt from *Sinful Rewards 1* copyright © 2014 by Cynthia Sax.

Excerpt from *When the Rancher Came to Town* copyright © 2014 by Gayle Kloecker Callen.

Excerpt from *Learning the Ropes* copyright © 2014 by Tina Kline-smith.

EPub Edition OCTOBER 2014 ISBN: 9780062292285

Print Edition ISBN: 9780062292292

JV 10 9 8 7 6 5 4 3 2 1

*For Tessa. Of course this one is for you.*

## ACKNOWLEDGMENTS

Always, always: my wonderful editor, Tessa, for all your patience and help with this whole project; Codi Gary for just being you when I need it the most; and Toby, your help is beyond description, often accompanied with wine and Archie Comics and always with glitter in your hair.

# CHAPTER ONE

*September, 1823*

The door slammed shut behind her, but there was no acknowledgment from the crowded room. Water dripped off her cloak and puddled around her feet; the wetness had long since infiltrated the materials of her cloak and boots, making her skin cold and clammy. Fighting against the shivers, her eyes adjusted to the light in the room, taking in the cheering men congregated in the center. Bets and encouragements were called out, but Louisa could not see what the spectacle was through the mass of male bodies.

Some of her hair had escaped her hood and she lifted a hand to push it back out of her face. Her fingers were freezing on her already cold skin and she clenched them in a futile effort for warmth. She could feel her stockings clinging to her legs and feet, wedging themselves uncomfortably between her toes inside her sopping boots. The holes in said boots had chosen to make themselves uncomfortably known today with a vengeance, letting in every drop of rain and mud they could. She did not look forward to cleaning the expected mess or to repairing her boots, if she could even find the means to do so. She forced herself to not contemplate the state of her dress or the possibility of her portmanteau not measuring up against the torrential downpour outside.

"Come on, Harry, put yer back into it!"

"Almost got 'im, Johnny. Stronger now!"

"A shilling says Harry comes back and wins it all!"

The shouts turned to roars, the excitement growing. Louisa could hear the desperate cries of those who had placed a losing bet on Harry. She still could not see what was happening, but it was clear from the spectators that Johnny had the upper hand in whatever they were doing.

Her eyes scanned the room. Several of the wall sconces had sputtered out, casting the pub in shadows. Discarded plates covered with forgotten food sat neglected on the tables, no one bothering to clean them up. Candelabras dripped wax on the tables and several of the benches were propped up with blocks of wood to steady them. The congealing food matched the odors coming from the kitchen, which Louisa dared not glance into. The room was all male; no serving maids scurried around to clean up the mess left by the patrons. Along one wall was the bar, separating the room from the casks lining the wall behind it. A large gray cat sat in the space between two casks, paws tucked under it, unblinking eyes on her; it was the only living thing to have noticed her entrance.

"Yes," Louisa muttered, glaring at the creature. "I look like something you dragged in."

The cat yawned, revealing its sharp fangs. Deeming the gamblers and Louisa beneath its notice, the cat shifted and began grooming itself, the small pink tongue darting out.

*Hmph.* It was illogical for her to be rankled by the dismissal of a cat, but such was her current mood.

Victorious cheers resounded in the room, mingling with the groans of defeat, and the crowd began to disperse. One man sat at a table, wringing and flexing his hand in obvious pain. Money exchanged hands; only one protested the fairness of the match and subsequent match, but was silenced by a large, beefy hand landing heavily on his shoulder.

Louisa's eyes widened as she saw the owner of the hand stand up. A true giant, he towered over all in the room, reaching above six feet in height. A thick neck supported a large, bald head that glistened in the candlelight. Dark eyebrows capped his dark eyes separated by a crooked nose, obviously broken at some point in his life. A neatly trimmed chin-strap beard ran along his jaw, accentuating the angles of it. A barrel chest expanded to shoulders so broad Louisa was sure she could sit comfortable on one; the white linen of his shirt did nothing to hide the enormity of his body. Arms like tree trunks bulged with muscles and his thighs strained against the material of his brown trousers.

"Now, George," the deep voice rumbled calmly in the now quiet room, "Harry here is not protesting the match. Why are you?"

"B—but Johnny—"

The giant interrupted, "Did you bet on Harry?"

"Aye."

"Did Harry win?"

"No." George's face took on a resigned look.

"Then there is no reason for you to not pay up, is there?" The giant smiled, revealing white teeth. None were missing, although some were crooked.

"No, Johnny."

"Good to hear, man." Johnny patted George's shoulder. The smaller man jerked involuntarily under the pressure, but Louisa had the feeling the giant had reined in his strength to minimize any damage. "You know how I feel about cheats. Now, who's thirsty?"

Louisa watched as the giant moved behind the bar and men carried their empty tankards over. He filled them, taking coin as he did so, laughing and talking with his customers. She swallowed when his eyes finally fell on her and Louisa flexed her grip on her portmanteau unconsciously. When he filled the final tankard thrust at him, the giant wiped his hands on a towel and walked over to her, his long strides eating up the distance.

"Good eve, miss," he greeted in his deep voice, nodding his head. "What can I do for you?"

Louisa flexed her grip again, otherwise not moving or dropping her eyes from his. "This is an inn, correct?"

"Aye. The Beefy Buzzard. The rooms are upstairs. You need one?"

"Hey, Johnny, that some new entertainment?" One drunken shout carried over the others.

Louisa's face flushed hot despite the earlier chill of the rain lingering on her skin. Giant Johnny half turned to the room and shouted, "Oi, respect the lady or get out! Yer wife will be happy to have you home early tonight, Charlie."

Ribbing followed that statement, Charlie getting jostled and hit by his friends. His scowl lasted only a moment before he was grinning again at whatever was said.

"Sorry for that," Giant Johnny said, turning back to her, a grin on his own face. "They're not always the best-behaved lot."

Louisa regarded him, silently weighing her options. The rain had not let up outside and there was no other inn in the vicinity. She truly had no choice but to stay at the Beefy Buzzard, God help her.

He thrust out a hand toward her. "John Taylor, proprietor and innkeeper, at your service."

Louisa hesitated a moment before placing her hand in his. It was immediately dwarfed in his large one as he shook it. Warmth surrounded her fingers and seeped in, warming her cold skin.

"Mrs. Brock," she replied, trying to not betray her reaction to the handshake. This alias had served her well these past months.

Mr. Taylor frowned and glanced at the door. "Your husband is seeing to your coach?"

"I am a widow," she said, sharing the story she had decided upon. It was less remarkable for a widow to be a solitary traveler than a young woman.

"My condolences," Mr. Taylor offered. "It is an unpleasant day to be traveling by oneself."

"To be traveling at all, to be sure."

"Indeed. Let's get you into your room and warmed up." He gestured to the stairs but Louisa did not move.

She felt her face flush again and she gritted her teeth. She lifted her chin in a gesture of challenge. "I am afraid I have few funds, sir," she gritted out. Mr. Taylor frowned but did not speak right away, so she continued. "I am willing to pay through other means." His gaze ran down her body at that statement and she felt her flush deepen, this time with anger. "Not that," she bit out. "Never that."

His eyes met hers again and his eyebrows twitched. "I am not in the habit of compromising women in need of shelter, Mrs. Brock. I was assessing what you would be able to do."

Louisa tilted her chin even more. "I can clean or do dishes or cook." Cooking might be a stretch, but based on what she smelled and saw coming from the kitchen, she was certain no one would notice the difference. "Whatever you ask me to do, within propriety of course, I will do my best. I am a hard worker."

Mr. Taylor shook his head. "We can discuss this in the morning. You are in need of a bed and a warm bath, it appears. Let's get that sorted first, shall we?" He relieved her of her portmanteau before she could protest and lumbered off in the direction of the stairs. The crowd parted at his large approach, leaving a wake of leering drunkards. Louisa lifted her sodden skirts and hurried after him up the stairs.

The corridor was darker than the pub below it, only three sconces lighting the entire area. He opened a door at the far end and disappeared into it. Louisa hesitated at the door, unable to see into the darkened room.

The sound of her portmanteau falling to the floor reached her ears. Footsteps came from the darkness, approaching her. Louisa swallowed when Giant Johnny stepped into the meager light, holding a candelabra. She stepped to the side when he didn't stop and watched him use one of the remaining wall sconces to light the brace in his hand. He returned to the room, the candles providing a faint circle of light around him. She watched as he knelt down and used one of the candles to light the coals in the hearth; light and heat began to creep into the room when he succeeded.

Giant Johnny—Mr. Taylor—straightened and looked at her, his ham-sized fists on his hips. He regarded her with serious, dark eyes. "You will be safe here, Mrs. Brock. I guarantee it personally. I will be closing the pub soon and will ensure the men do not bother you."

"Thank you."

"It will take some time, but I can get a bath up here. Hot water and all that."

"That would be lovely, thank you."

He kept his eyes on her, still standing in the doorway. "Are you in the area for long or just passing through?" he asked.

Louisa blinked. "I am uncertain. My plans are currently in flux." As they had been since leaving Ridgestone over two months ago.

"Well, you can have this room for as long as you need. We will make arrangements in the morning."

"Thank you."

He cleared his throat. "I cannot leave the room until you move from the doorway, Mrs. Brock. I need to return to my customers before they decide to attack the kegs on their own."

"Oh." Louisa quickly stepped into the room. "Of course."

With a crooked smile, he made his way to the door. "I suggest remaining in the room. I will bring a plate of food up shortly. Open the door for no one but me."

Louisa raised her eyebrows. "Is it that dangerous here? Hardly a ringing endorsement."

Mr. Taylor paused and looked back at her, displeasure at her comment clear on his face. "I guaranteed your safety, but even I cannot be everywhere at once. The advice I give you is prudent, but not mandatory."

Louisa swallowed, knowing she had been inexcusably rude. Even with that knowledge, her apology stuck in her throat. She turned her gaze to the door, unwilling to allow him to see whatever emotion there might be in her eyes, and nodded.

He cleared his throat, a deep rumbling that brought to mind what she thought a volcano would sound like. "It is late and you must be uncomfortable in those wet clothes. I will get a bath up here soon. Would you prefer that or food first?"

"Whichever one you can manage. I will accommodate you. There is no other helping you, is there?"

"Mr. Packard cooks, but that does not often allow for help outside the kitchen. A couple of boys come during the day, but return home early due to their age."

"As I said, I will accommodate you," Louisa repeated.

"Thank you." With a nod, Mr. Taylor closed the door behind him with a definitive click.

Out in the corridor, John released his grip on the doorknob and shook his head. The lady may look nice, but she had the tongue of a viper. Even dripping water on his floors and lips blue from the cold could not disguise her charms. Charms that were less appealing once she spoke.

Shaking his head again, he returned to the crowd below. Even a man such as him knew to stay away from such creatures, especially if he wanted to keep all his important parts in working condition.

# CHAPTER TWO

Louisa pressed her nose to her stockings and sniffed. They were still damp, but didn't have the musty odor from being wet inside her portmanteau. As she had waited for her food and the bath the previous evening—the latter of which had never appeared, despite the assurances from Giant Johnny—she had hung what items she could by the fire to dry out.

Setting the stockings by the fire again to give them a few more minutes, Louisa examined the room in a manner the darkness had not allowed last night. And she was glad it had not. Spider webs adorned the walls and ledges, a thick layer of dust covering the window hangings and floor; her footprints clearly marked every space she had stepped. The window glass was covered in such grime that she doubted the curtains were necessary. She had felt the thinness of the mattress, pillows and covers during her fitful sleep, but was still unprepared for the cold reality in the light of day. Indeed, she may have been just as comfortable on the floor.

The table where she had picked at her inedible supper was scratched and stained; one of its legs had been poorly replaced, which explained the wobble the night before. The chair was no longer matching, if it ever was, but at least it had held her weight steady. The tray remained on the table, more unappetizing in the morning than it had been when it first arrived, a fact that Louisa had not thought possible.

Grimacing, Louisa returned to the fire and repacked her portmanteau before pulling on her stockings. Standing, she smoothed the wrinkles out of her dress and stepped into her slippers. She pulled on her cloak and lifted her bag, intent on leaving. She may not have much coin to her name, but she did have standards. Surely there was another inn within walking distance.

Lifting her chin, she marched to the door and opened it with a yank. She let out a shriek as a large body and a chair tumbled toward her, arms and legs flailing. Jumping out of the way, she managed to not have her toes crushed as Giant Johnny sprawled at her feet.

"Ouch! Bleedin' hell," he cursed, curling up on his side and holding his head.

"Mr. Taylor!" Louisa dropped her bag and knelt beside him. "Are you injured?"

"What do you think?"

She blinked at the pained growl coming from him and sat back on her heels. "Well, judging from your ability to speak, I should think you will survive."

He glared at her from underneath his hands. "Would you?" His voice was flat.

"Whatever were you doing outside my room?" she asked.

Another glare and a grimace as Giant Johnny—the alliteration pleased her for some reason—rolled himself into a sitting position. "I told you I would keep you safe. I slept against your door to ensure none would bother you. I have no illusions of the morals of drunkards."

She blinked again, taken aback by his actions. "I see. I suppose you leaned the chair against my door, thus causing your imbalance when I opened it."

"You suppose correctly."

"Perhaps in the future you will find it prudent to lean against a more stationary object, such as the wall." Louisa rose to her feet and clasped her hands in front of her.

"Perhaps I shall."

"Nevertheless, is there anything I can assist you with?" she asked. "A cold compress for your head, perhaps?"

He moved his fingers gingerly to the back of his head. "I think that is unnecessary. I have suffered"—he winced as he fingered a sensitive spot—"worse knocks to the head than this."

"But not while in the service of my protection."

A little unsteady, he rose to his feet and righted the chair that he had fallen on. "The reason for the injuries does not increase them, Mrs. Brock."

"No," she allowed, "but my subsequent obligation is now a factor." Her eyes followed his movements as he straightened. Good Lord, but the moniker "Giant Johnny" was highly appropriate. The man was a mountain. A fleeting thought crossed her mind about what it would be like to have those large arms encompass her.

He waved his hand in dismissal. "Think nothing of it. You had no reason to expect me to see to my promise in such a manner."

"Still . . ."

He spied her packed portmanteau and looked at her questioningly. "You are moving on? I thought your plans were unconfirmed."

Louisa lifted her chin. "They are. But that does not mean that I must stay here in order to solidify them."

He put his thick hands on his hips, doubling his width. "But it also means that you do not have to leave in order to do so either." She opened her mouth to speak but he stayed her with his hand. "I understand what it is like to be adrift. If you wish, you can remain here. It is clear that I need help, a woman's help." He gestured to the room. "I have little notion and less inclination for cleaning. I need someone to take charge in this area. Will you do it?"

Louisa stared at him. *Help him by being a maid? In an inn?* Of all things she had considered doing, working in such a place had never crossed her mind. She was not suited for such work. A governess, companion, yes, but a maid? What would her mother have said about this? Or any of her family?

She pressed her lips together and lifted her chin. It had been six years since she allowed her family to influence her and this job would at least keep her protected from the elements. She would be able to protect herself from the more unruly patrons, she was certain. It would be hard-earned coin, to be sure, but the current condition of her moneybag would not object to whichever manner she earned more. It would indeed present the biggest challenge she had yet faced, but how hard could it be?

"What say you, Mrs. Brock?"

His voice drew her out of her thoughts. Regarding him

thoughtfully, Louisa knew better than to just accept his offer. "What sort of benefits could I expect?"

"Proper wage, meals and a room." His answer was quick.

"How many meals?"

"How many does the average person eat?" he countered. "Three by my count."

Would her stomach survive three meals of such fare? She nodded. "This room? Or a smaller one in the attic?" She had slept in her fair share of small rooms as a governess; she would fight for the biggest one she could get.

"This one is fine. This is not a busy inn, so it can be spared." He rubbed his bald head. "My room is behind the office, so you will never be alone on the premises."

*Hm.* "I see. Free days?" Not that she expected to need them. She knew no one in the area and had no plans to inform her friends—her *former* friends—of where she was.

"Once a fortnight."

"And my duties?"

"Cleaning, of course. Helping out in the kitchen and pub when necessary."

"Was last night a typical crowd?" she asked.

"Yes. Local men come here regularly. There are not many places a man in this area can go to."

"And the women? I am curious."

He shrugged his boulder shoulders. "None have yet to come in here. I don't cater to their tastes."

Louisa sniffed and glanced around the room. The condition truly was atrocious. If the other rooms were like this, it would take days of hard work to get them up to scratch. It would be an accomplishment to be proud of, if she succeeded.

*Ha—if I succeed? I always succeed.*

She looked back at Giant Johnny, watching her with his hands on his hips, legs braced apart. She eyed him. He stood like a sportsman, sure of his ground and his strength. A sliver of awareness slipped through her at the confidence he exuded. This man was capable of many things, she was certain of it.

And if she were to agree to his offer, she would be with him every day. This mountain, this behemoth, would have authority over her as her employer. It was not the proximity to the giant that worried her, it was that last fact.

It rankled. For so long she had wished for independence, had almost achieved it with her friends and the formation of the Governess Club, only to have it collapse underneath her. And now she found herself once again having to submit to a man's authority.

It was a bitter pill to swallow. She would have to trust that she would eventually be able to turn the situation to her advantage. Nodding, she said, "I accept the position, Mr. Taylor."

A large smile broke out over his face and he offered her his hand, engulfing hers when she placed it in his grip. "Excellent. Start with breakfast, will you? Packard is already in the kitchen and he can whip something up for you. Then we'll talk work. Find me in my office or in the pub."

*Breakfast?* Her stomach turned at the thought. *Good Lord.*

## CHAPTER THREE

*Good Lord.* Louisa sat down at the small kitchen table with a thump. The pail in her hand dropped to the floor, dirty water splashing onto the stone. The mop followed suit, giving a clang as it clattered next to the pail.

She hurt. Her muscles were sore and every inch of her body seemed to ache. The pain seemed to permeate her very being. Unable to even hold her head up, Louisa laid her head on the cool table and closed her eyes.

Inchoate respect for maids settled in her. After three days of furious cleaning, still less than half of the sleeping rooms had been cleaned. She had assured Giant Johnny—*Mr. Taylor*—that she would have the task completed within a week's time. What had she gotten herself into? Her fingers were red, the skin was beginning to crack around her fingernails and all her muscles were protesting their overuse. Never one to leave a job unfinished, it was her pride that continued to spur her on.

She did not allow herself to think of the pub room and the cleaning that it would entail.

*Good Lord indeed.*

"Packard, if that is you, bring me some bread and cheese and a pint."

Louisa bolted into a proper sitting position despite the scream of protest from her back. Giant Johnny was in his office and had heard her ignoble collapse. Thanks be to God, he had not actually seen that it was her. He had been watching her closely since she began her maid work and she felt he was searching for some reason to find her lacking. More of her blasted pride would not allow him to see any weakness in her.

Stifling a groan, she pushed herself up and prepared the meal Mr. Taylor had requested. The bread and cheese were some of the only edible foodstuffs in the kitchen, having been provided by outside sources. Louisa carried the tin plate and frothing mug into the office, where the giant was bent over some books. A pair of spectacles rested upon his nose, lending themselves to an incongruous portrait of a man at work.

"Put it there," he muttered, gesturing to the only free spot on the desk. Louisa obliged and the sound of her skirts caused him to look up briefly, then complete a double take as he realized just who had brought him his food. Giant Johnny—*Mr. Taylor*—shot to his feet and took his spectacles off and stuffed them into a shirt pocket. "Mrs. Brock. Good afternoon." He was wearing only trousers and a shirt with the sleeves rolled up past his elbows; the opening at his throat was held together by loosely tied strings, giving her a pleasing view of the top of his chest, and he wore no tie. He had the look of a laborer about him, not an innkeeper.

"Good afternoon, sir."

He glanced at the open door to the kitchen. "I am sorry, I was expecting Packard."

"I believe he stepped out for a moment before he needed to start the evening meals." Louisa looked at him with a demure smile, hoping it hid her shaking muscles.

"I see. Yes. Thank you. For the food."

"You are welcome."

He gestured to the food. "Would you like to join me?"

She was starving. "No. Thank you," she added belatedly.

"I insist."

"I must return to work." Her muscles screamed at her in protest.

"That is what I wish to speak to you about."

Louisa narrowed her eyes and pressed her lips together. That did not bode well. She would be damned if he found fault with her work, not after she had worked her fingers to the bone the last few days. "Is there something the matter?" she asked, her voice tight and stiff.

He rubbed his bald head and gave her an exasperated look. "Mrs. Brock, fetch some tea for yourself and come sit down. That is an order," he added when she opened her mouth to object.

Stifling an indignant huff, she did as she was bade and returned shortly with a small tea tray. Settling her skirts around her legs as she sat, she folded her hands over her lap and waited for the tea to steep. She met his gaze straight on, refusing to give him any hint of anxiety or intimidation.

Not that she felt either, but that was beside the point.

He had waited for her return to resume his seat himself, fingering the feathered quill in his hand. Once she was settled, he squeezed himself into his small chair. Louisa watched him do so, closely. He braced his large hands on the curved arms and gingerly brought his body down onto the seat as though he was afraid he would break the chair. His bottom settled as close to the edge as he could possibly get it before sliding back. He paused for a moment, holding his breath; she wondered if he realized he looked to be waiting for the furniture to collapse beneath him.

Once assured it would support him yet again, he released his breath and leaned back. He affected what she assumed was to be a calm pose, but the disparity between furniture and man was too great for him to be truly comfortable. She thought for a moment if the impending conversation also contributed to his discomfort.

Well, she was in no way going to make this easy on him. She maintained her solid stare and kept her lips pressed together.

"Where are you from, Mrs. Brock?" he asked, breaking the silence.

Louisa did not even blink at his opening salvo. "South."

"South where?"

"South England."

The corners of his mouth tugged. "I assumed you are from England, Mrs. Brock. Your accent betrays that much."

She did not reply. The less she said, the less he would know.

"And your family?"

"What of them?"

"Where are they?"

"I could not say."

"Your husband's family did not take you in after his passing?"

"What do you think?"

He lifted a hand. "Pax, Mrs. Brock. I am not your enemy."

Louisa busied herself in checking the steeping tea. It was not yet strong enough for her preferences but she prepared herself a cup anyway to prolong the silence. Milk and sugar were added, the clinking of the spoon against the cup filling the room.

Mr. Taylor tore a piece of bread from the small loaf on his own tray and popped it into his mouth, watching her closely. As he chewed, he cut slivers of cheese, his eyes darting between her and his task. When he had several slices, he added one to his mouth and took a gulp of ale. He grimaced and peered into his tankard before setting it aside.

When his mouth was clear, he asked, "Have you heard of the Five Hit Wonder?"

Louisa held her cup of tea close to her mouth. "No." She sipped her tea.

One side of his mouth tilted and he offered her the plate of bread and cheese. "I am not surprised. The Five Hit Wonder is a pugilist. In the fight that made him famous, he felled his opponent in just five blows."

Louisa took a piece of bread and cheese and nibbled on it. Her stomach demanded more but she restrained herself.

"Few women follow pugilism. It's a masculine domain."

She spoke up, not a flicker on her face. "Prizefighting is barbaric."

"Such is the chant of many a temperance march. It takes a special female to be able to be a spectator at a match. But that is another matter. The Five Hit Wonder is—was—the reigning champion. For years. The best since Jack Broughton, many said. Broughton civilized the sport, by the way, by introducing more rules to reduce the gore and chaotic nature of the bouts."

She tilted her chin. "I fail to see the civility of a sport where the object is to beat a man to a bloody mess."

Mr. Taylor drank more ale and held some bread and cheese in one of his large hands. "It can be quite lucrative. The prizes are monetary, some purses more than you would imagine."

She sniffed. "The slave trade is lucrative; hence the reluctance of the slavers for its demise. Yet you will not see me condoning that either simply because the color of the coin is pretty."

He popped the food into his mouth and waved a hand, indicating the room. "So lucrative, in fact, that it facilitated the purchase of this inn."

Louisa stared at him for a moment before a quick laugh escaped her. "Are you telling me that you are the Five Hit Wonder? Ridiculous." She continued to laugh, but misgivings began to tickle her spine. The man had the size to be a prizefighting champion.

Without speaking, Mr. Taylor stood and crossed to a door at the back of the room. He opened it and took one step inside the room. She could see a shelf of books and the corner of a bed as he pulled out a brown book with a plain cover. It must be the bedroom he mentioned. Closing the door behind him, he moved back to the desk and held the book out to her, and after a moment she had no choice but to take it. The misgivings grew into dread as she opened it to find playbills and articles pasted to the pages. The playbills proclaimed the coming bouts of John Taylor, the Five Hit Wonder. The more recent ones had pictures of him stripped to the waist, poised in a fighting stance with a fierce look on his face. The articles spoke of his accomplishments, his history, his revolutionary approach to the sport.

Louisa swallowed and focused on a piece of information in one of the articles. "You were in the army?"

He had resumed his seat. "The King's Twenty-sixth Grenadiers. But armed service is bloody boring when there is no active combat. It is where I started boxing as a way to amuse myself."

She shot him a disapproving look and said, out of habit more than anything else, "Your language is still in the prize ring, I see. Please be more mindful."

He raised his eyebrows in surprise and chuckled. "Oh, well done, Mrs. Brock. You would make a fine governess with that prim tone."

Louisa shut her mouth and pressed her lips together.

Mr. Taylor leaned forward and folded his arms on the desk. "Who I am is not a secret; I do not intend it to be. But I told you this story because I want you to know that I understand the need to begin anew. My questions are not meant to interrogate you. I merely want to know if an angry husband or some other family is going to appear and cause trouble."

When she didn't speak, he continued. "I have been watching you since you started here and I can tell that you have never been a maid before. Your language, your inefficiency, even your dress does not speak of life in service. I have no intention of holding it against you. Everyone can learn a new trade. But I am putting myself and my inn at risk if I am harboring a runaway wife or daughter or even convict. I need to know that my investment in you is sound and that there will be no issues."

Louisa swallowed and lifted her chin. "There is no husband, family or constable looking for me. There will be no such trouble." *I hope.*

A ghost of a smile tugged at his lips and he sat back. "Good. As I just said, I will be lenient as you learn your job. How goes the room cleaning?"

She hated to say it, but the man said he would be lenient. "I may need more time than a week. I have only managed to clean four of the rooms."

He nodded slowly. "Fine. There is not much need for them just yet, the customers mainly being the locals looking for food and drink."

She stood and he followed her. She picked up her tea tray. "If there is nothing else, sir, I should start getting the kitchen prepared so Mr. Packard can begin the evening menu."

"Of course." He watched as she moved to the door. "Just keep in mind, Mrs. Brock, a fresh start can be a good thing."

Louisa didn't stop as she exited the office, happy in the knowledge that she hadn't betrayed the state of her muscles. She took the tray over to the sink and washed up, thinking she would have to be careful where Mr. Taylor was concerned. He was more observant than he appeared to be.

# Chapter Four

Louisa sat back on her heels and wiped the sweat from her brow. This was the last room. She glanced around the small space, now glistening in the sunlight provided by the window. For the life of her, she could not feel a sense of accomplishment in completing her task. Now that they were all clean, she knew it was only a matter of time before the rooms were used and once more needed to be cleaned. To be certain, they would not likely need such focused attention again, unless there was a particularly inconsiderate guest, but still.

She was too tired and sore to revel in her success. *Good Lord*, she thought, rubbing her neck. *I was not meant for service.*

With a sigh, she pushed herself to her feet and collected the cleaning supplies. She tossed the dirty water out the window and carried the rest down to the kitchen. Mr. Packard gave her a nod when she came in, his pipe dangling from his mouth. "Mrs. Brock, I need the big pots from the office."

She forced herself to smile at the portly cook and nodded. "Of course, right away." It stuck in her craw to be deferential, but she needed the money. Mr. Taylor had given her wages yesterday, reduced due to her room and board, but it felt good to have her finances on the rise again, meager as her earnings were.

Depositing the cleaning supplies in a closet, Louisa went to the office and poked her head in before entering. She had avoided Mr. Taylor as much as possible since their encounter in here several days ago. She had succeeded surprisingly well, it being an average-sized inn and they the only three employees. Besides, if he wanted to see her, he knew where to find her.

Several casks inhabited one corner of the office, filled with what, she did not know. Above the casks was a shelf filled with dried spices, sugar, flour and other dry goods in clay pots. Above even those, several large pots hung from the ceiling. Stretching on her toes, Louisa could not even brush the lowest one with her fingers.

Pressing her lips together, she scanned the room for something to knock the pot off its hook on the ceiling. No broom or other such long-handled device was in reach to aid her. Spying Mr. Taylor's chair, she dragged it over and lifted her skirts to step up onto it, using her free hand on the back of the chair to steady herself. The chair itself wobbled, enough to give her a moment's doubt, but she persevered. She took hold of the shelf and reached up to the pots. Her fingers just managed to brush the bottom of the lowest one.

"How in the blazes did they get up here?" she muttered to herself before extending her arm again, this time going up on her toes.

Her fingers were nearly close enough to dislodge the pot.

If she were quick enough, she would be able to catch it as it fell. If not, well, after spending so long with children, her ears could withstand one loud commotion.

She stretched farther, wishing to get that extra inch that might serve her purpose. She tightened her grip on the shelf, hoping it might boost her farther. The chair wobbled beneath her, teetering to one side. "Come on," she muttered through gritted teeth. "Almost there." She shifted to balance the chair better, but the wobble worsened. She managed to lift the pot off the hook a bit, but lost her grip and it settled back down. "Oh no you don't," she growled at the pot and tried again. She placed her fingers in the same spot and lifted the pot again. One more half inch and she would have it.

But the chair had other plans. Too unbalanced, it tipped to the side and Louisa felt herself fall with it. Her hand on the pot flailed, trying to right herself and the chair, but to no avail. The shelf shuddered under the unexpected weight of her panicked grip, the clay pots jostling together, ringing in the quiet of the office. She gasped, "Oh no," before feeling all the support underneath her give way and she knew she was falling.

Just as the chair slid that final inch from under her and her fingers lost their grip on the shelf, quick footsteps came up behind her and strong arms circled her waist, lifting her to safety. The chair clattered to the floor and the clay pots settled, the office resuming its previous tranquility.

"Are you all right? Injured in any way?" Mr. Taylor's deep voice rumbled in her ear. He held her effortlessly against him, her legs dangling in the air.

The breath from his voice warmed her ear and neck,

causing a flutter to travel down her spine. Louisa blinked as she registered the hard chest against her back and the arms around her waist. They were strong, confident, and she knew that he would not drop her; it was beyond his ability to do so. Her back curved into his body, instinctively adjusting to him, and she had to fight the urge to lean her head back onto his shoulder. Good Lord, but he truly was Giant Johnny, easily surpassing his fellow men in both size and strength. The knowledge trilled through her blood.

*What in the blazes am I thinking?* she asked herself, shaking herself out of this surprising reverie. She cleared her throat. "Release me now." Her voice was clipped and she consciously softened it to add, "Please. I am fine."

She felt his hesitation, but he slid her down after a moment, holding on to her waist until her feet were steady on the floor. "You are certain you are uninjured?" he asked.

Louisa stepped away from him, the distance between their bodies welcome despite her skin itching to return to his embrace. That would not do. "Yes."

He was rubbing his head when she turned to look at him. "What were you thinking?" he asked. His tone was irate.

She lifted her chin. "Mr. Packard sent me to fetch him one of the pots." She gestured to the dangling instruments, still swaying from the incident.

"And you thought the best way to fetch one was to stand on a damaged chair?"

"I could not reach. What would you have me do?"

"Did it occur to you to find someone who is taller than you?"

"Why would it? The chair was convenient and was serving quite well. I had no need for anyone's help."

Mr. Taylor's eyes narrowed and they turned black with anger. "No need? Then what do you call falling off the chair and my keeping you from harm? Was that not needing help?"

Sniffing, Louisa looked away. "I did not say I needed you to rescue me."

"If I hadn't, you would likely be unconscious on the floor, perhaps even dead." His voice was laced with displeasure. Tension radiated off him. She would not have been surprised to see him assume a prizefighter's stance, his muscles were so tight.

"There is no call for such dramatics," she huffed.

"Packard!" Mr. Taylor bellowed, making her jump. He reached up and retrieved the pot she had risked her safety to get. A shot of annoyance ran through her at how easily he accomplished the task. The cook appeared in the doorway and Giant Johnny thrust the pot at him, his eyes not leaving Louisa. "In the future, Mrs. Brock is not to fetch these pots." He silenced her protest with a slash of his hand. "She is too short and it risks her safety. Either yourself or I will get them, or anyone who is tall enough, for that matter."

"Yes, sir." Mr. Packard gave a sharp nod, no question or hesitation in his voice. He didn't even shoot a look of irritation in her direction for being the cause of such a clipped command; he simply accepted it and returned to his duties.

"That was unnecessary," Louisa began.

Mr. Taylor cut her off, placing his fists on his hips. It made his presence in the room increase, if that were possible, taking every available inch as his own. "Mrs. Brock, you may have little regard for your own safety, but I will not have your injuries or your death on my conscience. So long as you work here, if there is any task that may risk your health and well-being, you will seek assistance."

"I don't need—"

"This is not negotiable," he clipped out. "If you feel you will have difficulty meeting this expectation, pack your things now."

Louisa hated him in that moment. Hated that he was commanding her, hated needing this position for the shelter it provided, hated knowing he was right. This hatred was visceral, bleeding from her bones and through her pores until she could almost feel the hot slime of it on her skin, burning her. The hatred wasn't a stranger, but it had been so long since she felt it that it took several moments for her to gain control of it.

She swallowed and nodded. "I will do as you say."

Mr. Taylor visibly relaxed, his arms and shoulders lowering. "I am glad to hear that. I should not want any harm to come to you."

Louisa gritted her teeth. "I am not your responsibility, Mr. Taylor."

"So long as you are in my employ, you are."

For a moment, she was in serious contemplation of leaving. True, here she had a roof over her head, food—despite how questionable it was—in her belly and something to occupy her days. But Giant Johnny was turning into a domineering man, one used to ordering people about and not anticipating any refusal, merely taking what he saw as his right. She had spent her past few years fighting against such men, leaving when it was a better option than losing. She had no desire to find herself in yet another situation like that.

She thought she had found her sanctuary with her friends and their Governess Club. For a brief time, they were their own masters, making their own decisions regarding their lives and their futures. True, Jacob Knightly lived at Ridgestone with them, but for the most part he remained out of the Governess Club's business. The estate and his marriage were his concerns; the Governess Club, the ladies'.

And it had been wonderful. Difficult, but wonderful.

But now she found herself yet again in the situation of submitting to a man. Did she need this position that much? Would she be able to survive like this? Odds were low, as she had yet to succeed in that. How long would she be able to suffer this? How long before he would demand the sacrifice of her dignity, her self-respect?

Did she want to find out?

Mr. Taylor continued speaking, his tone more gentle now that he had gotten her to accede to his wishes. "I just want you to be safe. I would feel horrible should anything happen to you. It's for your own good."

She couldn't stop the snort. "Of course it is. Isn't it always?"

He was taken aback by the sarcastic vehemence of her tone. "What?"

She couldn't stop herself, didn't know if she wanted to. "Men like you are always making decisions for a woman's own good. We're too weak minded and flighty to be considered capable of determining what our own good is, so we must depend on men to determine that. Why does no one recognize that men are selfish and will manipulate the situation to serve their own needs? At what point did 'what's best for the woman' become entire acquiescence to man's desires? Why is it that no one can see that disparity? And those who do are scoffed at, ridiculed and shunned for being 'unnatural' females, merely for wanting the acknowledgment that they are in possession of a working mind and are capable of using it just as effectively as a man."

John blinked, feeling as though he had taken an unexpected punch to the kidney. He didn't know what to do: respond to her words—*what was it she said anyway?*—or marvel at the ferocity on her face. He doubted she knew what she looked like: eyes snapping, brows lowered, face red—even her golden hair seemed to resonate. Gone was the harpy and in her place was this woman caught up in a passion. He recognized that it was anger driving her, but there was a fine line between anger and lust and he knew which one was driving him now. He took a breath to ensure control over his body.

His mind belatedly processed some of her words. His brow lowered in confusion and he crossed his arms over his chest. "Are you saying that you want to get hurt?"

For some reason that made her angrier. "No," she snapped. "I don't want to get hurt. I want the respect afforded to men that I know what I can and cannot do and make decisions accordingly."

"But you didn't," he pointed out. "You were about to fall from the chair. You could have been seriously injured."

"Oh, and you never made a mistake once in your life? Never so close to accomplishing something that a little risk is worth it?"

"I highly doubt a pot is worth the risk." He was still confused.

"Oh!" He wondered if she would stamp her foot, but she

restrained herself. John watched as she took a deep breath, her breasts straining against her dress. She closed her eyes, her lips pressed together into an almost invisible line, and she was clenching her hands into fists and then relaxing them. When she spoke again, her voice was calm and flat. "Pray excuse me. Mr. Packard needs assistance."

John automatically stepped out of her way, the woman sweeping by him in a regal swish of skirts. The hairs on his arms stood up as she passed him, every nerve wishing to touch her in some way. Yea gods, she was a firecracker. One of the world's worst maids, but a firecracker nonetheless. Her anger had turned her brown eyes to an alluring dark mahogany, snapping with fire. Her pale cheeks had flushed with red, contrasting with her wheat colored hair that taunted him with its tempting softness. Her bosom had heaved with her furious breathing; his eyes were torn with where to look: at the rise and fall of her breasts, her delicate cheeks flaming with fury, her lips rounding on each word with deliberation or her eyes, the fire drawing him in with its promise of passion.

This was a woman who would do well in bed. In *his* bed.

Her pause at the door was infinitesimal. "And it is not about the pot, sir." She finalized her parting shot with a sniff and disappeared from the office.

A large grin burst out on his face. Oh yes, she would do very well in his bed.

# CHAPTER FIVE

"Mrs. Brock?"

Louisa turned her head at the young voice that called her name. "Yes, Timothy?" Suds were up to his elbows as he scrubbed the pots from the morning's cooking.

"Kin I asks ye a question?"

She closed her eyes briefly at his grammar. "Of course."

"Yer smart, right? Me mam's day is coming up and I been saving bits of me wages to git her somethin' pretty. Kin ye tell me what mams like?"

Louisa looked up from the tray she was preparing for Mr. Taylor. She had taken to bringing him a board of cheese and bread along with a pint. He worked in his office every afternoon and invariably grew hungry when he did.

And it always happened when Mr. Packard was out of the kitchen.

"You want to buy your mother a birthday gift?" Louisa asked. "That is very sweet of you, Timothy."

He blushed and scratched his cheek, leaving some suds on his skin. "T'aint nothing. I only gots a few pennies."

"Well, what ideas have you been thinking of?"

"Mebee some flowers, buts she kin get those in any field 'round here. Mebee a pretty dress? Or one them bonnets that them ladies wear. Buts I can't go into one of them girl stores."

"Are you asking me to go shopping for you?"

Timothy shrugged. "How much do them dresses and bonnets cost?"

Louisa's eyes were sympathetic. "More than a few pennies."

His face fell. "Well, what else do mams like?"

Louisa lifted the tray. "They like nicely behaved, handsome sons that do the dishes instead of going out and playing after dinner."

A cheeky grin covered his face. "I got the handsome stuff down pat!"

She smiled back at him. "That you do, Timmy boy." She turned and carried the tray to Giant Johnny's office. "I will keep thinking about your mother's birthday gift."

"Thank ye, Mrs. Brock," Timothy called out, the cheeky grin still on his face.

Giant Johnny looked up with a frown as she entered the office. "What was that about?" he asked.

Louisa shook her head. "Nothing important. Timothy wants to buy his mother a birthday gift."

"Hm" was all the response she got as he turned his attention back to his books, rubbing his head.

She stood in the doorway for a moment, looking at Giant Johnny hunched over his desk. He looked awkward, uncomfortable, as he scratched away at the paper. He didn't normally ignore her like this. Usually he stood and offered her a smile and a seat. She had become used to these offers, even put more on the tray when she was of a mind to accept.

She didn't often get the opportunity to watch him. Her days were too busy and in the evenings he was dedicated to the pub, serving and entertaining the customers. Regulars, mostly, all men. None came who expressed interest in needing a room; she had yet to clean the rooms again, for which she was thankful.

Now as she stood here, looking at him, she wondered at the tiny ball of disappointment at how he barely glanced up and didn't even smile at her.

Louisa watched his hand running back and forth over his bare pate. She had run her hands through a man's hair before, and she was curious about how her hand would feel in the same place as his now. Would his skin be soft? Smooth like the skin on her stomach or more rough, given the hair follicles that covered a human scalp? Would it be warm or cool? Would she be able to determine just by touch if he was naturally bald or if he maintained it that way?

She imagined herself standing beside him and sliding her hands along that bare skin, down his neck to settle on his broad shoulders. She had never seen a man of his size. Serving in the pub, she noticed how the men instinctively cowered when near him, but she found it intriguing. Ever since the pot incident when he had effortlessly held her by the waist, a part of her longed for it to happen again. Her skin tingled at the thought of being held in his arms again where she could lean into him and learn his body, his heat, his smell. Her shoulders ached to be surrounded by him, her throat drying at the prospect of being able to lean into him and pull his head down for a kiss.

She was not a maiden, having indulged with two footmen since becoming a governess. They had both been pleasant and attractive—she would have nothing less—and, most importantly, discreet. She never would have considered them if she had thought they would spread tales about her. The experiences had been enlightening, if dangerous. She gave a brief whisper of thanks she had never been caught with child. She was not a stranger to feeling lust, but the force of this particular lust for the giant sitting awkwardly at his desk took her off guard.

She was torn between indulging her lust and denying it. She was unsure if he was feeling the same attraction to her and he was her employer; that alone could complicate matters. As a governess, she had never allowed her employers any possibility of a sexual relationship, but those gentlemen had all been married with children. Such an arrangement would have made her more than uncomfortable in regard to her dignity and having to face his wife.

But her giant here was unmarried, no children in sight save for the two boys he employed. And if things became awkward, she had more freedom to leave than she had felt as a governess. She did not have a formal contract to stay at the inn and he paid her on a weekly basis instead of monthly.

If anything, it would rid her of the ache between her legs and along her skin whenever he was nearby. She was certain that even if he didn't exactly feel lust for her, he would be able to perform when the time came.

She just had to decide what it was she wanted.

"I've brought your tray, Mr. Taylor," Louisa said and moved to put it on his desk.

He muttered absently, "Thank you."

"Is something the matter?" she asked, glancing at him.

"Nothing you can help with," he replied.

She stiffened at the dismissal in his tone and turned on her heel to stalk out of the room. His voice stopped her.

"Wait, please, Mrs. Brock."

Louisa looked back at him. Mr. Taylor stood, the chair scraping loudly against the wood floor. He ran his hand over his head again. "I apologize. I should not have spoken like that to you. I only meant that it is an accounts issue, one that a maid does not need to be concerned over."

She lifted her chin. "A maid can have some knowledge beyond cleaning." At least *she* did. Not many others she had met did.

He nodded. "Of course."

At his agreeable tone, she took a step forward, softening a little. "I do, for instance."

A smile tugged at his lips. "I did notice that you were not the regular run-of-the-mill maid. Perhaps you can help me with this?" He gestured to his desk.

She looked at him warily before glancing down at the books. He shifted and held the chair out for her. Keeping her chin in the air, she moved and sat down, settling her skirts around her legs. He helped her shift closer to the desk and she peered down at the books.

"Good Lord, these are a mess!" She looked up at him.

He gave her a sheepish shrug. "I didn't think they were that bad."

"Do you even know how to do accounts?"

It was his turn to look offended. "I kept my own accounts from my fighting days."

She sniffed. "That is hardly the same as accounting for an inn, sir."

His offended look turned to a cajoling one. "I have become aware of that. Hence my asking you for help."

She blinked at the sudden rush of warmth that washed through her at his smile. There, that was what was missing when she first entered the office.

But she was foolish to give him any indication of pleasure at such a thing. She looked back down at the books. "Well, if I am going to make any sense of this, I am going to need some tea." She looked up at him and pierced him with one of her governess looks. "Please bring me some."

His cajoling smile turned into a full-fledged grin and the warmth exploded into a fire inside her. He sketched her a bow. "As you wish, my lady."

She sniffed and turned her attention to the books, watching out of the corner of her eye as he left the office. When his back was turned, she took a longer glance at his retreating form, her eyes settling on his bottom.

Good Lord, but the man was finely built.

Hours later, Louisa dropped the pencil on the desk and leaned back in the chair, rubbing her eyes. "Well, I think I managed to save the accounts from your mismanagement."

John was in the chair on the opposite side of the desk. His posture was relaxed, leaning back with his chin in his hand and one ankle over the other. He had enjoyed this, watching her wrestle with the accounts. Once it became clear it would be a long, tedious job, he had not waited in the office but popped in from time to time to check on her. Evening customers would be arriving shortly and he had stolen a few minutes to just sit and watch her.

She was always flitting about the inn doing this and that and he had yet to observe her being still; even their occasional teatimes had been brief and awkward, with his tongue more often than not glued to the roof of his mouth. It had been pleasant to look at her, completely with her knowledge, for she was aware of his presence, and not have to worry about making conversation. It was a novel experience for him, to not know what to say around a woman.

He milked this opportunity for all he could get, from her wheat colored hair glowing in the light to the expanse of her bosom revealed in how her dress gaped open as she leaned over the desk and account books.

Oh, how he stared. He had never wanted for a woman, especially as a champion. He had made the choice several years ago to be more discerning in his choice of bed partners and it still surprised him to know that he had yet to end the spurt of celibacy that decision had precipitated. Seven years ago, if someone had told him he would not bed a woman in so long, he would have laughed his head off, for women had always made themselves available to him. Only after purchasing this inn several months ago did he find himself without access to the fairer sex. The women of Grompton-Upon-Tweer did not frequent the Beefy Buzzard and none had approached him outside the premises either. Add to that to the decided lack of maids working at the inn and he found himself staring unabashedly at Mrs. Brock's lovely bosom.

Fine apples they were, perhaps even as big as some oranges

he had once seen at the docks in London. His mouth watered now just as it had when he had bitten into one of those orange slices. Thinking about pulling the chair out from the desk and kneeling between her legs to nuzzle the creamy mounds had his free hand gripping the arm of his chair tightly to keep him from doing so.

He wondered how she would react if he did that. Or more, lifted her up and carried her through the door in the corner to his room to let her have her way with him.

John forced himself to look at her face. It had simply been too long since he had had a woman, although he had always been able to control himself during his celibacy before now. Perhaps it was Fate or God telling him it was time to end his self-imposed penance. Mrs. Brock was a widow and generally widows were open to discreet arrangements once the cold loneliness of their beds seeped into their bodies. True, she had thus far shown a decided lack of interest in such an arrangement with him, but after seven years he could wait. It could be that she had not yet reached that point in her widowhood; a lack of black clothing did not necessarily indicate an end to grief, as he well knew.

His eyes met her brown ones, noticing the shade of mahogany tinged with gold around the pupils. Lovely eyes they were.

He recalled her statement. "You are successful?"

She nodded. "I believe so." There was a hint of red on her cheeks, a flush of pleasure at her accomplishment.

"What was the issue?"

"There were many, but the largest one was the confusion between credits and debits. Comparing the entries

in the columns with the receipts showed the inconsisten-
cies. See here"—she turned the book around for him to see
better—"you had even mixed up the different accounts. This
entry here is for the candles, but the only receipt I could find
to match the date and number was for the butcher. And many
of the entries were not entered properly. They had the same
numerals, but in different arrangements than the receipts.
Had you not noticed this?"

He shook his head. "Maths never was a strong suit of
mine." Even as a child, he had confused his numbers. He
managed to get by, but it was never easy or a pleasant task.

"Well, it is sorted now." She closed the book and sat back
in the chair, giving no sign of relinquishing it to him. She
gripped the arms, curling her fingers around the wood and
pressing her lips together. Her gaze did not leave his and he
got the impression she was gathering her courage.

John raised his eyebrows in question. "You look like you
have something to say, Mrs. Brock."

She lifted her chin. "I do."

"Then speak."

Her grip tightened on the chair. "You were right before."

"I was? On what?"

"I am not a maid. I have never been a maid. It has been . . .
a challenge to adapt to such a position."

He grinned and a spark of pleasure pulsed in his chest
when he saw her blink and momentarily lose her focus. "I assumed as much. You are the worst maid I have ever seen."

Her lips pressed together and the focus returned to her
eyes, this time accompanied by anger. "I believe I have done
the best I possibly could."

John held up a hand. "I am not holding it against you. I could tell you were working hard and that is enough for me."

"Yes, that is what I wanted to speak of." She flexed her fingers on the chair, but did not release her grip. "I have been watching you too and I have noticed things."

More pleasure sparked at that statement. "Such as?" *My physique? My stature? My hands? My shoulders? Women like my shoulders.*

"You are good with the customers, quite good."

The pleasure dissipated. He had not been expecting that.

She continued. "True, they are intimidated by your size, but they do not actually fear you. You make them laugh and feel comfortable here. That is why they keep coming back."

He gave her a wry grin. "I rather think the ale is more of a reason for their loyalty."

She shook her head. "The Rose and Crown is a half-hour's horse ride away and I heard their prices are similar to ours. If it was a better pub, they would not hesitate to go there. They choose to come here, despite all the flaws."

John raised his brows at her words, but she continued, gesturing to the books. "One of your obvious weaknesses in management is your bookkeeping. It is atrocious, yet I see you working on them every day. They should never have achieved this state with the amount of effort I have seen you put into them."

He linked his hands together and settled them on his stomach, curious as to where she was going with this. "Your point?"

Mrs. Brock took a deep breath. "I have been raised and trained to run a household, including the bookkeeping. I could be your partner. I would handle the details such as employees, accounts, things similar to a house. You would be in charge of customers, running the pub and being the face of the inn. I would be the housekeeper to your butler."

He looked at her for a moment. The idea had merit. And appeal. If it meant he never had to look at those damned account books again, he would just about hand over the keys to her entirely. "My lord to your lady," he said.

A small flush covered her cheeks at the implications of such a metaphor. She lifted her chin. "Not in a true sense of the words, however."

"Of course not," he demurred. He still needed some convincing, though. "Tell me, what would be your first action, were we partners?"

"Remove Mr. Packard from the position of cook." Her response was so quick and automatic John had no doubt she had been thinking of that for some time.

"Why? He does the job competently."

"Have you actually tasted his food?"

He shrugged. "I have had worse."

"The point is that you do not want a merely competent cook," she replied. "One's cook is an attraction to visitors; a bad one will give people doubts when considering a stay. You want a stellar cook."

"But he cooked for Captain Wallace for four years before coming here. He cannot be that bad."

She cocked an eyebrow at him. "And who is Captain Wallace?"

John shrugged, having not asked Packard about it.

"He was captain of the HMS *Liberty*. A naval captain. Mr.

Packard is used to making due with hardtack and fish heads. He does not belong in the kitchen of an inn."

He took a deep breath and contemplated the situation. He was beginning to see his folly now. "What do you suggest? I have no wish to dismiss the man, for he is a reliable employee."

"Move him to assist you in tending to the bar. He is a large enough fellow to discourage rabble-rousers and to assist with the casks and whatnot. As for the cook, I am sure there are some large houses around here. We could entice an undercook or two to come run the kitchen. It won't have the prestige of nobility, but they will have their own kitchen to oversee."

John looked at her, at the remaining flush on her cheeks now accompanied by an excited light in her eyes. Her lips were pressed together, but he thought it was more because she was trying to contain her enthusiasm than displeasure.

Her excitement was contagious. He felt himself responding to it, being drawn in. Her ideas were strong, the logic was sound. He felt like a half-wit for not researching Packard more thoroughly, but at the time he had just wanted to open as soon as possible. And look to the large houses for employees? Again, he was a half-wit.

He felt a smile grow on his face. "Maids too can be lured away from their positions."

Mrs. Brock nodded slowly. "They might be more difficult, but we can try. To give up the training to be a lady's maid is more difficult than that of a cook. There is only ever one head cook in a kitchen, whereas there can be several lady's maids. Farms would be a better starting point, I think. Those girls are used to hard work and their families can use the money. We can split them between the cleaning and serving duties."

"That makes sense."

"We would need an ostler for the horses and carriages. That may be a bit more difficult. For grooms we can look to the farms as well, but they work with their fathers, so it may be challenging. Sons of the merchants may do as well. But we can make do with Timothy and Alan for now to serve both as grooms and kitchen help."

"Ostlers and grooms?" he interjected. "But we have no need for that. No overnight guests save yourself have stayed who might need carriages or horses seen to."

"But that will change," Mrs. Brock said confidently. "The weather and daylight are changing and you will have travelers such as I who will need shelter. You do not want them to move on to the next inn."

"But just like you, they will have no choice but to stay here if the weather is so unpleasant. The next closest inn in any direction is at least an hour away, even in a carriage."

"But you don't want people to stay here because they have to, you want them to stay because they want to. The first time they will have no choice, but when the weather improves, we will have a good enough reputation that travelers will deliberately seek us out for accommodations. It will only grow from there."

Yea gods, when she spoke like that, it was easy to believe her. With those ideas and enthusiasm, John could clearly see the Beefy Buzzard in a year's time, two and three, thriving and successful, just as he wanted it to be. It would prove to the naysayers that he could be successful outside the boxing ring and justify what they had said was his ill-advised retirement.

He loved his inn, loved his patrons and the stable community it had provided him thus far. But he was intelligent enough to recognize that he was not meant for the responsibilities of running an inn. As Mrs. Brock said, he was good to be out front, being the face of the operation, but his skills in other areas were lacking.

Which made her partnership proposal so alluring. It would allow both of them to focus on areas they were good at while bringing the inn to the thriving establishment he knew it could be.

And it would guarantee her staying in the area. One more benefit to the arrangement.

"What do you expect in return?" he asked.

"Half of the profits and that cottage I saw out back."

He raised his eyebrows. "Seventy-five, twenty-five. This is my inn, after all."

"It will become our inn. Fifty-fifty."

"You are getting the cottage out back, I get the tiny room right here. Seventy-thirty."

"That cottage is run down and will need much work and effort to make it habitable. Fifty-fifty."

"It is all of my money invested into this establishment. Sixty-forty."

Mrs. Brock stuck out her hand. "With the option of renegotiating in a year's time."

John leaned forward and wrapped his hand around hers. It engulfed her smaller one, her fingers barely managing to peek out around the side of his. He held it in a carefully firm grip, ensuring he contained his strength so as not to harm her. "Deal, Mrs. Brock. I will draw up an agreement."

"I can do that. It is something that will fall under my purview, after all."

He nodded. "Fine. We can start enticing those employees away tomorrow."

"I will continue to see to the maids' duties until those positions are filled. You will not regret this, Mr. Taylor." She tried to extract her hand from his, but John held firm, enjoying the softness against his palm.

He smiled at her, enjoying how her eyes dipped down to his lips and lost some of their focus. "Neither will you, Mrs. Brock," he murmured. "I am certain we both will be pleased with our new arrangement."

# CHAPTER SIX

---

"You want to what?" John barely kept his voice at an appropriate level.

Louisa sniffed. "It is not asking much."

"I hardly think buying four linen sets per room qualifies as not asking much."

She put her hands on her hips. "Trust me, it will make things easier for everyone."

"How?"

She ticked off her fingers as she listed her reasons. "It will guarantee fresh linens for guests. It will space out the need for laundry. If one set gets dirty, there will immediately be clean ones. It will reduce the wear on any single set, thus making them last longer and saving money. It will help establish our reputation for being a clean inn." She looked at him triumphantly, daring him to contradict her.

"But four each? And of the quality you are suggesting? The expense is too high."

"It is an investment, Mr. Taylor."

"An investment of *my* money. Of which there are not copious amounts."

"You will recoup your losses, you will see. And I know the state of your finances. You can afford this, along with the tea services and private dining room."

John sputtered. "Tea services and private dining room?"

She nodded. "Yes. Offering tea will appeal to the ladies of the town and travelers who just need a place to refresh themselves. And a private dining room will appeal to those of quality who prefer not to mix with lower classes as well as offer a place for meetings, such as the town council and ladies' charity."

John rubbed both hands along his head. "And where would this private dining room go? There is no room."

"I know. That is why I took the liberty of talking to some carpenters in town and they quoted me a price. It is most inexpensive." She lifted some papers off the desk and presented them to him.

John took them from her, giving her a glare. He glanced down at them and felt the blood drain from his face. "No. Absolutely not. This is too expensive."

"It is necessary."

He thrust the papers down onto the desk and folded his arms across his chest. "Perhaps in a year or so, once the inn starts to show a profit. But not now. The linens, yes to three sets each, and the tea services. But not the private dining room."

He blinked when she burst out into a grin. "I was hoping you would say that. For now you cannot object to the carpenters repairing the tables and chairs in the pub. Here is that quote." She held out another paper to him.

"What?" He was reeling from her abrupt change.

Louisa's eyes twinkled wickedly. "I thought the private dining room was too expensive at this time as well. But we do need to repair the furniture. The chairs are weak and tilt and several of the tables look as though they will collapse after one more round of heavy cheering. I thought if I showed you the higher quote first, you would be more amenable to this."

He stared at her. "Why did you not just consult me?"

"This is me consulting you."

"By manipulating me?"

She frowned. "That is an unpleasant word. I prefer guiding or directing."

"And I would prefer if you approached me with the respect afforded to me as the owner of the inn."

"We are partners."

"The word 'partner' calls to mind working together. Which won't be us for much longer if you choose to continue to manipulate me."

"You would terminate our agreement? That would be breach of contract."

John pressed his fists into the desk and leaned in toward her. Something flickered in her eyes—he didn't think it was fear—but she mimicked him, a move that sent his blood pulsing.

"There is no formal contract, Mrs. Brock," he gritted out, staying focused on the issue at hand. "You cannot breach what does not exist."

"We have a signed document," she countered with a hiss, her voice as tight as his. "It may not have been written by a barrister, but it is still legally enforceable, such as IOUs between gentlemen."

He smirked. "I have been around gambling enough to know that such IOUs are only enforceable by the gentleman's honor, not the law."

"Then you would admit to having no honor?"

"Funny to hear that word come from you after what you just did."

"I want this inn to be the best and will do whatever is necessary to achieve that."

A loud knocking on the door interrupted them and John realized how much their voices had risen. He glanced back to see Packard standing there. "What?" he barked.

The man stood straighter, bringing to John's mind Packard's naval experience. How had John not seen it before? Every time he spoke in an authoritative tone, Packard sharpened up. "The new casks of ale have arrived, sir."

"Thank you, Packard."

"With all due respect, sir, all the shouting is making the boys jumpy." Packard jerked his thumb in the direction of the kitchen where Timothy and Alan were likely working.

Louisa straightened, suddenly feeling foolish and ashamed of her behavior. To think she had been screaming at Mr. Taylor like a fishwife. She had not been able to stop herself after his accusation of manipulation. Which, in hindsight, she had been doing. It had seemed like a clever idea at first, but she could see now the error of her thinking. He had yet to display the unreasonable behavior she expected of men, so she had little reason beyond her prejudices to treat him so.

The apology she knew he deserved stuck in her throat.

She swallowed, trying to find a way around it. "I just have the best interests of the inn in mind," she finally managed, staring at the wall.

In her peripheral vision she saw him straighten and put his hands on his hips, hanging his head for a moment. He let out a big sigh, one that would have heaved any other body. "As do I. We are supposed to be working together. Trust me enough to approach me directly regarding changes. I will listen, as I expect you to listen to me, and we will determine the best course of action together."

She nodded her agreement. She did not speak but transferred her gaze to the desk, fiddling with some of the papers there.

"Where did the idea of serving tea come from?" he asked, breaking the silence.

Louisa glanced up. "From Timothy, really. He wanted to do something nice for his mother's birthday and I was thinking it would be a treat for a farmer's wife to come to a place where she would be served just like she was a lady. It wouldn't take much to add a high tea to the menu."

He stared at her for a moment before nodding with a small smile. "That is a very good idea. A smart one."

Pride and pleasure warmed her chest at his acknowledgment. "Thank you."

He shuffled his feet. "I ought to go help Packard with the ale delivery."

"Could you ask Maisie to send in some tea for me, please?" she asked.

"I will. She was a good choice for cook, I think," he said. "I don't think my stomach has been this happy since I bought the inn."

Louisa smiled at him and sat back down at the desk. "Yes, she is working out fine."

Mr. Taylor pointed to the door. "Well, I am going to help with the delivery." He turned and moved to the door.

"Mr. Taylor," she called out, stopping him. When he looked over his shoulder, she said, "About the ale . . ."

"Yes?" He sounded wary.

"I think the brewer is cheating you. Us, I mean."

"How so?"

She indicated a pile of receipts. "Based on what we are paying, the quality does not appear to match."

"What do you know of ale?"

His comment held a note of teasing, but she bristled at it still. "Enough to know when it tastes good or not. I am surprised the men don't complain about that horse—"

He held up his hand. "I will look into it."

Louisa nodded, grateful he had saved her from another less than ladylike display. When he disappeared from the doorway, she sat back in the chair and wondered why she was concerned about appearing a lady for him. It had been years since she thought of herself as such and to have the idea resurrect itself now was unsettling.

Louisa fell into bed, willing to lose the battle against exhaustion. Oh, but it was a good exhaustion. Two weeks had passed since she and Mr. Taylor began their partnership and the improvements were already noticeable. The rooms were clean with new linens on their way; the carpenters had repaired all the pub furniture and were now making a new large hidden closet on the sleeping floor to store linens and cleaning supplies so the maids would not have to fetch these things from the ground floor; the new cook, Maisie, was proving to be worth the price it took to lure her away from the large house; and the new maids were settling in decently well.

She and Giant Johnny had not fought since that first time; disagreed, yes, but no outright fights or arguments. One that she was glad to have won was in regard to the services the maids were to provide. Insistent upon the inn not being labeled a brothel, Louisa had convinced him that any such services would be at the maid's own discretion and preference, and not promoted by the inn. Even that had been a compromise, as he had pointed out that the possibility would draw male customers. After their decision, she had spoken with both Rose and Fanny individually, emphasizing the matter of their choice and that they would have the protection of the inn should they refuse such attention at any time. Giant Johnny had not been privy to that aspect of their agreement, but she felt confident he would agree if he knew.

But her days were long. Not as physically demanding as when she was working as a maid, but more required her attention, from the accounts to menus to supplies to training and directing employees. It seemed that from the moment she left her room, people were demanding decisions from her.

It was lovely, having people look to her for leadership and seeing the inn evolve under her guidance. Under *their* guidance.

She could not in good conscience deny the efforts John Taylor was contributing to the inn. Now that he was free of the paper encumbrances of management, he was flourishing even more in regard to customer satisfaction. He had consented to putting a sign in the window stating that the Beefy Buzzard was home to the Five Hit Wonder and already business had increased. They even had their first overnight guest this evening, a well-heeled gentleman traveling to London. The gentleman had appeared to enjoy his evening in the pub, listening to Giant Johnny regale them with a story of one of his early victories, blow by blow. Not that she would admit it to him, but she had enjoyed watching him tell the tale, if not the tale itself. He had become so animated, using his fists to punch the air in embellishment. A part of her had been mesmerized, rooted to the spot where she could watch him in his element. Thankfully she had managed to push that part of her down so she could focus on her duties, even if her eyes and attention kept drifting back to the large man, graceful and captivating in his storytelling.

And tonight was her last night in the inn itself. Tomorrow she would begin making the cottage livable, starting with her bedchamber.

She drifted off to sleep, a smile on her face, and dreamed of a bald gentle giant telling a story just for her.

John hammered in a shingle on the cottage roof and accepted another one from the carpenter, Robbie. Mrs. Brock had inspected the cottage for residency earlier in the week and the disappointment on her face ate at his gut. He directed the carpenters to halt whatever project she had them currently working on and to begin repairs to make the small residence habitable. He contributed when he could step away from the inn to help the project along. He decided the entire roof ought to be reframed and replaced, given the amount of leaks and rot they had found. They had already completed the reframing and were now laying the slate shingles.

It felt good to be doing physical work again. He enjoyed tending to his pub and inn, but after a decade of living by the strength of his body, the inaction of his new profession was difficult to accustom himself to. The ringing of hammers filled his ears, proclaiming to the world that men were at work. Robbie Brown and Joseph Smith were good at their jobs, working with conversation and laughter. Joe, the older one, was married with a third child on the way and Robbie was betrothed to a young lady in town.

Robbie handed John another shingle with a grin and a nod toward the inn. "We have a Peeping Tom over there."

John glanced in the direction Robbie indicated and saw Mrs. Brock standing at the rear entrance, her arms crossed and her lips pressed into a line even visible from here. He paused in mid-swing and took in her green dress and hair pulled back into a simple knot. He enjoyed looking at her slender stature, his eyes drifting to her curves with mouth-watering enthusiasm. She was taller than the average woman, which would aid in their intimacy. He knew that if he were to pull her back against him, her head would be able to rest on his shoulder and her bottom would nestle into his groin. In such a position, he would have easy access to that spot just below her ear that he longed to kiss and make his way down her neck to her shoulder, pulling away the fabric shielding her skin from his attention. She would lean back into him, perhaps even wrap an arm back to hold his head to that place where her shoulder met her neck and allow him to pay homage to her beating pulse. He wondered if she would be the type to give breathless sighs or heartfelt moans or . . .

"She's a piece of work, ain't she?" Robbie said, breaking into his fantasy.

John tore his gaze away from the object of his lust and reined in his wayward thoughts. "Eh?" He finished nailing in the shingle and shifted over, accepting a new one.

"Mrs. Bristly, some are calling her." Robbie grinned at him.

"Bristly?" More hammering helped him regain his focus. He stole a glance back to see that she had disappeared.

The younger man shrugged. "She's just so prickly. Like a hedgehog, I figure. Can't get close to her without risking your blood." He held out another shingle. John took it, but did not resume work. Robbie kept speaking. "I mean, she looks good and all, but as soon as she starts talking to you, your little boys curl up and hide, know what I'm saying? What man wants that? You must have balls of steel to be working with her."

Never mind that his initial impression of her had been similar. John took issue with the man's comments. "Oi, that's a bit much, don't you think?"

"Come on, mate, you telling me she ain't a fishwife to you?"

"Quit your jabbering, Robbie," Joe called from down on the ground with a fresh load of shingles.

"Aw, Joe, ain't no secret 'bout it," Robbie complained, lifting the load up by a rope. He untied the bundle and carried some back to where they were working, walking along the frame. "Likely nagged her husband to death, Mrs. Brock did. Glad my Amelia is biddable. All I hears from her are

'Yes, Robbie, oh, Robbie, yes, yes, oh yes!'" The young man grinned and laughed at his crude joke.

John dropped the shingle and hammer and rose to his full height. Even tilted on the roof of the cottage, balancing on the frame, he was hard to ignore. He stepped closer to the young man just barely out of adolescence, using his height to maximum intimidation advantage. He spoke softly. "Listen well, boy. I don't want to hear no disrespect of Mrs. Brock or any other woman, you get me? I'm not keen on ending my retirement on the likes of you."

Robbie bent his head back to look at John's serious face. His face paled and he visibly swallowed. "Sorry, mate, I didn't know she was your woman."

John shook his head in disgust. "Didn't your mother teach you no manners?"

"Excuse me, gentlemen!"

Mrs. Brock's voice interrupted them and they all turned to see her walking across the yard with Timothy and Alan carrying tankards and a tray laden with food. She called up as they moved closer. "It is nearing time for luncheon and I thought you might be hungry."

John turned back to Robbie and said with a growl, "Would a fishwife or hedgehog do that?" He made his way to the ladder and climbed down, Robbie following him. He met Mrs. Brock as she was nearing the cottage and took the food tray from her. "My thanks. We were just talking about taking a break."

She gave him a strange look, but he ignored it and set the tray on a nearby log. Joe and Robbie made their way over to the food, but when Robbie reached to take a tankard from

Timothy, John pushed him away. "You're last," he muttered with a glower. "When we're done, you can eat. And thank the lady for her consideration in bringing your ungrateful ass food."

"Yer joking!" the boy exclaimed.

John glared in answer and Robbie shrank down, shuffling away from the tray. He muttered what passed for a thanks.

John took a long drink from his tankard and felt her move to his elbow. "What was that about?" she asked quietly.

He wiped his mouth with his sleeve. "Nothing. Just a boy growing up."

"You will inform me if there are any problems, correct?"

"Of course."

Her fingers lightly touched his elbow. John stilled, his senses honing in on the light pressure. He turned his head to look at her, his body following suit when his gaze met her mahogany eyes. They had the strange effect of both calming and exciting him, to be the recipient of her focused attention.

She spoke, keeping her voice at a discreet level, well aware of Joe and Robbie sitting not too far away against the wall of the cottage. "I want to thank you, Mr. Taylor, for seeing to my cottage."

He felt a surge of pleasure at her thanks, but tried to dismiss her gratitude. "It is part of our arrangement and no bother. I enjoy this type of work. Gets the kinks out and all that."

"Nevertheless, I appreciate it. This is something I do not have the skills to see to myself and must then depend on others."

He grinned at the disgruntled look on her face. "Poor

Mrs. Brock," he teased. "Forced to depend on the kindness of others." She lowered her brow, creating creases along her forehead. She opened her mouth to speak, but he forestalled her by running his thumb along those creases, smoothing them out.

He did not know why he did it. It was more automatic than anything. Under his thumb, her skin was smooth and soft, its creaminess contrasting with his own tanned skin. His eyes narrowed in on where his thumb came in contact with her forehead, focusing in on the spot. He rubbed her forehead a few times before trailing his thumb down to her cheek, learning the texture of that skin as well until he was caressing her chin with his thick digit.

Mrs. Brock's eyes had widened when he touched her forehead, stared at him unblinkingly as his thumb traversed her cheek. Now her mouth gaped open slightly and her shoulders rose and fell with her breathing. Her tongue darted out, licking her lips and his eyes were riveted by the sight of it. When not pressed into a thin line, her mouth was pale pink, nicely shaped with her lower lip more lush than the top and the small bow along the top lip just large enough to catch a man's attention.

But John's attention was currently on that lush lower lip. It begged him to kiss it, draw it into his mouth to nibble and suck. Heat flooded his body at the thought of closing the small distance between them and doing just that. Based on the look on her face and her breathing, Mrs. Brock would welcome his kiss at the very least. He shifted, preparing to do just that.

A clatter broke the spell. John dropped his hand and

turned to look at Joe teaching Timothy and Alan about the
shingles, the boys throwing them onto the growing pile to be
pulled up to the roof. Robbie had moved to the shade of a tree
and was stretched out for a nap, his cap covering his face.

The sound of skirts moving reached his ears and John had
to watch Mrs. Brock return to the inn. She strode quickly and
did not glance back over her shoulder. He ducked his head
ruefully, his body pricking with want. He had to content
himself with watching her hips sway back and forth until he
couldn't see her anymore.

## CHAPTER SEVEN

---

Giant Johnny stuck his head into the office. "Come with me."

Louisa glanced up from the accounts. "What for?"

He sighed. "Just come. I only have a few minutes. Please," he added.

With a frown, she stood and followed him out through the noisy kitchen towards her cottage. The carpenters had finished for the day, the sun already beginning to set. "What is it, Mr. Taylor? Dinner patrons will be arriving shortly. I still help to prepare and serve meals, as you well know."

"First off, I think being partners means we can address each other by our Christian names. John is mine."

"I know what your name is. And I disagree, as the use of our Christian names implies an intimacy that does not belong in a business partnership."

"Doesn't it?"

"No."

"What about all those husband-and-wife partnerships? We are hardly the only couple to run an inn together."

Louisa lifted her chin. "You have hit upon the difference. We are not married."

"No, we are not." He had stopped next to the ladder up to the roof and looked at her, his dark eyes smoldering. She knew what that look was for and it sent a wave of heat directly to her womb. Good Lord, it had been some time since she had had such a reaction to a man. She couldn't remember it being so powerful.

She crossed her arms over her chest, hoping to hide how her nipples had tightened. "Why did you bring me here? Is there something the matter with my cottage?"

Giant Johnny shook his head. "Nothing is the matter. I just thought to show you something."

"What is it?"

"How to shingle a roof." He gestured to the ladder. "Up you go."

Her eyes widened and she felt her jaw drop. She just stared at him for a moment before regaining her wits. "I beg your pardon?"

He grinned at her, making her stomach tighten. "You looked so unhappy to not be able to repair your own roof. I thought you might like to learn the basics, at least."

Louisa glanced warily at the ladder. "You expect me to climb that thing in a dress?"

"I would lend you some of my trousers, but I doubt they would be your size. Even with a belt, they would be so big on you they would be a danger." He leaned into her with a cheeky grin. "I won't look if you don't want me to."

Her face reddened and she pressed her lips into a thin line. "You will proceed before me," she stated.

"Have you climbed a ladder before?"

She sniffed. In stables, yes, but not for many years. "How difficult can it be?"

"The ladder wobbles."

"Thank you for the warning. I am sure that I will be fine, if it holds you. Now if you please." She nodded at the ladder and waited.

With a shrug, he scaled the ladder until he could swing up onto the roof. He leaned over to watch her ascent. Pressing her lips together, she held her skirts up by one hand and with the other clasped the wood of the ladder. Leaning in to compensate for her one-handed rise, she climbed up rung by rung, using the heels of her shoes to secure herself more firmly to the ladder. When she reached the top, he offered her his hand, which she refused until she noticed that half the roof was missing. Deciding the loss of pride was preferable to the loss of her life, she took it.

When his fingers encircled hers, the sensations from earlier that day came rushing back. His calloused skin scraped against hers, making all of her nerves stand at attention, focused on him. Thoughts of how his hands would feel against her belly, her breasts, her thighs and she felt a tingle tease her core.

He didn't release her hand, instead pulled her closer to him, his arm sliding around her waist. "Be careful."

"I am fine," she said, but didn't pull away, not when his hand felt so nice against her hip.

"Allow me this," he murmured in her ear. "It is dangerous up here for even the most sure-footed of men."

She nodded, still focused on the heat coming from his side

and seeping into her body. A part of her mind whispered that she should move away, that she did not need to lean against him so, but the instinct to survive had her relishing his support.

Giant Johnny gestured with his free hand, covering the whole roof and pointing at the exposed wood. "We had to reframe most of the roof. The wood was rotten and you would have found yourself with one big hole, hopefully one that didn't fall on your head."

"I know what happens to rotten wood." She found her voice again.

He ignored her and continued explaining their progress on the roof to her, carefully maneuvering her toward where shingles had already been laid, watching to see that she stepped carefully along the exposed wood and providing her support.

He glanced down at her and smiled. John released her to pick up a hammer and held it out to her. "Want to shingle your roof?"

Louisa stared at him. He could not be serious? She had never shingled a roof before. It was a task reserved for m—

On that thought, she took the offered tool and lifted her chin. "Tell me what to do."

A grin covered his face and he led her to the laid shingles, walking onto the roof. She followed, holding her skirts in one hand, stepping cautiously. She eyed him walking confidently and forced herself to relax. If the wood supported his weight and size, it would do the same for her. Except that statement was something her logical mind failed to communicate fully to her still tense body. A part of her wished he still held on to her hand. *Just for the support,* she told herself.

He bent down and picked up a shingle. He knelt down and showed her the layering. "When it rains, you want the water to be able to run unobstructed down the roof. By layering the shingles, it keeps the water from entering the house, but if the first layer was at the peak—"

"The water would pool in the ridges instead of flowing down," Louisa interrupted. "Yes, I see. That is quite logical."

He grinned at her. "Yes, we men are known for our logic."

She glared at him. "Do you really want me to respond to that?" She belatedly recognized the tease.

The grin remained. "The shingles are to be nailed down, like so." He crouched, overlapped the new shingle over the top half of the already placed one and put a nail in each of the four corners, ensuring they entered both wood and shingle. "Easy as that."

She eyed the shingles uneasily and glanced down at her green dress. She would have to be careful if she did not want it ruined. She hunched down beside him and took four nails from the nearby bag. He handed her a shingle, which she adjusted to overlap as he had. Nailing it in was challenging, as she did not want to hit her fingers. But when it was done, she looked up at him with a smile. "Easy as that."

They continued that way, John handing her the shingles to nail in. Their progress was slower than it had been with Robbie and Joe, but he did not mind the view of her crouching on the roof and swinging a hammer.

It was oddly arousing, watching her confidence with the task increase. He gave a brief prayer of thanks that she hadn't helped them during the day; it would have been difficult to explain the allure of a hammer.

Their pace picked up. "Not so hard, is it?" he said after several minutes.

"So easy even a woman could do it, is that what you are saying?"

"Easy, don't get all prickly." He spread more tar around. "It was just a comment. I happen to like conversation."

"We can converse about the inn. I had some thoughts about the drink selection."

"What about it?"

"We could purchase a variety of alcohols and different qualities as well."

He glanced at her and checked her placement of the new shingle. "Make sure you cover as much of the laid shingle as possible. Don't leave any spaces. What would having different drinks accomplish?"

She fixed the mistakes he indicated. "It would create an exclusivity. We could charge more for the higher-quality drinks. The color of money is all the same, so anyone with coin could purchase it, but the chances of a farmer being able to afford a dram of fine-quality Scotch is rare. It would cater to a higher class of client and keep the inn from being a gin-and-ale-only establishment."

"You have thought this through."

Louisa turned her head so he wouldn't see her blush with pleasure at his comment. "Yes. We could even do the same with the gin and ale. Have different brands and qualities, charging more for the good stuff."

The bare wood was now out of reach. John moved the nail bag and some shingles over and Louisa followed, hobbling over in her hunched position.

"You might be more comfortable if you kneel." He indicated his stance.

She shot him a look that said *Don't be foolish.* "I have no wish to ruin my dress."

John threw his head back and laughed. "That is such a womanly thing to say."

She glared at him. "I am a woman, in case you have failed to notice."

"Aye, that is one thing I noticed about you straightaway." His voice dropped and when she looked up at him, his eyes had that smolder in them again. Of course her body responded with an ache between her thighs accompanied by a rush of wet heat. He continued. "Getting a little dirty can be pleasurable."

She turned her attention back to the tar. "There is no excuse for not taking care of one's clothing, be they male or female. A little caution is a more affordable expense than new clothing." She deliberately misunderstood his innuendo.

"I would buy you a new dress."

"No, you would not."

He fell silent at her quick response and Louisa could feel him looking at her. She kept her attention on the task. When he resumed his painting and spoke, it was something she was not expecting. "Did your husband refuse you new clothes?"

She froze, panic rising up in her. *Dammit.* She had never fully developed the story of her marriage, having never stayed in one place long enough for people to inquire about it. Her mind raced, trying to construct a plausible story.

At her silence, he continued speaking. "I did not mean to distress you by mentioning him. You have never mentioned him, so I am curious. But I would buy you new clothes; I don't think I would be able to refuse you, were you mine."

She cleared her throat, focusing on one part of his statement and keeping her eyes on her task. "That is a foolish thing to say. One should not make needless purchases simply because another has stated a desire for it. There are other factors to consider."

"Like finances."

"Yes. And need. For instance, if I already had ten dresses, I would hardly need another one, correct?"

"Do you have ten dresses?" The tease was back in his voice. She was beginning to recognize it.

"That is not the point."

"Just like how the pot was not the point. Do you ever speak directly to the point, or is the extent of your conversation oblique allusions?"

"Oblique allusions? That is quite fancy coming from a prizefighter."

"I have been known to read a book or two." He handed her another shingle. "So if you had ten dresses, and the new one you wanted was in a new color, you would not buy it?"

"Not if I could not afford it. And did not need it."

"Does any woman need ten dresses?"

"It has been many years since I needed or desired more than ten dresses."

"Were you a governess at one time? You wear a lot of dull colors, green and gray and brown."

"Can I not simply like them?"

He chuckled. "Not in my experience with women."

Her hammering paused and John felt he was stepping into

unwelcome territory. "You are very inquisitive about my past," she said.

"We have worked side by side for nearly a month now, Mrs. Brock, two of those weeks as partners. Shouldn't we know something about each other?"

"Can we not keep our relationship professional?" While she allowed her attraction to him, Louisa did not want him to know too much about her. It would raise awkward questions.

"I knew things about my manager's personal life and no one doubted our professionalism. You won't even let me use your Christian name."

She took another shingle from him and secured it to the roof. She did so with four more shingles before she spoke again. "I was a governess once. It did not last."

"Was that when you married?"

It was close enough to the truth. She did not invent her late husband until after she left Ridgestone. "Yes."

"What was his name?"

She shot him a look. "Mr. Brock."

His look in turn was exasperated. "My late wife's name was Amanda."

That made her stop working. "You were married?"

"Yes. She died seven years ago in childbirth."

Louisa sat back on her heels and looked him directly in the eyes. "I am sorry to hear that."

John shrugged. "We married because I got her with child. By the time of the birth, we had already acknowledged that we would not suit. She wanted to be with the champion at all times and not the everyday man. I wanted a wife who liked it when I stayed home. More than that, though, I did not want any child of mine to be born a bastard."

"The child died, I assume." At least there was none around calling him Father.

He nodded, appreciating her matter-of-fact tone. "That is what I mourned most."

They stayed silent for several minutes, kneeling on the roof, not quite looking at each other. John had not realized before the comfort of shared silence, how it could soothe. Finally, she took a deep breath, her shoulders rising and falling, and lifted her chin.

"My name is Louisa."

He looked at her, her raised chin and lips in a firm line. A smile tugged at his lips. "Is that a pity gift?"

She glanced at him. "Whatever do you mean?"

"You feel pity for me, so you are allowing me the use of your name. You're tossing me crumbs, hoping it will make me feel better."

Her face showed her exasperation. "You don't have to use it if you don't wish to. Hand me a shingle." She held out her hand.

He held one out to her, not releasing it when she would have laid it on the roof. "It is my pleasure . . . Louisa."

Was that a blush? He could not quite tell in the fading light. John chuckled as she hammered in the nail. "Let's hurry it up, Louisa. The light is fading, Louisa. It will be time for dinner soon, Louisa. Maisie needs help preparing the meals, Louisa. I will tend the pub with Packard tonight, Louisa."

"Oh, would you just stop already!"

His laughter echoed over the yard.

## CHAPTER EIGHT

*Late October, Ridgestone Manor*

Jacob stepped out of the carriage to see Claire, Bonnie and Sara all standing in the drive. Even in the twilight, he could see the anxious look on their faces. Claire pulled her shawl tighter when Stephen and Nathan exited the carriage.

Without Louisa. Their disappointment was palpable.

Grooms and footmen were already seeing to the luggage and Jacob strode to the waiting women. He kissed Claire on the cheek and put his hand on her growing belly. "You should not be outside in such cold weather, sweetheart. Not with just a shawl."

"You didn't have any success?" Bonnie asked.

Sir Stephen shook his head, his face grim. "I must echo Jacob's sentiment, wife. You must take care."

Bonnie glared at him, even as she accepted his embrace, angling her body to accommodate her large stomach. "I cannot think of such things at this time."

"You are nearing your time," her husband pointed out. "You will not have a choice regarding what to think about. Where are the boys?"

"In the nursery, preparing for bed. I was about to go lumbering up when we received word of the carriage. You would not believe how difficult it is to carry all this around." She rubbed her stomach.

"I will accompany you." Stephen left his arm around Bonnie, supporting her as she walked.

Sara stood with Nathan's hand entwined around hers. "You must all be hungry. I will see if Cook has something warm for you."

She moved to do that, but Nathan tightened his grip on her. "Send a maid." He nodded at Greaves, the butler, to do so. "I wish to not have my fiancée run away just as I arrive."

"Is the fire in the drawing room lit?" Jacob asked.

Claire nodded and linked her arm around him, bringing their bodies close as she led them inside. "It is nice and toasty tonight."

"Your leg is paining you?" Sara asked as Nathan leaned on his cane more after divesting his cloak.

He grimaced. "Just the cramped coach ride. And it is going to snow soon, or so my leg tells me. I will be fine . . ." He leaned in and whispered the rest of his sentence in her ear that had her face turning scarlet.

"I missed you too," she said softly, fingering the lapels of his coat. "I just wish you had returned with Louisa."

"As do I. I do not relish leaving you behind as I continue on to Windent."

Her blush did not lessen. "I am sure we can have a room prepared for you tonight. Claire and Bonnie would serve as chaperones."

Nathan flashed a grin at her. "They are worse than we are. You hear how they encourage us."

Sara stopped just outside the drawing room and looked up at him with worry lining her face. "Nathan, I know I said I wished to postpone our wedding until Louisa was found. And—and I thank you for your patience. But if you wish—I mean, if you need—want to, it's not that import—we could—"

He placed a finger over her mouth. "Stop. We will wait. There is no issue. The purpose of the wedding is to tell the world what we already know: You are mine and I am yours. If your friend is not there, then not all the important people will know."

Relief flooded through her and she pressed her forehead to his chest. "I am so concerned for her. It has been four months and we still have heard nothing. I feel as though we drove her away, you and I, with what we did. This is a punishment."

He rubbed her back. "That is foolish thinking. Come into the drawing room and hear our news. It is not encouraging, but the good side of it is that we still have not uncovered anything to indicate she is not enjoying good health. We will resume our search next week once we hear from some inquiries we made."

He led her into the drawing room to join their friends.

"Pull your hat down more," Louisa whispered. "We don't want to be recognized."

"I would think my size is revealing enough," John muttered, obediently tugging his brown cap down as much as possible to hide his bald head. The fake mustache she gave him itched like the devil, but he was glad to have won in not wearing a wig to match it.

She adjusted his clothing, standing so close to him that he could smell the soap she used. Lemon. Tart, just like her, but able to be sweetened with the right ingredients. She said, "I ensured the clothing was purposely large, even on you, to give the impression that you are smaller than you actually are. As I am dressed as your ladybird, I think our disguises are foolproof."

He glanced down her body. "Your right breast is falling down."

"Oh good Lord." He watched in fascination as her hand disappeared down into her bosom to adjust whatever it was she put in her dress to increase the size. The dress itself was a dark blue with lace trim along the hems and bosom and clung to her curves. Her blond hair was arranged in artful disarray, giving the impression of just rising from bed—or coming from a back-alley tup. Her face was heavily adorned with rouge and other coloring, a mole patch placed jauntily below one of her eyes. Seeing her display herself in such a manner, John had to fight the urge to hide her under his coat or, better yet, drag her back to the cart and return to the Beefy Buzzard.

"I thought we were supposed to be making ourselves unremarkable. That"—he indicated her bosom—"is guaranteed to catch every man's interest."

Louisa rolled her eyes. "Yes, but they will not be looking at my face, will they?"

He had to give her that. "Yea gods, she will be the death of me," he said under his breath. Louder, "Remind me again why we can't just go into the Rose and Crown all normal like."

She gave an impatient huff. "They are our closest competition for a pub. They don't offer rooms, so we have the advantage there. But from what I have heard, their ale is superior. I want to find out what they serve. I told you I suspect our brewer is cheating us. Perhaps we can discover something here."

"But why must we resort to subterfuge? Why can we not just go in as though we are ordinary customers?"

"Because," she said, as though he were a young child, "we are not ordinary customers. What do you think would happen if word got out that the proprietors of the Beefy Buzzard were frequenting another pub?"

"That we needed a diversion?"

"No, that the quality of our inn is so low we won't even partake there."

He frowned. "You don't drink ale. How do you know it's bad?"

"Because I serve it. I hear the men making comments about it. And they drink it more slowly the more sober they are."

"Every man drinks more slowly when he is sober, regardless of the drink."

"And I see you grimace into your pint every time."

True, he did that. John heaved a big sigh. "Let's get this over with then." He wrapped his arm around her waist and held her close, enjoying the feeling of her soft curves molding into his side.

"I think this part is unnecessary," she protested.

"No one will believe you are my ladybird if I don't hold you like this," he pointed out. "You are too beautiful not to be touched."

She fought to ignore the blossom of pleasure in her chest

at his compliment. "Remember to hunch, make yourself shorter."

If she didn't know better, Louisa would have sworn he just huffed like a little girl. They approached The Rose and Crown, the chatter and laughter already spilling out into the street. John swung open the door and led her in, quickly scanning for a table where they could sit as unobtrusively as possible. Finding one, he pushed through the crowd, holding her close to his side. He told himself it was for her protection, but he knew better.

As they walked, he noted several men turning their way. But, as she predicted, their eyes were not on either of their faces. John felt his blood simmer with annoyance when he saw the lust in the men's eyes. One was foolish enough to grab Louisa's arm to halt their progress.

"Hullo, honeypot," the man slurred, his eyes and words directed at her bosom. "Lemme git ye a drink."

John pushed the man away, causing him to stumble and fall onto another man. "She's with me," he growled and resumed their progress through the room. When the overturned men tried to make a fuss, he discouraged them with a dark look and they went back to their own business.

When they reached the table, he sat with his back in the corner and maneuvered her onto his lap before she could get her own chair. He wasn't about to give any man in the room the impression she was still up for grabs. Having her close and learning the feel of her body was merely an added bonus.

She gave a little squawk. "I know this is unnecessary."

He held her firmly, forcing her to stay. "Ladybird, remember. Put your arm around my neck."

With furious eyes that promised retribution, she obeyed. "You must at least try to look like you're enjoying yourself, Louisa," he muttered. It's not like he enjoyed having an erection in public, but with her bottom nestled nicely against his member, it would soon be unavoidable. His thighs could easily discern the shape and softness of her buttocks and his hands ached to explore and massage the cheeks.

A serving wench approached them. "What's it to be?" She eyed Louisa up before settling her eyes on John. They held more than a hint of interest and invitation.

"Well, luv, what do ye fancy?" John asked Louisa, patting her hip possessively.

She didn't even notice the pat on her hip, so focused was she on the wench's interest in the man underneath her. *Hmph, two can play at that game.* "Anythin' ye want, Johnny," she purred in his ear, caressing his chest. She glanced at the serving wench, the challenge clear in her eyes as any good ladybird would do.

"Two pints of yer best 'n a nibbles board. 'N quick too," he ordered.

"One pint," Louisa corrected him. She ran a finger down his cheek to under his chin, following his beard to make him turn his face toward her. She leaned in closer to him and gave him a sultry smile, lowering her eyelids seductively. "We kin share."

John didn't look at the wench. "One pint," he amended. The girl turned away with a twirl of her skirts and disappeared into the crowd. He swallowed, his mouth dry as she looked at him with that hooded seductiveness.

She immediately leaned back, peering around the room.

"It's a smaller space than ours, but it has the same number of tables. But that makes it more cramped."

*How in blessed Mary's name can she think of business right now?* John was struggling to keep his physical awareness of her under control. "There's a private dining room down that hallway." He used his nose to push her gaze in the direction he meant, using the moment to inhale her tasty scent again. All he could seem to think about was how her mouth would taste.

"Hm, I wonder how often it is used," she said absently. "We are too far from Grompton for the town to use it." Did she notice she was still caressing his chest? The small circles her fingers made burned through his waistcoat and shirt and onto his skin.

"But they do have an assembly room above stairs," he pointed out. He wondered how she would look twirling down a dance line with him.

"Yes, that is an advantage of theirs. I wonder what the cost would be to add one."

"I disagree that we should have one. There is no space, not unless we eliminate the rooms, which would be a larger source of revenue than an assembly room that is only occasionally used."

She grimaced and tilted her chin to the side. "You are right about the revenue. But we can discuss it again in the future. They don't have as much light as we do. It's easier to hide the uncleanliness." She wiped the table with her finger to prove her point.

"But sometimes people prefer an atmosphere with less light," he said. The corner they were in was decently dark and

John knew that he could fondle her without being seen. The thought shot straight to his cock and he shifted his hand from her hip up her rib cage until his thumb was nestled under her breast.

Louisa looked at him, her lips pressed together in displeasure. "None of that, thank you very much." Her words belied her interest. Sitting on his lap, she could not help but be aware of the solid body beneath her. Her experience was with well built, but slender footmen, and she could feel the full-bodied strength of the man she was sitting on. He was big, but any doubt she had in regard to his muscles was now banished. She had to fight from leaning into him and reveling in that physical power. She was thankful the padding around her breasts prevented him from noticing how tight her nipples had become.

His free hand brushed some of her hair away from her face, the long ends trailing along her bared shoulder. "Ladybird, luv. We must act our parts. I am just demonstrating the advantages of a darkened pub."

She was distracted for a moment by noticing a small faint scar that ran from the corner of his lip and disappeared under his beard. She never would have seen it if their faces weren't so close together. "This is—"

"Don't be alarmed, but I am going to kiss you now. The wench will be back at any moment and I don't want my manhood questioned." His hand slid into her hair, holding her head in place.

"You—"

John cut off her protest by pressing his lips to her and sliding his tongue into her open mouth. Yea gods but she tasted sweet. Smooth like honey, this sweetness was what he was looking for to balance out her tartness. He delved in again, eager to draw more of it out of her, eager to have her flavor fill his mouth.

He held her head firmly as he explored her, holding her to him, learning the crevices of her mouth, the contours of her lips and teeth. She held herself stiffly, but didn't attempt to push him away; he thought it may have been from the surprise of his kiss, but he didn't care, so long as she allowed him to continue in his quest. His first kiss in more years than he would publicly admit and he wanted to draw out every moment of it. With this woman, none other. John yearned to know her more, to study the nuances of her pleasure. He touched her tongue gently, coaxingly, and a thrill ran through him when she finally responded.

It likely hadn't taken long, moments really, but he felt he had been begging for her response for hours. The relief when she finally did coalesced in his bones and intensified the kiss. Her body sighed into his and she tightened her arm around his neck, letting out a small moan he felt all the way down to his cock. Her tongue lifted up to meet his, touching it fleetingly over and over as she learned its texture. Her free hand came up to settle against his cheek, her fingers lightly running along his beard down to his chin and up again, sending shivers down his neck and spine. She teased him, this woman did, teased him with her quick touches and soft lips, inflaming him beyond reason.

Their breaths mingled as they kissed and they grew bolder the longer it lasted. She drew his tongue into her mouth again and sucked on it, eliciting a deep groan from him. The wet heat of her mouth reminded him of her lower regions, of how her softness would surround him, welcoming him. His half cockstand graduated to a full one, straining against his breeches as it became hard as granite, seeking the sweet delicacy it knew existed between her legs. He shifted her bottom on his lap, positioning her to leave her no doubt about how she affected him.

His blood was racing through his body to pool at his groin. For so many years he had denied himself and knowing his self-imposed celibacy could soon end sent his mind scattering. He did not know how long she had been a widow, but her kiss clearly spoke to him of loneliness and desire. This was a woman who had been denied a pleasure her body knew and craved, and now together they would find relief.

John moved his hand from beneath her breast and closed it over the supple mound, intent on learning its shape and weight, intent on feeling how hard her nipple had become. He growled in frustration when his hand encountered a foreign material between her dress and flesh and his fingers worked at dislodging it.

She pulled away. "No," she gasped.

"What?"

"My disguise!"

Reality descended upon him as her words registered. His mind had been so addled by their kiss he had completely forgotten that they were in a public place, and for what reason. A quick glance at the room showed the wench making her way to their table with a tankard of ale and their cheese board. He captured her mouth again, keeping the kiss more innocent than their previous one, and he adjusted her disguise back into place, making it look like a fondle.

The tankard and tray thumped down onto the table and they broke their kiss, both breathing heavily. Louisa stared at him, taken by surprise at her disappointment that the kiss had ended. Her breasts ached, wanting to know his touch. She glanced at the wench who was glaring at her and felt a surge of primal satisfaction at knowing she had properly staked her claim on this man.

Not that she truly wanted to claim him. It was the principle of the matter. No woman should seek to steal a man, not when he clearly had another woman already on his lap.

Shooting the wench a victorious smile, Louisa ran her thumb over his lips, smearing away the lip rouge. She gave him a mock apology look. "Sorry abou' the rouge, Johnny. Yer just too eager."

He blinked, still dazed. She didn't blame him. Her insides were still quaking with arousal, lust pooling at her core. Swallowing, John fumbled for the payment. "What ale do ye serve here?"

The wench turned to leave. "That there's Black Duck."

"Same as we serve," Louisa murmured, her wits returning.

He lifted the ale to his nose and sniffed. "Seems about right." He took a long swallow and nodded. "That is one smooth ale. Tasty."

Louisa rummaged in her reticule and pulled out a metal flask. "Now compare it to ours."

John looked at her with incredulity. "You actually brought a flask of our ale?"

"Will you just drink it?" she whispered.

So much for the nice haze of the kiss. Shaking his head, John tilted the flask back and grimaced. "That pales in comparison," he said. He washed the disgust out of his mouth with the fresh ale.

"I knew it," Louisa said triumphantly. "We are being cheated."

"Normal people don't sound so happy about that."

She took a piece of bread and cheese and popped it into her mouth. "I am not happy at being cheated. I am happy at finding the proof that we are. Now you can talk with the brewer and straighten this situation out." She handed him some bread and cheese, which he took.

John fiddled with the food for a moment. "Louisa, about that—"

"It was just business," she interrupted him. Now that her body was once more normal, it was easy to put that kiss into perspective.

"Just business?" he echoed. Did she truly believe that? He still had a raging hard-on and she said it was business? She was a widow; there was no way in hell she was ignorant about what was poking at her ass.

She nodded. "Yes. Nothing more. I understand why you had to kiss me."

*Oh, I doubt that.*

"But we can't allow that to complicate our partnership."

"Of course not," he muttered darkly. *So much for my luck tonight.* He popped the bread and cheese into his mouth, chewing roughly to keep from making an ass of himself.

They ate in silence for several minutes, John focusing on the table and counting in his head to regain control of his body and emotions. Louisa picked up the tankard of ale and frowned into it. "What does it taste like?"

"Try it and find out," he said.

"Could we get some water? Or tea?"

He snorted at her. "At this time of night? Some ladybird you are."

She sniffed. "We both know the truth."

He shrugged. "If you would prefer tea, then I will have the wench bring some. Ale is more for men, anyway."

John raised his hand to catch the serving wench's eye, but Louisa lifted the tankard to her mouth and drank.

And drank. Without stopping. His jaw dropped as he watched her gulp it down, her throat working as she swallowed large quantities at once. As the ale disappeared, a part of him lamented that he hadn't gotten more than those few sips. Any remaining displeasure toward her disappeared with each gulp she took.

She finished with a gasp, dropping the tankard back onto the table. "That was disgusting," she proclaimed, wiping her mouth.

"You don't have to guzzle it like that," he pointed out. "You can take smaller sips."

She nodded. "I will do that next time."

"Next time?"

She nodded and stood. She stumbled a bit, her head dizzy and stomach wavering, and John grabbed her arm to steady her. *Oh good Lord.* "Next time. But not here. I'll be damned if I spend more of our hard-earned money from the Beefy Buzzard at the Rose and Crown. Take me home, Johnny."

She made it to the cart before losing the contents of her stomach.

## CHAPTER NINE

### November

Louisa left the office. "Where is Mr. Taylor?" she asked the kitchen. Her voice was clipped.

"Don't know, ma'am," Maisie said, lifting a tray of buns from one of the ovens.

Alan was stirring a pot of stew and Timothy was peeling potatoes. Both shook their heads. "I've not seen 'im in an age," Alan said. He and Timothy exchanged a glance as she turned on her heel. "I wager 'e's in trouble agin," he whispered.

"I heard that, Alan," Louisa called over her shoulder. "No wagering unless you want to be the one in trouble." The boy ducked down, stirring the stew vigorously.

She stepped out into the pub just in time to see some new arrivals enter with luggage, snow coating their boots. Glancing around, she did not see Giant Johnny anywhere, so she welcomed them and after they signed the register, sent Rose to see them upstairs to their rooms and settled.

She moved to speak with Mr. Packard at the bar, her boots sounding her determination against the floor. "Where is Mr. Taylor?"

Mr. Packard finished pulling some ale. "Last I heard he was going into the cask room for some inventory."

"Thank you." She turned on her heel and made her way down a small corridor behind the bar that led to some storage rooms. The door to the cask room was open and she could see several sconces lit once she stepped inside. His head was in a corner, floating above the casks. She moved to see down the aisle created by the untapped barrels. She looked at him, his back to her, mumbling softly as he marked things in the notebook in his hands. His spectacles were in place and he was wearing his standard trousers and shirt, his head covered by a red kerchief.

"John," she said.

He jumped, jerked out of his engrossment. "Yea gods, Louisa, you scared the bejeezus out of me."

"John," she repeated.

He turned, his brow furrowing at the tone of her voice. "What is it?" He placed the inventory book, the pencil and his spectacles on one of the casks and put his hands on his hips.

Louisa fought to control her smile. "I checked four times. All four times it was the same."

"What?"

She took a step toward him. "A profit. We made a profit last week."

He stared at her for a moment. "You are certain?"

She nodded. "Four times. I am more than certain."

"We made a profit?"

"A small one, just twenty pounds, but a profit."

His eyes widened. "Just twenty pounds?" he exclaimed.

"Just twenty pounds? Do you have any idea what we can do with that?"

She nodded. "We can buy some new dishes and cutlery or more tea sets or start the private dining room or—"

"Yea gods, woman!" he said. "Stop thinking of the inn. On twenty pounds I could rent a gig and take you to Bath for a night at the Assembly Rooms, pay for a nice hotel and still have some quid leftover."

She frowned. "That would be foolish." To spend their money on such a frivolous thing would be folly when the inn needed so much attention. She had the fleeting thought of running into some old acquaintances there. She had avoided fashionable centers for a reason.

"Foolish be damned," he said, walking toward her. "We made a profit!"

A grin replaced her frown. "We made a profit!"

He danced a little jig in front of her, looking absolutely foolish, being such a large man in a contained space. She laughed joyously and clapped her hands until he grabbed her and spun her around in quick dance steps. With a squeal, she threw her arms around his neck and he lifted her in a big hug, twirling her around the cask room.

"We made a profit," she murmured in his ear.

John stilled, holding her close to him, becoming fully aware of the woman he held in his arms. Her breasts pressed against his chest, her length running along his, her feet dangling between his legs. Her hair was soft against his cheek and smelled of the stew that had been simmering in the kitchen all day mixed with her own lemon scent. Her arms were warm around his neck, her hands gripping his shoulders with a strength her slender frame did not reveal upon observation. He pressed his nose into her neck, still smelling the stew mixed with lemon.

He could feel the stillness in her frame, feel how her nipples hardened even through the layers of fabric that separated them. John pulled his head back to look at her. Her face was flushed and the gold in her rich brown eyes shimmered with awareness. She licked her lips, staring at his mouth.

"We made a profit." His whisper was hoarse.

She met his eyes. "Yes."

John ducked his head closer, stopping with just inches between their mouths, giving her a chance to pull away. But it was she who tightened her arms around him and closed the distance, pressing their lips together.

It was a heated fusing, born out of excitement and the lust that had simmered the last several weeks. Their mouths devoured each other, their breathing rapid. She gripped his head with both hands and pushed her tongue into his mouth, tangling with his in the familiar erotic motions. He adjusted his grip on her, one arm hooking beneath her bottom to secure her body closer to his. She wrapped her legs around his and the last coherent thought to run through his mind was *Door is open*. He stumbled over and shut it loudly, fumbling with the lock, triumph rushing through him when he heard it slide into place.

He turned them back into the room, staggering around until their bodies jerked to a stop when her back met a cask. A puff of breath was forced out of her, but she did not stop kissing him, did not stop herself from dominating his mouth. Her hands tugged his kerchief off his head until her fingers gripped the bald skin, running along the sensitive surface.

John drew away slightly, slowing the kiss, teasing small moans out of her as he nibbled and sucked her bottom lip. Using the cask to support her, he lifted a hand to bury it in her hair. The strands were silk around his fingers and the sound of pins hitting the floor joined their heavy breathing and moans. He captured her mouth again, sliding into it to caress her tongue, licking and dancing together.

Louisa's head was spinning, her blood cascading from her body to between her legs, instinctively preparing for the man who was currently kissing her senseless. She moaned as he stroked her tongue with his, the action sending tingles down her spine. His beard scraped her chin with the deep kiss, the prickly hair sending sensations swirling from her mouth and down her neck. Her body recognized the hard discomfort of the cask at her back, but all of her attention was focused on the man at her front.

Her nipples were painfully tight, her breasts aching for attention. As if he could read her mind, his hand left her hair and tugged down her bodice and he palmed one of her breasts when they sprang free. Pleasure made her head tilt back, breaking the kiss. Her breath came in gasps as he molded and kneaded the round flesh, his coarse skin causing slight abrasions and increasing her delight. It had been over two years since her last affair and she had not realized how much she had missed the feeling of a man's hand on her.

He kissed his way to her neck, his back hunching over and forcing a separation from hers. She did not appreciate that and grasped his head to bring it back up. She claimed his mouth, invading it, and tangled their tongues together again. Her hands fell down to her skirts and pulled them up to her waist, freeing her legs to properly wrap around his waist.

John was beyond thinking. All he knew was the tantalizing woman in his arms was opening up to him and he needed no encouragement to take what she was offering. He stepped in between her legs, grinding his granite-hard cockstand against her. Being this close to her intoxicated him. He reached down to her knee and followed her leg up underneath her skirts and cupped her mound, feeling her wet heat throb from under her unmentionables. A growl of frustration rose up in him. He wanted—he needed to be closer to her. He gripped the material separating his fingers from her core and pulled, the sound of tearing material reaching his triumphant ears.

He stroked her as he thrust his tongue into her mouth, mimicking the action he knew was only moments away. His blood pounded through him, each throb making his erection harder and more desperate to settle into her heat. Her wet arousal coated his fingers, allowing them to slide along her outer lips before he pushed one into her.

She gasped against his kiss, her arms gripping his shoulder and her legs tightening around his waist. As he moved his finger in and out, she ground her hips against his hand, unable to keep herself from moving. He pushed a second finger into her and rubbed her clit with his thumb, feeling her inner muscles tighten around his fingers. He had not been mistaken—this woman was a firecracker in his arms.

She broke the kiss and sank her teeth into his shoulder, small moans and gasps heating his skin and shirt. Louisa was overcome with a desperation to have him inside her, filling her completely. She reached down and her fingers frantically worked at the buttons of his falls. When they were done, she freed his cock and whispered the hot command.

"Now, Johnny."

Without delay, his fingers left her and his hands gripped her hips, holding her in place. He pressed closer to her, the head of his penis nudging at her entrance. Deeply kissing her, he thrust inside. *Yea gods*. Seven years and how many weeks of this woman teasing him and he was finally inside her, her smooth muscles encasing him, her wetness welcoming him in.

His mind emptied of everything, his entire being focused on where the silky heat surrounded him. He couldn't hold back. One hand grasped the cask above her head to give himself more leverage as he thrust, feeling his cock slide in and out with long-denied lust and vigor. Her nails bit through the linen of his shirt and into the skin of his back and once more she was biting his shoulder, the soft keening escaping her spurring him on. He grunted with each thrust, pushing harder and harder into her, wanting to fill her as much as he possibly could. Her ankles were locked around his waist, keeping him close and digging a heel into the small of his back. Her muscles squeezed him tight each time he pulled out as though trying to keep him inside. The sound of him sliding against her juices filled the room, accompanying the dull thud of their clothing crashing together.

A small part of him registered how her grip around him tightened and her shudder as she gasped out her release, her inner muscles contracting around him. He followed her scant seconds later, his seed flooding into her. His climax rushed through him, forcing out grunts from deep inside him, and he slowed his thrusts, bringing their coupling to an end.

Faint laughter and conversation floated down the corridor and snuck into the room, becoming more audible as their breathing and hearts slowed. John pressed his forehead to hers as he caught his breath, dropping soft, slow kisses on her lips and cheeks.

Her grip on him relaxed. Legs releasing his waist, she gently nudged his chest. He had no choice but to step away, his cock sliding out of her. John gave her a quizzical look, but she adjusted her dress and retrieved her hairpins from the floor without looking at him. Following her lead reluctantly, he tucked himself back into his falls and picked up his kerchief, long having fallen to the floor. Without asking her permission, he moved back to her and lifted her skirts.

"Stop—" she exclaimed with surprise and tried to push his hands away.

He pressed the kerchief to her core, cleaning up their lovemaking. "Allow me this," he said. "I would not have you uncomfortable or embarrassed."

Louisa stood awkwardly, her legs pushed slightly apart as he tended to her, her hands hidden in her raised skirts. She didn't know what to do or where to look, so she directed her gaze to the row of casks beside her. Somehow having him clean her up was more intimate than what they had just done. The material was soft against her sore flesh and the way he pushed against it was soothing.

When he was finished, he stuffed his kerchief into a pocket and tucked some of her hair behind her ear. At that, she brushed around him and left the cask room, hurrying back toward the office. She pushed through the growing crowd of the pub and into the kitchen, distractedly noting how smoothly things were running. Timothy was still peeling potatoes, Alan now helping him, telling her that it had not been all that long since she had last been in here.

"Did you find 'im, Mrs. Brock?"

She pulled up short at the sound of her name and blinked at Maisie. "I beg your pardon?"

The cook scooped stew into two bowls and placed them on a tray already laden with buns. Rose, one of the serving maids, took the tray out into the pub. "Mr. Taylor. Did you find 'im?"

"Oh. Yes. I did." She continued to the office and closed the door, shutting out the kitchen and noise. Rubbing her forehead, she leaned against the door and the reality of what had just transpired hit her.

*Well, that was unexpected.*

## CHAPTER TEN

Louisa poured herself another glass of wine and sat back in the chair, staring out her window into the darkness. She had moved into her cottage shortly after completion of the roof; her chamber was still the only habitable room, but it was all hers and it afforded her the privacy she craved. She had moved a table and chair from other rooms to provide more functionality and was pleased with the result.

She took a long sip of the wine she had pilfered from the inn, enjoying how it slid down her throat. She would leave Giant Johnny a note in the morning so he could balance his inventory. The inn was dark across the yard, the pub long since closed and all the guests abed, the moonlight casting shadows over the property. Only half the rooms were occupied tonight, but it was a great improvement from a few weeks ago. One of the rooms was a repeat customer, a fact that pleased her—repeat customers would tell their peers about their favorite places to stay.

She sighed, annoyed at how sleep would not come. She had prepared for bed several hours before, intending to rise early to help Maisie begin the day in the kitchen, but sleep still eluded her. And the wine was not relaxing her as she had hoped and she did not like the reason why. She glared at his bedroom window at the bottom corner of the inn, annoyed that he clearly had no issues with his sleep.

Three days had passed since she had allowed Giant Johnny to tup her in the cask room. The memory had her squirming slightly in her chair, her nerves aching for his attention again. They had not spoken of it or of much at all, and that was how she preferred it.

He was so different than her footmen. Those two she had chosen after careful deliberation, a planned pursuit—even though they thought they had been the pursuers—and detailed expectations. She did not regret her selections or the loss of her virtue; since leaving her family home, she had not felt so bound by society's strictures as she used to. It was her choice who she gave her body to, her choice alone, and she would not be made ashamed of it.

Yet she was not foolish about it either. Posing as a widow had been a conscious decision, as had her footmen selections. Both had been slender, capable and discreet, neither having expectations beyond their brief liaisons; she would not be caught in the same situation Claire had been. She had even approached a midwife for information on preventing conception and obtained several sheaths, insisting on their use. Both footmen had easily acquiesced to her requirements.

But Giant Johnny was so different. Large and brawny, they had had sex in the cask room of all places instead of a quietly planned rendezvous in her room. No sheath had been used, as the whole thing had been entirely unexpected. *Unplanned,* she rephrased her thought. Her attraction to him was not a surprise, but she had not yet determined her course of action in approaching him about it. She had some doubts whether or not he would agree to her conditions—he was so much *more* than the footmen had been—but she was confident that in the end he would capitulate. After all, he was a man and she knew without arrogance that she was an attractive woman.

That was all some men needed. Or desired.

Any initial hesitations she had had over his size had been banished with the cask room. As a rule, she avoided larger men, but she had to admit that he had never used his size to intimidate or impose upon her. Her skin began to tingle and she closed her eyes, allowing the memory of being completely supported by his strength and the power of his thrusts to wash over her. Tilting her head to the side, she imagined the scrape of his beard as he kissed her neck and the feel of his hand as it cupped her mound. Her breathing grew agitated and she licked her dry lips as arousal began to take over her body.

Louisa was about to lift the hem of her nightshirt to see to herself when Giant Johnny's face was replaced by that of Lord Darleigh, his young face twisted with angry lust.

Her eyes flew open and she gripped the wine glass tightly. It had been so long since he had invaded her mind that this appearance took her by surprise. It was a malicious joke of God that while she had survived, his attack would be revisited upon her time and again in her memory. An acquaintance of her brother's, he had been so congenial to her on the occasions they had met, and in her innocence, she had not suspected anything sinister behind the glances he would send her. Until she had to defend herself against him and flee the house, leaving him bleeding to death on the library hearth.

She hadn't returned or spoken to any of her family or friends since that day six years earlier. She had realized that she needed to take control of her own life and depend on no one.

It had been a struggle. Changing her name, finding a position in service, earning her own keep, not speaking of her past—everything she did was on her own and for her survival. There had been a few moments of caution, when her old life threatened to catch up with her new, but she managed to evade them and move on. The closest had been two years ago when one of her brother's friends had attended a house party where she was working as a governess. He hadn't quite recognized her, had accepted her story at face value—it was easy to fool people with a change in wardrobe, lack of cosmetics and a convincing story. He had tried to force his attentions on her as well at that party, but at least this time she was better prepared to defend herself.

It was then she came up with the idea of creating a private school with her friends and convinced them to join her, creating the Governess Club. The plan had gone well and had been well on its way of accomplishing exactly what she wanted— independence and control. But then Claire had gotten married, followed by Bonnie. That had not been in the plan.

The final straw was Sara, the one she thought she could rely on to remain constant. It was likely uncharitable of her, but Louisa never thought Sara would attract the interest of a man; she was too meek and mild to draw any of that sort of attention. She had had visions of the two of them becoming spinsters together, working and becoming successful with the Club until they retired together to a nice cottage somewhere warm. She had always wanted to see the Continent and Portugal had a nice sound to it. But then Mr. Pomeroy had proposed, the final rock that had shattered her dreams of independence.

There was no possible chance of the Governess Club surviving, not with three of the members married and one of those living so far away. Even if Claire and Sara declared themselves committed to the club, the nature of marriage would soon change that. Their husbands would demand more and more of their time, children would come along and require their attention—in short, the club would have died a slow, agonizing death and she was damned if she would remain to watch it.

So she left. At Sara's wedding to Mr. Pomeroy, Louisa slipped out of the church during the vows and made her way to the coaching inn. She had it timed perfectly and had boarded the mail coach just as Mr. and Mrs. Pomeroy would be introduced to the world.

And she hadn't looked back. Her next three months had been spent moving from place to place, introducing herself with variations of her name, often even sneaking into stables and shacks to avoid registering at public inns. It wasn't until she entered the Beefy Buzzard that she had been tempted to remain. Giant Johnny's offer had given her a reason to hope once more that she would be able to realize her dream.

Louisa drained her wine glass, attempting to wash away the vision of Lord Darleigh. Her hand shook as she placed her glass back on the table, a heavy ball gathering in her stomach.

Taking deep breaths, she tried to calm down by reminding herself that no authorities had caught up with her yet. All she had to do was continue in her ruse and she would be fine.

She gazed back out of the window, desperate for something to focus on, something to distract her from her memories. She was about to pour herself another glass of wine when movement in the yard caught her eye. The kitchen door had opened and someone left the inn. Leaning forward, she squinted to get a better look.

His size was unmistakable, even if his features were too shadowed to see. John moved across the yard toward the stable, his footsteps sure and confident. Nothing deterred him, his focus on his destination clear. At the stable door, he paused to light a lantern and disappeared inside, the light disappearing the farther into the building he went.

Why was he going there at this time of night? Was it an illicit rendezvous? Her gut churned at how he could roger her in the cask room one day and then meet another in the stable. Such was the nature of men.

Her mind controlled itself after a moment down that path. Over the past months, she had seen no indication that he was involved with any woman, herself excepted. It could be that he was the most discreet man alive, or there could be another reason for his late-night visit to the stable. She wondered if one of the guests had requested something or he had heard a commotion.

The thought of him putting himself in danger did not sit well with her. He may be a foolish man, but he was her surest way to independence and she did not want anything to risk that. If she went to the stable, she could help him with any possible trouble there might be. If it had merely been a guest requesting something, well, as a partner in the inn, she had a right and a duty to know everything that went on there.

With that thought, she tightened her wrapper around herself and slid her feet into her boots. She was going to the stable.

Louisa slowed as she approached the stable. She had not brought a lantern, having none in her cottage and not wanting to alert any potential criminals to her arrival. As she drew near, the sound of something—or someone!—being punched reached her ears. She froze, the sound continuing. Who was being beaten? John? He was a big man, but even he could be overpowered by numbers, weapons or even taken by surprise. *Blast*, she should have thought this through better and brought some sort of weapon. All that wine had muddled her head.

*At least it's not an illicit affair*, a small voice in her head informed her. Ignoring the relief that statement brought, she pressed herself against the wall and edged her way toward the open door. Twisting her head, she darted a quick look inside before retreating to the safety of the dark night. No one had been in the aisle, the light coming from one of the smaller stalls in the back. She chanced a longer look. Shadows on the wall clearly showed someone punching, but the distortion of light and shadow made it difficult to determine who. The sound continued, no cessation indicated. Whoever was getting beaten must already be unconscious, for no grunts or moans filled the stable.

She crept in, crouching below the stable walls to avoid being seen. Only about half the stalls were in use and all the horses were calm, something that appeared odd to her. Wouldn't they be more agitated if a fight was happening nearby? However a horse should react, it was clear what was happening and she pushed on.

She paused at one stall, spying a neglected plank of wood. Reaching in, she grasped it and lifted it, holding it as she had the hammer last week. It would have to do. Pressing her lips together, she continued, approaching the back stall. Her heart was hammering in her ears and she tried to keep her breath slow and even so as not to draw attention to herself.

Reaching it, she took a deep breath before standing and rushing around the wall, brandishing the plank of wood over her head as she charged the attacker.

John turned just as she swung the plank down and dodged it, catching it in his hands as it whistled by his shoulder. "Yea gods, Louisa, what has gotten into you?" he demanded.

Her eyes took in the scene. He was the only one in the stall, a large cylindrical bag hanging from the ceiling by a chain. There was no injured man on the floor, no blood oozing out of any wounds, no evidence of a fight. Taking in the man standing before her, she saw he was shirtless, his sweaty skin glistening in the light of the lantern. Her heart was now hammering for different reasons.

Riveted, she stared at one drop of sweat as it drifted from his shoulder and down his chest, catching in the curly hair that covered it. Her eyes took in his large, dark nipples and then roamed down to his abdomen. The muscles were more defined than her footmen's had been and there was not an ounce of fat. His dark hair continued to trail down and disappeared into his trousers in the most tantalizing way. She had the urge to run her fingers through that hair and discover the treasure it promised.

Jerking her gaze away at that thought, her eyes landed on his arms, also covered in hair. While his abdomen had been flat, here his biceps were clearly defined, the bulges larger than she had ever seen on any man; she knew both her hands would not encircle them. She had felt the strength and power of those biceps as they had easily hefted her off her feet and the thought of them doing that again made her knees weak.

Drifting down slightly, she saw his hands wrapped up in cloth mufflers, his fingers protected by the soft material. She met his gaze again, saw the angered confusion in them. "What are you doing?" she babbled, recovering from the surprise of—everything.

He wrested the plank of wood from her and tossed it to the side; the sound of it hitting the floor reverberated throughout the stable, disrupting the horses slightly. His glare did not abate. "I am using my practice dummy. Now answer my question."

Louisa straightened and adjusted her wrapper around her shoulders. "I saw you enter the stable and was curious. When I heard sounds of a fight, I thought to help."

His brow lifted with incredulity and a half smile pulled at his mouth. "You thought to help me in a fight. With a plank of wood."

She sniffed and lifted her chin. "It was all that was available. And I can fight just as well as the next man."

That inspired a bark of laughter. "I doubt that."

She narrowed her eyes at him. "It is true."

"Very well. Prove it." He gestured to his punching dummy. "Hit the dummy." He placed his hands on his hips and she was hard-pressed to keep her focus on the conversation.

"I don't need to prove myself to you."

"Prove it to yourself then. Hit the dummy."

Glaring at him, she stalked to the dummy, wound up her arm and hit it for all she was worth. The bag hardly moved, but she danced away from it, shaking her hand. "Ow! You could have warned me it was going to hurt."

He intercepted her dance and took her hand in his, forcing it to open. "Come here," he said when she tried to pull away. He massaged her fingers, easing the pain. "You said you can fight as well as the next man. I am the closest next man around, so I would think you could handle it."

She glared at him again to hide how much she was enjoying the hand massage. "All you proved was that I am not a champion brawler."

"Pugilist," he corrected. "Or prizefighter."

She sniffed. "Little difference."

"Much difference. A pugilist fights by rules, with honor; it is about besting his opponent, not pummeling him. A brawler does not abide by such strictures, as his fight is solely about physical dominance."

"The end result is the same: blood and injury. Both are barbaric."

John grinned at her. "There are times when you sound every inch a lady."

She froze, shocked he had picked up on something she took for granted. Her mind raced. "I had a good governess," she finally said. It was the truth. He didn't need to know the full nature of her upbringing.

"Now," he said, releasing her hand, "the first thing you need to know is to make your fist like this, without curling your fingers around your thumb. Tuck it under like this, keeping it outside." He curled her fingers into the position he meant. "This will keep your thumb from breaking. And don't hit with your knuckles unless you actually want to cause damage. Hit with the front of your fist, like so." He demonstrated a soft hit against the dummy. "Now you try."

Looking at the bag warily, Louisa made a fist as he had shown her. Winding back, she stilled when he stepped close and his fingers lightly took her arm. "No, pull your elbow back behind your shoulder," he said, his breath warm against her cheek. "It gives you more power. And keep it up, like so." He directed her arm with his fingers. "Now release."

She did as he said, causing the bag to shudder. It wasn't a swing, but movement just the same. She looked at him. "It doesn't hurt as much, but it's difficult."

He steadied the bag with one hand. "That's because this is my bag. It is made to withstand my punches while still being heavy enough to develop my power. This is a champion's bag. I could have a smaller one made for you, if you like."

Intrigued for just a moment, she shook her head. "Why didn't it move when I hit it correctly?"

"It's not really supposed to move much," he explained. "This is a resistance tool. If it swings too much, then it won't be withstanding punches and therefore building power. My trainer would stand and hold the bag still to provide even more resistance."

"Show me how you use it." She tried to keep the interest out of her voice.

He gave her a half smile. "Of course. Step back a bit." When he ensured she was safe, John stood at the bag within arm's reach in an upright stance, raising his hands to hover just below his chin. He moderated his breathing, taking slow breaths in through his nose and out through his mouth. He wound up his right arm and jabbed at the bag, the dull thud of his muffler hitting the canvas meeting his ears. He did a few more right jabs before bringing in his left for combination hits. The bag shuddered where it hung, swinging slightly as the force of his hits increased. The thuds picked up their pace, mingling with his grunts whenever he hit the dummy. He shuffled around the bag, imagining an opponent in front of him and hitting him.

His exercise lasted several minutes, his mind and body achieving the mindless state of repetition and exertion. When he finally stopped, his breathing was haggard and his muscles were beginning to ache, especially around his shoulders. He had been a prizefighter for a decade and it had taken a toll on his body.

Panting, he glanced over at Louisa standing at the edge of the stall. Her mouth was slightly open and her eyes had a glazed look to them. Her fingers absently played with the edge of her wrapper, but he could see her tightened nipples through her nightshirt.

John turned his attention back to the bag, steadying it with his hands, fighting his reaction to the woman. The last thing he wanted was another relationship like his marriage, where his wife only had use for him when he boxed. Even though Louisa's obvious arousal had his cock stiffening into a full-fledged salute, he resisted it.

His caveman side was screaming at him. This is why he had come into the stable so late at night, unable to sleep because of this woman. She had avoided him for the last three days, so he turned to a proven method to work out his frustrations, both sexual and otherwise. And now here she was, clearly open to getting into bed—or a stall—with him.

But his seven-year celibacy gave him strong control over his primitive side. And he would not be made a fool of by a woman again.

"Johnny," she said, her voice quiet and throaty. The sound of his name spoken in such a way shot another arrow of lust to his groin, but he continued to resist. "John," she repeated, so he turned his eyes to her. "About the other day—I understand—I don't have expectations. It was just—"

"So help me God, Louisa, if you say it was just business, I won't be held accountable for my actions." He turned back to the dummy and gave it a few hard punches.

"What?" she asked, startled by his interruption.

He was incredulous when he turned to face her fully, hands on his hips. He didn't miss how her eyes scanned his chest again, but he remained focused. "What kind of man do you think I am? To make love with a woman I work with, a woman I respect, and consider it just business? If you were a prostitute, yes, but yea gods, Louisa, give me credit for having some semblance of honor."

She looked at him with solemn eyes. "I was going to say that it was just unexpected. We need not place any more ideals upon it. We both were involved in what happened; I do not place the blame at your feet."

"Oh. Well." He blinked. "Not that I think we did anything worthy of blame," he muttered.

"In fact," she continued as though she hadn't heard him, "that is something I wished to speak to you about."

He watched as she pressed her lips together and lifted her chin, actions that amused him. She did those things when she was going to make a declaration of some sort or was unhappy about something and trying to save face.

She did not disappoint. "We are both healthy adults, obviously with needs that are not currently being met. I propose we make an arrangement between us to see to those needs."

John rocked back on his heels. "You mean to have an affair?"

She nodded. "A discreet one. It would not do for our inn's reputation should word of it get out; women are just beginning to feel comfortable here. We would meet late at night, in my cottage when I indicate you will be welcome. A sheath would be used, something I must insist upon, as I have no wish to conceive a child. You must never spend the night but return to your room soon after we are finished with each other and ensure none sees you enter or exit the cottage. Outside of that, our relationship would remain as it is, professional and courteous. No sneaking touches or kisses, no needlessly seeking the other out, nothing to indicate anything untoward is happening between us. While I understand my widowed status allows me a modicum of freedom, I will not be fodder for gossip."

During her delivery, he had turned back to the dummy

and traced lines on it. When she was finished, he resumed punching it.

"Well, do you agree?" she asked over the noise of his exercise. When he continued his punching, she raised her voice. "Do you have nothing to say?"

He stopped and shot her a hooded look. "I wasn't aware my participation was required in the conversation. You clearly have it all sorted. Am I even necessary to see to your needs?"

She sniffed. "There is no reason to be crude."

He barked out a laugh that had the horses shifting. "You just outlined the most bloodless affair known to man and you think I am being crude?" He shook his head. "What makes you think I would agree to any of this?"

"Well," she sputtered, "you are a man. I am offering an arrangement with no expectations. I should think that would appeal to you."

"The fact that I am a man means I should be grateful for your offer? What am I to expect when I enter your room—will your nightshirt already be pulled up and your legs spread, and ten minutes later I take my leave of you?" He shook his head again. "I am a man, not a savage. Such a cold arrangement has never held any appeal to me. I am not controlled by base desires nor will I beg for your favors or attention. If I enter any sort of affair with you, I will not be afraid of any expectations placed upon me. And it would be an affair that leaves us both satisfied, not this fumble-tumble idea you have."

"A simple *no* would suffice." Her chin was in the air again.

John walked up to her until she had to tilt her head to keep her eyes on his face. "That wasn't a no," he murmured, enjoying how her mahogany eyes widened. "It was a request for us to actually discuss this like reasonable adults who are attracted to each other. I won't deny it, kitten, I want to make love with you again, but not at the sacrifice of intimacy and affection."

She shook her head and her voice was firm. "It would just be sex, not making love. No intimacy or affection."

He looked at her, trying to see beyond her words. "How long ago did your husband pass away?"

She stilled and there was a brief flare of panic in her eyes. "Long enough for this to not be a scandal."

"You loved him, so much that it hurt when he died?"

"What business is it of yours?"

John reached out and tucked a loose blond strand of hair behind her ear, trailing his fingers down her neck and to her shoulder. "I would not seek to hurt you. It is not wrong to seek happiness, even when one you loved is gone. I would do all in my power to assure you find it."

That was the wrong thing to say. He could see it in the way her face darkened and closed off, a formidable wall erecting between them.

"My *happiness* is not your responsibility. It is mine alone, dependent on me and no one else, least of all any man. Forget I ever mentioned anything." She spun on her heel and marched out of the stall.

## Chapter Eleven

Louisa barely paid Rose's chatter any mind as they cleaned the vacated guest rooms. This was not something she usually assisted the maids with, not after training them, but she wanted to avoid the office today. She knew it would be the first place Giant Johnny would look for her and wanted to delay that confrontation as long as she possibly could.

The humiliation from the night before still burned in her. The crudeness of his words, the way he rejected her proposal—it had been unexpected and embarrassing. Neither of her footmen had put up any fuss, which was how she liked it.

But Giant Johnny had to be different, didn't he. Why couldn't he be like every other red-blooded male and just take the sex she was offering? Why did he have to make things so difficult?

It hadn't helped that she had been so aroused after watching him with his punching dummy. The play of his muscles in the candlelight, the way they bunched along his back, how his biceps tightened and released; she had felt the impact of his hits deep inside her and it thrilled her. She hadn't realized before that moment how incredibly controlled he was and she wanted to have that leashed power in her bed and between her legs.

If only he hadn't refused, she could have her satisfaction whenever she wanted.

She and Rose gathered their supplies and moved on to the last room. Rose began pouring out the used water basin while Louisa stripped the bed of its dirty linens. She was about to retrieve the clean ones when heavy footsteps sounded in the corridor and Giant Johnny appeared in the doorway. His face was tight and grim.

"Mrs. Brock, a moment if you may."

She stood her ground. "I am busy." She held a pillow in front of her, a pathetic shield.

Without speaking, he stalked over to her and yanked the pillow from her, tossing it on the bed. He grasped her elbow and pulled her out of the room. She resisted, squirming to get out of his hold, but he just tightened his fingers.

"Unhand me," she demanded as they neared the stairs.

He ignored her and descended the stairs.

"You have no right to manhandle me! I will make a scene, I swear."

He didn't stop, but pulled her through the pub. "Go ahead. No one will care and you will only look foolish."

She shut her mouth and pressed her lips together. She knew he was right. She lifted her chin and tried to walk regally for all he was propelling her through the room. She did not make any eye contact with patrons or employees, feeling the burn of her earlier humiliation compound itself at this display of chauvinistic imperialism.

They entered the kitchen and he led her without hesitation to the office. Expecting him to release her once they arrived, she was surprised when he continued into his room and closed the door behind them. When he did release her, she took several steps away from him and rubbed where his hand had been, although he hadn't actually hurt her.

Louisa glared at him. "If you think that display of prehistoric—"

He closed the distance between them, his face dark, and covered her mouth with his hand. "Stop," he growled. "You had your turn to speak last night. Now it is mine."

Her glare continued over his hand until he dropped it. She raised her chin. "You did manage to say plenty last night," she pointed out.

"Yea gods, woman, do you never cease?" He ran his hands over his bald pate.

She thrust her fists onto her hips. "You drag me into your room, most inappropriately I might add, and then have the audacity to be put out with me? If anyone has a right to be—mmph!"

John cut her off the only way he could think of. He caught her waist and pulled her flush against him, his mouth descending quickly to take her mouth in a wet kiss. She struggled for a moment, but he held her close and followed her movements with his head, not letting her get away. Finally, she sighed into him, her arms sliding around his waist.

Yea gods, but he would never tire of kissing this woman. He sank into her mouth, tasting the sweetness he knew lay beyond her tart words. Their lips met and molded into each other, teasing and exploring the other. He kept it slow, savoring the way she kept sighing, her body relaxing against his, giving herself up to him in a timeless instinct.

Breaking the kiss, he lifted his head, pleased to see how slowly she opened her eyes and blinked at him. He smiled at her. "Allow me to speak," he murmured.

Anger flashed in her eyes when his words registered, but she pressed her lips together and nodded.

"I brought you in here because I did not want you to use any excuse to avoid me. Do not belittle either of us by claiming otherwise," he said when she opened her mouth. She clamped her lips together and glared at him, telling him he had been right. "I also did not want anyone interrupting or eavesdropping.

"I said last night that I would discuss your proposal as reasonable adults. I will not accede to all of your wishes, just as I am aware you will not with all of mine."

She looked at him warily. "What wishes are those?"

"I will be upfront with you. I have no intention of entering any such arrangement with you without knowing that marriage will be the end result."

Louisa pulled out of his arms and took several steps away, turning her back on him. "I will not marry. It is out of the question."

"I am not saying that it needs to happen now or even soon, but eventually."

"No."

"I will give you time to grieve your husband and to adjust to the idea of marrying me, but I will not risk the possibility of a child out of wedlock."

"There will be no child. I insist on using sheaths." She began to pace the length of the short room.

John was still surprised for a woman to speak so bluntly about such things, but he kept it to himself. Louisa was not a usual sort of woman. "I agree to that, but sheaths break, kitten. I will not have a bastard."

"You don't even know if I am still open to having an affair with you."

Her voice was betraying a hint of panic and desperation. He furrowed his brow, wondering what had her so set against the institution. "I would say the way you just responded to my kiss says otherwise."

She made a dismissive gesture. "I am sure I would have done the same with Mr. Packard." Her pacing did not falter.

John let out a bark of laughter. "I find that hard to believe."

She lifted her chin and sniffed. "Men find women interchangeable. Why can women not do the same?"

He walked up to her and stood in front of her, halting her pacing. Louisa tilted her head back to glare at him. He smiled at her. "You would be comfortable with Packard doing this to you?" He trailed his fingers down her neck. "Or this?" He stepped closer and nuzzled her ear. "What about this?" He placed hot kisses just below her ear in a sensitive spot that had her inhaling sharply. "Or this?" His hand slid down her back to cup her bottom, pulling her against his groin.

With a huff, she pushed him away. Her body screamed at her to step back into his embrace, but she resisted and stepped around him, resuming her pacing. "You made your point. That is hardly the issue, however. I have no intentions of marrying. Not you, not ever."

John frowned at her. "Why are you resisting marriage again? Was your first one so horrible?"

She missed a step, but recovered. "Yours wasn't ideal, so why are you eager to marry again?" she countered.

"Because I know that no marriage is normal. Each one is unique to the people in it. A marriage between us will be much different than our previous ones."

She started rubbing her arms as she walked. "Why are you so insistent upon this? Do you offer marriage to every woman you tumble?"

"Since my wife died? Yes."

Louisa halted and stared at him. "Well, that puts this into a better perspective. I had no idea you were so cavalier with your proposals."

"I am not."

"But you just said—" Her voice trailed off as his statement sank in. She shook her head. "No. No, it—you—"

John nodded, his face serious. "I have proposed marriage to every woman I have been with since my wife passed. There has only been the one."

Her head continued in its slow shake, her eyes wide. She started rubbing her arms again. "That cannot be true." She kept staring at him. "Please tell me it's not true."

He shrugged, a frisson of hurt blossoming in him at her rejection.

"Oh dear Lord," she said. She was now rubbing her arms furiously. "Oh dear Lord."

"Louisa?" he ventured cautiously.

"Oh dear Lord, I need to get out of here." Panic had overtaken her entire body. He could see it in her eyes, a frightened wildness in them that unsettled him. Her breath came in choked gasps and she stumbled toward the door. "I need to leave," she repeated.

John beat her to the door, blocking her way and holding it shut. "Calm down, kitten."

"Let me out." She struggled to get past him.

"You can't leave like this."

"Let me out, let me out!" She clawed at the door, trying to pry it open, but he was too strong and too heavy. She turned her attention to him, pummeling his chest with her fists. "Let me out, damn you!" Her face was turning red with her exertion and labored breathing.

"Louisa, calm down," he said over her frantic words. "You can't go out like this. You will frighten everyone."

She didn't hear him, just kept pummeling him and repeating herself. Out of options, John grabbed her by the shoulders and pulled her into him, wrapping his arms around her, halting her movements. Her body shuddered and struggled against him, but he did not lessen his hold.

"Please let me out," she whimpered.

"Hush," he said, keeping his voice and embrace gentle. He rubbed her back, willing her body to calm. When he felt it begin to relax against him, he let out a long breath he hadn't known he was holding. Her shaking subsided to faint tremors and her breathing was a consistent tattoo playing on the linen of his shirt. Her cheek rested against his chest above his heart.

Bending slightly, he scooped her up into his arms and carried her the few steps to his bed. Laying her down as softly as he would china, he pulled off her boots and covered her with a blanket. Her lack of protest showed how deeply she had exhausted herself. The look on her face reminded him of men who had taken hard knocks to the head and couldn't think straight.

Without another thought, he climbed in beside her and settled around her, his arm resting over her protectively. Her eyes fluttered closed and he watched as she drifted off to sleep. He frowned as he took in the dark circles under her eyes and the worry lines creasing her skin.

Something had happened to her, something traumatic. John had never been so certain about anything in his life. To react this way to his wish for marriage? Yea gods, it hadn't even been an outright proposal. What would she have done if he had gotten down on one knee with a ring?

A dark anger built up inside him when he thought about what her husband must have done to her. He knew depraved men existed, thankfully had not encountered any of them, but he had heard talk about what some men enjoyed doing to women and it made him sick inside. The thought of what Louisa must have suffered at her husband's hands made his arm tighten around her, drawing her farther into his protection, even though he had the ugly thought that his protection was too little, too late.

It explained things about her. Her anger, her wish to be in control, her unwillingness to accept help. Given how she might have been broken, John was thankful she instead persevered, showing a strength he could only admire.

He knew he would have to go slow with her, build her trust in him. If it took years, he would accept that if it meant she would be healed from whatever wounds she carried.

He would not leave her side for a moment of it.

**Chapter Twelve**

Louisa sighed and cracked open her eyes. Her head and bones ached and she raised her hand to brush hair out of her face and rub her forehead. She opened her eyes more, taking in the unfamiliar room. Shafts of light filtered through the cracks in the curtains and she guessed it was early evening. What was she doing sleeping in the middle of the day? And which room was she in?

She sat up, the blanket that had been wrapped around her falling down. Glancing around, she saw she was alone in a bed and it came rushing back. *Oh good Lord.* Giant Johnny had brought her in here for a marriage proposal. To which she had panicked in a most embarrassing manner.

She flopped back down on the bed, her arm covering her eyes. Had he really tucked her into bed as though she were a child? She recollected feeling his arm lying across her stomach and the warm length of his body alongside hers. She supposed she ought to be thankful that he had not stripped her of her clothes, although she noted her boots were not on her feet.

How in the world could she face him again? It was embarrassing enough to know he had witnessed her spectacle, but to treat her as an invalid, incapable of seeing to herself? Her mortification knew no bounds, despite the accuracy of his assessment.

What had even happened to her? She could recollect only one other experience like it, when she had fled from Willowcrest. The panic had utterly consumed her, to the point where she was no longer in control of her body. It was odd, watching oneself with a sense of detachment, unable to do anything. When the enormity of John's proposal had sunk in—the man had ended a seven-year abstinence for her!—all she could think of was fleeing, getting away from him, but he had not let her. The panic had eaten at her, crawling out of the recesses of her soul, until it debilitated her, leaving her spent and exhausted.

Taking a deep breath, Louisa sat up again, determined to push through. He could think what he liked, but he would never see her in such a state again. All she had to do was lift her chin and pretend it had never happened and she would be fine.

Swinging her legs over the side of the bed, she located her boots on the floor and put them on. As she went through the mundane routine of buttoning them up, her eyes scanned the room. She hadn't been in John's room prior to this afternoon and it intrigued her. What sort of personal articles did her prizefighter have? She frowned at that brief thought, telling herself that he was by no means *her* prizefighter.

The bed she sat upon was high—her feet dangled off the side—and long, giving her the impression it had been custom made for its owner, for it was certainly large enough for Giant Johnny. The linens and covers were of decent quality—not what one would find in a noble house, but remaining comfortable while durable. A small candelabra ordained a bedside table, the candles half-used. The top book on a pile was *The History of Tom Jones, a Foundling*, which brought a smile to Louisa's lips at the thought of the big man reading a romantic story. A good-sized vanity stood against the wall opposite the window, sporting a mirror and the various grooming implements one would expect any man to have. Eyeing the razor, she wondered again if his baldness was a choice or natural.

Her eyes fell on a miniature sitting beside the mirror and Louisa moved to take a closer look. A young, dark-haired woman with a sultry smile gazed back. Running her finger around the frame, Louisa supposed this must be his late wife to hold a place of such prominence; he would be able to look at her every day as he completed his ablutions. She thought back to what he had said about his marriage and wondered why he would want the daily reminder of an unpleasant union. Sympathy slid through her when she realized that this miniature was likely the closest link he had to the child he lost and mourned.

She caught her reflection in the mirror and her look turned to one of horror at the state of her hair. Taking out the remaining pins, she purloined the brush from the vanity— *why on earth does a bald man need a brush?*—and quickly raked it through her hair before pulling it back into some sense of order, retrieving from the bed what hairpins she could find to help.

Patting her hair in its final place, she looked at the items on his vanity more closely. His shaving kit, including the brush she had used, was made from dark cherry wood with gold trim. They seemed out of place for the man who preferred to dress in trousers and a shirt, keeping his wardrobe simple. Yet as she reflected on it, the quality of his clothing was fine, if not quite up to Bond or Jermyn Street standards. She glanced back at the custom bed, at the quality of the linens and the size of the pillows; even the candelabras were of decent quality. All this attested to a man of means.

Louisa fingered the handle of the straight blade, tracing the gold. A man's personal wealth meant little to her. In her experience, the state of a man's purse did little to determine his character. What spoke to her was the way he spent it. John was subtle, choosing items that brought him comfort without declaring his wealth to the world; those that did were personal, private. Even buying this inn spoke to his character. If he could afford it, as well as these items, then he likely could have afforded a nice cottage to spend his retirement reading about the Tom Joneses of the world instead of counting casks and serving steak-and-kidney pies to strangers.

He was a complex man, her Giant Johnny. Another frown at that reappearing thought. Unhappy with it, she patted her hair one last time and moved to the door. It was time she resumed her work, having already slept the afternoon away. She paused at the door, wondering if he would be on the other side in the office. Knowing there was little she could do to avoid him if he was, Louisa took a deep breath and lifted her chin, twisting the knob in her hand.

Giant Johnny stood as soon as the door swung open, wrenching his absurd spectacles off his face. He tried to catch the chair from falling, but he was not fast enough and the furniture shattered, sending splinters of wood careening across the floor. Louisa jumped out of the way to avoid her feet getting hit by one of the arms.

"Damnation," he cursed. Immediately his face turned red with contrition. "My apologies, Louisa. I did not mean to curse."

A small smile tugged at her mouth. "Perhaps the situation warranted it. I doubt you were expecting the chair to break. I suspect your reaction was more out of surprise than intent."

His face remained red, the color stretching to cover his head. "True, that." His eyes turned to concern. "How are you?"

She glanced down at her feet. "I am uninjured. I managed to dodge the flying debris."

"No, I meant—hell." He rubbed his head before putting his hands on his hips. He gestured to the desk. "Are you hungry? I have a tray here. And tea. Or I can get more ale, if you prefer. I finished my tankard but it is readily available. As you know." He muttered that last part, his face reddening once more.

Warmth bloomed in her bosom, spreading to her stomach and head. It was almost dear to see him fumbling and nervous. "Where will I sit? We have a lack of chairs in here now."

He missed the tease in her voice. "I can stand, it is no bother." He moved and held out the smaller chair on the far side of the desk for her. Stepping over the debris, she settled herself into it and prepared herself a plate of cheese, bread and meat from the tray. Without being asked, John lifted the dainty teapot and poured her a cup, fixing it as she liked. Her eyes watched as his thick fingers handled the tiny sugar tongs, then set the small cup and saucer close to her plate.

"Thank you," she said. "How has the afternoon gone? Any concerns or mishaps that need to be addressed?" She took a bite of bread, eager to focus on work and not how he was hovering nearby.

"Um, no. It was a slow day, so I spent it in here."

Louisa nearly choked on her bread. "You spent the day in the office? You hate the office."

He cleared his throat. "Yes, well, I wasn't needed anywhere else and there was someone in my room."

It was her turn to go red. She lifted her chin and looked him straight in the eye. "I apologize for the inconvenience."

"No, no, no bother at all," he assured her hurriedly. "I, um, it's just—"

"Yes?"

"I did not mean to cause you any distress," he said. "I had no intention of causing you harm."

"I know that."

"Louisa." He crouched down close to her and took her hand. "You must know that I greatly respect and admire you. I have come to care for you."

She tried to tug her hand out of his, but he wouldn't let go. He continued. "All I am saying is that you have no need to be afraid of me. I will never intentionally do anything to harm you."

"Thank you," she said, struggling to keep her voice normal.

"I do wish to be with you, but I can't have a bastard. Life is hard enough without having to live with that. If I have to choose between not having you and having a bastard, I would choose to not have you. Not because I don't desire you—yea gods, kitten, you just have to look at me and I stand at attention—but because a man must have some code, some honor, and therein lies mine."

Louisa stared at the man at her knees, his head bowed as his fingers traced over her knuckles. She looked at him and thought of his room and his behavior toward her. This was a complex man before her, a subtle man, but one who lived honorably. It was true—she had no fear of him. It was what his desires represented that repulsed her. To marry would be to completely surrender who she was, to lose whatever identity she had scraped together, and that was something she could not tolerate.

She understood his dilemma. She agreed that life was hard enough—how much more difficult would it be if she gave birth to a daughter out of wedlock? What sort of life could that child expect? But the thought of marrying him squeezed her throat shut. For a brief, absurd moment, she understood how Sara felt whenever she experienced one of her anxiety attacks.

She cupped his cheek, pulling his head up to look him in the eye. Her eyes begged him to understand. "It's not you, John. It's marriage."

He nodded. "I understand. I know. I mean, I don't know, you don't have to tell me, but I understand. I can be a patient man. All I ask is a chance to prove myself to you."

Louisa shook her head. "You don't have to prove anything to me. You are a good man, John Taylor. It is I who have the problem. If I were different, we would be having a much more favorable conversation right now."

"I don't want you to be different. Just give me time. We will be cautious, but I need your assurance that if you find yourself with child, you will at the very least consider marrying me."

She took a deep breath. He wasn't actually asking for much. She would get what she wanted and he would have his assurances. Considering marriage was much different than actually marrying. She hadn't conceived with either of her footmen, so it was even likely that she was incapable. What sort of risk would she be taking to agree to this? Not much, by the looks of things.

Louisa gave him a small smile and traced his cheekbone with her thumb. "I can do that."

Relief flooded his face and he turned his head into her palm, kissing it. "Thank you."

"We still need to be cautious and discreet," she warned him. "And the inn must always come first."

"Of course." John grinned at her and tugged her forward to lean closer to him. "Now to seal our bargain with a kiss."

"If you insist," she said, licking her lips. Her eyes were already riveted on his mouth.

"On this, I do insist," he murmured, his eyes twinkling. He held back a space, giving her time to pull away if she so chose.

She did not disappoint. Letting out a sigh, she pressed her lips to his in a gentle caress, capturing his lips with her soft touch. She guided their mouths in the intimate dance, taking her time as she explored him.

It was a feeling she had never experienced before, this desire to learn about a person. Her footmen had been calculated decisions meant to broaden her own knowledge of lust, desire and the act of coupling. But with John it was different. When she licked his lips and dipped her tongue into his mouth, it was because she wanted to feel his groan vibrate against her. When she sucked on his lower lip, it was because she wanted to feel his breath quicken on her skin. When she traced his neatly trimmed beard, it was because she reveled in the scrape of the hair between her fingers. Above all, she did all these things because she knew it brought him pleasure.

When she kissed this man, it was about him, not her.

John broke the kiss and pressed their foreheads together. "The door is open, kitten," he panted. "Let's take this into my room."

She caught her breath and sat up, shaking her head. "I cannot. We cannot. I have already slept the afternoon away and dinner will be starting soon. We must prepare."

He sat back on his heels, linking their hands together. "Tonight, then?"

She nodded. "I will leave my cottage door unlocked. Come once the pub has closed for the night."

He frowned. "I dislike the thought of your door being unlocked."

"It cannot be helped. Chances are I will fall asleep waiting for you and knocking on the door will be disruptive. And there is only the one key."

"Don't get your back up, kitten," he soothed. "Allow me to be concerned for you. I would feel this even if we hadn't just decided to have an affair."

She was still disgruntled. "Either way my safety is my own concern."

"But it doesn't have to be. Gather some of your things and you can wait in my room for me tonight." He grinned suggestively at her. "After all, we've already determined you are quite comfortable there."

"Hmph." She lifted her chin and returned her attention to her food. "I suppose that would be feasible. For one night, at least, but you must see to having a second key made tomorrow."

He stood. "Of course." He leaned back down and kissed her cheek, inhaling her scent. "I shall count the minutes until tonight, kitten." He straightened and left the office, a spring in his step.

Louisa sat for a long moment, staring at the desk without really seeing it. She had just agreed to embark on an affair with this man. Her footmen had been prudential, but this she feared bordered more on an affair of the heart. She would be foolish to let either of them think in such a way, but she was at a loss as to how to prevent it. She was worried at least one of their hearts was already engaged, and she wasn't sure that it was his.

She shook herself out of her reverie and the noises from the inn surrounded her again. "Alan," she called out. The boy came to the office door. She indicated the broken chair. "Clean that up please and then go and fetch the carpenter, Mr. Smith. I need to speak to him about fashioning a new chair."

## Chapter Thirteen

Louisa woke slowly, the sound of scraping reaching her ears. She squinted in the early morning sun and rolled over, seeing John at his vanity, his face half-covered in shaving cream. His head was tilted as he drew the straight razor over his neck. He was wearing only his trousers and even those were hanging loosely around his hips, giving her a splendid view of his profile and a hint of his nicely rounded buttocks. She watched him in silence for a moment, enjoying it.

Somehow one night in his room had turned into three. And now a week. Even though a second key to the cottage had been made, she conceded to herself that his room was likely best, with his custom-made bed built to hold his large frame. She doubted he would be comfortable in her bed.

She sat up abruptly, the time of day sinking in. "Good Lord, I've slept in."

His reflection furrowed its brow as he wiped the blade on the towel draped over his shoulder. "I doubt that. I haven't heard anyone in the kitchen yet." He angled his head the other way to scrape the stubble off his cheek.

"But it is already light out. Anyone who is up might see me return to my cottage. They would know I spent the night elsewhere." Her shift falling over her head muffled her voice. Once her head poked out, she scanned the room for her stockings. Finding one, she pulled it on. "Where is my other stocking?"

He picked it up from where it hung off the wardrobe and handed it to her. "Would it be so bad for people to know?"

"Of course it would be. I have no wish to marry."

"It's not like we were caught in bed together," he muttered before splashing water on his face and wiping it dry. "They can't force us into marriage based on suspicions alone. For all they know, you could have been with one of the guests last night."

"Yes, that would be much better," she said, her morning sarcasm strong. "I would much prefer to be known as the inn-keeper who goes above and beyond to ensure all the needs of her guests are met."

"I didn't mean it like that."

"But that is what you said."

"Louisa," he sighed. "Would it be so bad to marry me?"

She glared at him as she picked up her dress. "You said you were fine with this, that you wouldn't say anything more about marriage unless I am with child."

He raised his hands and moved toward her to help her with her dress. "And I am not. I am just asking what makes marrying me so unappealing."

"I've told you, it's not about you."

"It must be, as you obviously had no compunction about marrying before."

She clamped her mouth shut, her eyes blinking as he tugged her laces together. When he was finished, she marched over to his vanity and began to unbraid her hair. She picked up his brush and pulled it through her blond tresses. "Why do you even have a blasted brush?" she muttered.

"It came with the set." He watched her, hands on his hips. "You know that I am not Brock, correct? That I am not like him?"

She was silent for several beats, the brush pausing in midstroke. "How do you know that?"

John shrugged. "I don't, as you have never breathed even a word about him. I am assuming your jitters have to do with him."

"You haven't told me anything about your wife." Her tone was defensive.

"You haven't asked. What do you want to know?" When she didn't reply, he continued. "The difference is that I am not trying to hide her. I will tell you anything you like, but every time I ask about your late husband, you change the subject."

Her brushing resumed. "It has nothing to do with him. You just don't understand."

"Yea gods, Louisa, I am trying to. Can't you see that? Can you understand that your refusal would be easier to stomach if you would just explain yourself to me?"

She twisted her hair into a simple bun, hairpins sliding in to hold it in place. "That's the thing, you will never truly understand."

He stiffened at her insinuation. "I see. The prizefighter is good for a tumble, but heaven forfend he should attempt intelligent conversation."

"No," she snapped. "You will never understand because you are a man."

His feeling of offense remained. "That is not much better, kitten. What does that have to do with anything?"

Louisa turned to face him, crossing her arms over her chest and glaring at him. "If we were to marry, what would people call you?"

He frowned, feeling as stupid as she had implied moments before. "I don't understand. John Taylor."

"And what would they call me?"

"Mrs. Taylor."

"Mrs. *John* Taylor. In marrying you, I lose everything. My property becomes yours, my money becomes yours, my very name and identity become yours. Even those children you desperately don't want to be illegitimate won't truly be mine, but yours."

"What of it? It's the way of things. All those things come to me because I am your husband, who is expected to provide for you and our children. Makes sense to me."

That was the wrong thing to say. Her face darkened as her mouth pulled down into a ferocious scowl and her skin flushed with anger. She was seething. "Of course it makes sense to you, as you are not the one who loses everything. Marriage is legalized degradation and exploitation of women; once married, a wife has no rights, no recourse should she need it. She becomes her husband's property to use and abuse as he sees fit."

"A husband's duty is to care for his wife, not abuse her," John pointed out.

"And how many husbands actually abide by that? How

many put their wives in danger through infidelity or their fists? And if a man is seen to be abusing his wife, well, that is merely his legal right. None interfere with a husband's discretion, even when it is so blatantly wrong. There is very little difference between marriage and slavery and those who fight against either is considered seditious.

He was incredulous. "I hardly think you can equate marriage with slavery."

"Why not? Slaves are seen as savages based on the color of their skin and their inability to speak our language when first presented with it or to wear clothing like ours. They are not seen as sentient beings, capable of providing for themselves and making sound decisions. Wives are viewed the same way and I will not subject myself to it. Slaves cannot leave their masters and wives cannot leave their husbands; it is prettied up with a romantic notion, but the intent is the same. It is ludicrous to consider a man like Charlie Drover, who can barely recognize his own name, capable of voting and owning property, yet deny me that right. I am a sentient human being, capable of running an inn, of educating children, of making intelligent decisions in all aspects of life, and I refuse to be denigrated into the role of wife merely to appease some societal concept of propriety that was created by men!"

Yea gods but she was beautiful when fired up. Her eyes flashed with angry passion and her bosom heaved with her rapid breath. John was hard-pressed to keep his eyes off her breasts, but even the fire on her face aroused him.

He crossed his arms over his chest and tried to focus on what she was saying. "So you think I am just like every other man in England? That is why you don't want to marry me?"

She threw her hands up in the air in frustration. "I've told you, it's not about you. Haven't you been listening, you big galoot?"

A bark of laughter escaped him. "Big galoot? Is that what you really just called me?"

"Yes, and I'm not sorry for it." Her chin was in the air.

He scratched his freshly shaven cheek. "I don't think I've been called a galoot since I grew a foot in one week."

She huffed, chin still high in the air. "I can't imagine why not. You can be exceptionally obtuse."

John couldn't help himself. He walked over to her, a smile playing at his lips, eyes roaming over her still flushed face. He stopped when he was more than close enough to touch her, awareness of her prickling along his skin. "Say it again," he murmured.

"What, *galoot?*"

He gave a mock shudder. "Oh yes, again."

A smile tugged her lips. "You are being ridiculous."

"Because I am a—" he prompted.

"A big galoot."

He took a long breath through his nose and fluttered his eyes, smiling at her. "You certainly know how to sweet-talk a man, kitten."

"You—"

"Big galoot," he finished and put his hands on her waist to pull her to him. Once her body was flush with his, he lowered his head and kissed her.

He had spent a week studying her body, two months before that studying her personality. He was still learning the nuances of her pleasure, the softness of her skin, the valleys and slopes of her body, and hoped he would be allowed to explore them for the rest of his life. He knew that she was a fighter, one for whom control was important, even as she was trembling with ecstasy. So her initial reluctance to his kiss didn't surprise or discourage him, but made the moment her body sighed into his all the more sweet.

Her hands landed on his chest, sliding up to his shoulders and down to clutch his biceps, pulling herself even closer to him, his legs pushing into her skirts. Louisa felt her breasts pressing against his chest, her nipples hardening at the feel of his heat through the fabric of her clothing. She opened her mouth, welcomed in his tongue and met it with her own, the feel of his beard against her chin sending swirls of desire down to her stomach.

How could it be that her head still spun after a week of enjoying his kisses? How could it be that with each one her desire for him grew? A lust, a need was growing inside her to clamber into his skin and burrow herself as deep as she could inside him, making them one. This took her beyond her experience, as her footmen had been short-lived affairs, a hot lust that burned out rapidly and was easily dismissed unless deliberately brought to mind. With John Taylor she found herself watching him more and more during the day, leaving the safe confines of the office more and more just to be around him, reliving the moments in which he touched her, kissed her, made her laugh.

He had become an obsession, a flame she could not keep herself away from.

John moved his kiss down her neck, paying homage to her beating pulse, and she angled her head to give him more access. The tugs on her laces on her back brought a small dose of reality. "No." Her protest was weak. "I must go."

"You can wear this again today," he murmured against her skin, his hot breath skimming her nerves and making her eyelids flutter. "You have done it before."

"John—"

"Allow me this, Louisa. Allow me to love you."

She wanted to correct him, wanted to tell him that what they were doing had nothing to do with love and that she ought to get to work. What she did was cup his face to pull him in for another kiss. As she devoured his mouth, he pushed her dress off her shoulders, the garment sliding down her body to pool on the floor. His trousers needed little encouragement to follow suit.

John bent slightly to wrap his arms around her waist and lifted Louisa up. She obliged by holding on to his neck, securing herself more tightly as he carried her over to his bed. The moments he carried her, lifted her as though she weighed no more than a cat, sent thrills through her, knowing her giant contained a strength beyond what she could measure and he used it to bring her pleasure.

He sat on the bed, Louisa straddling his hips, their mouths still fused. Her shift was bunched at her waist, her stockinged thighs cradling his. Above her stockings, where their bare skin met and his erection throbbed insistently against her belly, fire coursed over her nerves and she knew without even feeling it that she was wet, her core weeping in anticipation of being filled by him again. Her inner center ached with loneliness, its wail echoing in its emptiness, only to be appeased by his penetration.

"Ah, kitten," he moaned against her lips. In one fluid movement her chemise was relieved and chucked to the floor. He buried his face in her breasts as one questing hand sought the wet warmth underneath her curls. Her fingers ran down his back, marveling again at his muscles and strength. When two of his fingers found her nub and rubbed circles over it, her nails gripped his skin, threatening to draw blood. His mouth closed over a nipple and his tongue ran around it, puckering it into a hard point.

Her head fell back, small gasps escaping her in time with his suckling. She caressed his head, holding him to her breast, her fingers running over his bald head.

He shifted his hand, his thumb replacing his fingers so they could slip inside her, stroking the walls of her core. "Johnny," she moaned.

"You are so hot," he muttered against her breast. "So wet. Hot and wet." His fingers moved in and out of her, coiling the familiar tension inside her.

"Harder, Johnny, harder."

He obeyed, quickening the thrusts of his fingers and increasing the pressure of his thumb. "I love it when you say my name like that," he growled.

"Johnny," she repeated. He growled against her breast, the vibrations coursing through her. "Johnny."

Another growl and he removed his hand from her mound. "Enough of this." He held her close as he twisted and lay her on her back on the soft mattress. He knelt on the floor, using his body to separate her thighs. His hands ran lightly over her skin, drifting from her stomach to her inner thighs, running along the creases that separated leg from hip.

"So beautiful," he crooned. "Beyond measure."

Louisa sat up and grasped his shoulders, guiding him down. "Don't make me wait, Johnny."

His eyes glinted up at her as he neared his destination. "I am going to make you purr, kitten, so much you will scream."

"Words are meaningless. Put action to them."

His face disappeared and he breathed on her moist skin, adding his warmth to her already boiling core. His tongue flicked out, its tip running along her length before his mouth fastened on her clit. "Oh yes, Johnny, finally," she murmured and lay back on the soft mattress.

As he worked his magic with his tongue, the coil inside her increased its tension. "Right there," she gasped when he hit a particularly prime spot. Her hips jerked when he returned to it, not hiding her pleasure in the slightest. She pressed her head back into the mattress, arching her back as he suckled.

He growled against her, sending shafts of delight through her core. She set her heels on his shoulders, opening herself up even more to his attentions, pressing herself against his face. She was getting close, her body's trembling more difficult to suppress.

He lifted his head for a breath. "You taste so sweet," he muttered. "The finest honey." He dove back in.

She arched her back again and gasped. "Fingers." She barely managed to get that word out but it was enough. His two fingers slid back in, stretching her once more, forcing her closer to the edge of the abyss. He skillfully maneuvered her closer and closer, his mouth and fingers working in tandem to drive her there. Her heels slid down his back, digging in below his shoulder blades, trying to draw him in even closer. His pace quickened and moments later she arched her back, choked gasps escaping her as her body climaxed.

John eased away from her, dropping light kisses on her thighs as his fingers slowed their pace, prolonging her orgasm until her body relaxed and she released a deep shuddering sigh. He sat back on his heels, one hand rubbing circles on her stomach, and smiled at her. "You are amazing when you come."

She smiled at the ceiling, her eyes closed. "I can't take all the credit. But don't think I am excusing your prize-ring language."

He moved to lie on the bed next to her. "You enjoy it, admit it."

"I admit nothing, sir."

"I can make you admit it."

"Never."

He chuckled, his hand still caressing her stomach. It drifted up to include her breasts, but remained light and attentive. Louisa opened her eyes and smiled at him when she saw he was watching her. She rolled on to her side to press up against him, his hard cock between their bodies. She trailed her hand down his firm chest to grip it, her thumb spreading the bead of moisture that had already escaped. He groaned as her fingers closed around his shaft and tugged gently.

"I suppose you now want me to return the favor." The look she gave him was sultry.

He shook his head, propped up on one elbow. "No favors here, not in my bed," he said. His eyes shut as her grip firmed and her strokes became more confident. "Nothing I do is out of expectation of receiving the same. I ask only that you do what you wish, whatever brings you pleasure."

Her movements stopped, her fingers remaining around his cock. John nearly begged her to continue. "You mean to say," she spoke, "that if I were to leave this bed now, leaving you like this, you would have no objection?"

"Oh, I would object wholeheartedly," he replied. He looked at her, cupping her face in his large hand. "But I would not force anything on you that you did not wish. True pleasure and intimacy cannot be achieved without trust, and making demands on a person in bed does not breed it. This is what I give to you, my trust, and with it, my affection."

Louisa looked at him in a long silence, still holding his member at her mercy. He did not waver from her scrutiny, but held it, confident she would see the sincerity of his words.

When she spoke, it was with a small frown on her face. "You are an odd man, John Taylor."

He gave her a small smile. "An improvement from a big galoot, I am sure."

She did not react to that, but tightened her grip on him enough to make him inhale, but not with pleasure. It didn't exactly hurt, but his body instinctively reacted to the possibility of that appendage being in more pain. "I could hurt you," she said.

"Yes." He refused to break her gaze, recognizing she needed this.

"I have seen grown men scream like little girls when this is hurt. I could do that to you with just a squeeze of my hand."

Yea gods, but if he didn't deflate just a little bit at that thought. "Yes."

"Do you still trust me?"

"Yes." He did not hesitate, his tone firm and sincere, his gaze still not leaving hers. This was vital to both of them.

Her grip eased and she began to move her hand up and down, her touch pleasurable once more. "You make yourself vulnerable to me."

"I just had my head between your legs. We make ourselves vulnerable to each other."

"That seems foolish."

"Such decisions can be, at times. I think this is not one of them."

Louisa leaned into him, kissing his chest before resting her cheek over his heart. His words made her feel inadequate, unworthy of the trust he was bestowing upon her. He claimed she made herself vulnerable to him, but she couldn't agree. Even now she was feeling the weight of everything she had been running from, all the lies she had told, knowing they ensured her survival. Did that justify telling them, if it meant she could live?

He threaded his fingers into her hair, tilting her head to gaze upon her face. His questioning eyes roamed over her as though trying to see inside her mind. "Louisa?"

She did the only thing she could think of, the only thing that would ensure his distraction. She gave him a smile and kissed his chest again, making a trail down his sternum, pausing to pay homage to his nipples. When her teeth nibbled on one, a deep groan rumbled up from his chest. With slight pressure, she had him lying on his back, her hand encouraging his cock to impressiveness.

When her trail of kisses grew closer to their destination,

his hand on her head stopped her. "You don't have to." His words were not very convincing.

She pushed his hands away and held his wrists to the bed. "You will lie there and make yourself vulnerable to me, Johnny. And you will enjoy every moment of it."

He smiled at her. "If you insist, madam."

"I do."

"My kitten has claws," he said, linking his hands behind his head. Her dominance aroused him even further.

"And you need to watch yourself that you don't get scratched."

Louisa dipped her head and ran her tongue along the length of his cock. He inhaled sharply, his shaft quivering as more moisture beaded at the tip. She flicked it with her tongue, the salty taste seasoning her mouth. Grasping the base of his shaft, she closed her mouth around only the head and sucked.

A strangled whimper escaped him, sending a surge of power through her, and she took as much of him into her mouth as she could. She kissed him as thoroughly as she knew how, using the reactions of his body as a map to his pleasure. Her hand worked with her mouth and his body twitched and writhed. When she curled her tongue around his shaft, adding the rough friction to the fray, his hips began to make little thrusts. One of his hands came to grip the back of her head, but she batted it away, intent on this being from her alone. She increased the suction of her mouth.

"God, Louisa, I—I want—I need to be inside you."

She didn't stop, didn't acknowledge his words. She was in control and she would decide what would happen. She cupped his balls, fondling them, feeling them harden in preparation.

"Kitten, love, I'm going to—"

His cock throbbed in her mouth and she lifted her head, rapidly pumping him with her hand. "Not yet, Johnny, not until I say."

"Please," he begged.

"Hold off." Her pace increased.

"Louisa!"

A few more hard pumps. "Now."

A guttural groan accompanied the hot spurt of his seed. It arched onto his stomach, pooling on his skin. She continued to stroke him, easing her pace and pressure as he emptied. His chest rose and fell with his deep breaths as he recovered.

Grasping one of her arms, John tugged her down to settle against him, kissing the top of her head. "You, kitten, are beyond words."

Louisa smiled into his chest, her equilibrium restored. She was safe again, once more in control of herself and her situation. Order was restored and his words could be forgotten. She wasn't vulnerable in the slightest.

## CHAPTER FOURTEEN

John climbed to the top of the stairs, seeing Louisa speaking with Rose and Fanny about the rooms. Watching her, his body tingled with the memories from that morning and his cock stirred just thinking about what she had done to him. Even that little conversation when his manhood was literally in her hands—yea gods but she made his blood boil.

Marriage equates slavery? Now that he had time to think about it fully clothed, he could understand her perspective. Didn't agree with it—he doubted Amanda had felt like she had been in slavery—but he could see her thinking it was true. Her first marriage must have been horrible, even worse than his.

He leaned against the wall and crossed his arms, watching her. He wasn't actually complaining about their relationship—hell, if that morning was any indication, she had no qualms either. Why did he feel like something was missing? He didn't intend on marrying her right away; he just wanted the option for the future.

He would have to work on convincing her otherwise. At

least with him marriage would be different. He didn't understand how she couldn't see that yet. After all he had done for her—how many men of her acquaintance would give her a partnership in an inn? Teach her how to shingle a roof? Drink ale with her? What was it about him that reminded her of her first husband? Yea gods, if it was something he could stop doing, he would; he just needed to know. If she didn't talk to him about it, how could he know what to do to change her mind?

"Winter weather is approaching," she was saying to the maids. "We must ensure all rooms have extra towels. I have already informed Alan and Timothy to keep the coal reserves stocked in the rooms as well; you will have to keep the fires at a low burn starting mid-morning. If the rooms are not let by late evening, we can let them go out and can light them again if there are any last-minute guests without losing too much heat."

The girls nodded and she sent them on their way. Louisa turned and looked surprised to see him standing there, but recovered and walked toward him. "What are you doing here?"

"Watching you."

She raised her eyebrows. "You have work to do. You don't have time to be watching me. Why would you even say something so foolish? What do you truly want?"

John pushed himself off the wall and straightened. "Lunch. I've asked Maisie to get some plates ready for us. Rose will bring them out. And I tend to say nice, complimentary things to the people I care about. I know, it's strange, but that's just the way I am. I like it when you feel good about yourself."

She frowned. "You are being ridiculous. I don't appreciate this kind of teasing."

"Do you appreciate any kind of teasing?" He took her hand and walked down the stairs with her.

She had pulled her hand out of his grasp by the time they reached the bottom. "Teasing is a waste of time. People should just say what they mean."

"I did say what I meant. I was watching you. You are quite watchable. Ale?"

"Please." She sat at a table in the corner while he pulled two pints and brought them over. "How can someone be watchable?"

John smiled at her and shrugged. "Don't you watch me?"

"I don't."

"Liar. I've noticed it."

"I deny everything." She couldn't help but smile back at him.

He chuckled. "There you are, kitten."

Her smile disappeared. "You need to be more careful," she warned him. "We don't want people to know about us."

"We don't?"

"So you have to stop it with the hand-holding and the 'kitten' in public."

They were interrupted by Rose bringing out their food, ham sandwiches and apple pie for dessert. "Anythin' else, luv?" Rose asked, her eyes on John. He shook his head and bit into his sandwich, the maid tossing her hair over her shoulder and a smile at Louisa.

Louisa stared hard at John as he ate, picking at the bread of her sandwich. He reached for his pint and glanced up. "What?" he said around the food in his mouth.

"Nothing." She lifted her sandwich to her mouth. "So you will stop? We are agreed?"

He thought for a moment. "No."

"What?" She nearly choked on her food. "What do you mean? We don't want people to know about us."

"No, *you* don't want people to know about us. I am fine with them knowing. If you allowed it, I would marry you and shout it from the rooftops."

She frowned fiercely at him. "Stop this. You are being ridiculous."

"Allow me to show you the respect of not hiding you."

"John, we discussed this."

He shook his head. "I remember more of a diatribe on your part, not a discussion."

"Why do you have to do this? Why does everything have to be an analysis of our relationship? Why can't you just accept what we have?"

"I don't know." John gave her a sad smile. "I'm not trying to force you, not trying to make you into my slave. I just think you deserve more than something we have to hide. I think *I* deserve something more. It makes me feel like you are ashamed of me."

Louisa stared at him, swallowing her food, and washed it down with some ale. "You are an odd man, John Taylor."

"So you've told me."

"I am not ashamed of you."

He shrugged, taking a big bite from his sandwich.

"John—"

"Johnny Taylor!"

They both looked up to see a scrawny man with unwashed

hair standing across the pub from their table. His clothes were worn, with holes in some places and stains on the lapels. A tattered red scarf hugged his neck loosely.

The man walked slowly toward them, slightly hunched and his hands in fists. "'ere comes the Five Hit Wonder, ladies 'n gents. Bigger'n a mountain, stronger'n a bear, no man alive can beat 'im."

John grinned and stood up, heading toward the man with his hands up in fighting mode. The man kept talking. "Watch 'im, gen'lemen, 'e is big but 'e is fast. Lightnin' quick, wot wit' a one-two"—John feinted two punches—"'e starts his attack, an' then th' ol' three-four-five"—three more feints—"an' 'is opponent is down for th' count." The man made an elaborate show of falling into a chair to much laughter from the patrons.

John grabbed him by the arm and hauled him up into a hug, pounding his back. "Alfie Spike, ye old wanker, wha' brings ye here?"

"Well, who else is gonna make sure yer not scarin' proper folks wit' yer unnatural height?"

"Me? Folks ain't scared of me when they've got yer ugly mug to look at."

The two men embraced again with more back-pounding and laughter. When they separated, John gestured to the pub and Louisa. "Welcome to th' Beefy Buzzard, Alfie. We're doin' fine. And ov'r here be Mrs. Louisa Brock, me partner in th' enterprise." He led the smaller man over. "Mrs. Brock, Mr. Alfie Spike, my old manager and all-'round scoundrel." He laughed, clapping the man on his shoulder.

The man bent at the waist, smiling at Louisa and bringing

her hand to his mouth for a kiss. "Pleasure, Mrs. Brock, I'm sure."

"Mr. Spike. Welcome to the Beefy Buzzard."

"Ooh la la, ye've got yourself a nice soundin' one for a change there, John."

John cuffed him on the head. "Watch yerself. Packard, another ale and sandwich. Sit." He pulled out a chair and Alfie slumped into it. "What brings ye to Grompton?"

Alfie yanked his ratty top hat off his head and tossed it on the table, scratching his head before pulling some leaflets from his jacket. "Wot else, mate? Boxing. There's a mill in a fortnight. Here, in Grompton. Where's th' privy in 'ere?" He scratched himself, caught Louisa looking at him before removing his hand sheepishly.

John gestured. "Back that way." He finished off his sandwich as the man disappeared down the corridor to the privy.

Louisa watched him leave as well and frowned deeply at John when they were alone again. "Who is that man?"

"I told you. Alfie was my manager. Arranged my fights, took care of business."

"Why did you speak to him like that?"

John grinned. "I've known him for years. We've always talked to each other like that."

"No." Louisa shook her head. "Ye old wanker? Yer ugly mug? Folks ain't scared? You're talking like you belong down on the docks."

"What?"

"You do it with the customers as well. When you're talking with anyone but me, you speak as though you're in Seven Dials. You talk like a prizefighter to everyone but me."

"I do?" John looked at her with a blank face. "I had no idea."

"Why do you do it?"

"Well, I am a prizefighter, kitten. I suppose there are expectations that go with it."

"Expectations to make yourself sound unintelligent?"

John sat back. "I'm a prizefighter. I'm good at it."

"You *were* a prizefighter. You are retired and have been successful at making this inn flourish."

"It wasn't flourishing until you came along."

Louisa shook her head. "You would have made it work without me. You are an intelligent man, John. You don't need to hide it."

He gave her a small smile. "Why not? I have to hide what I'm doing with you."

Louisa pushed herself up from the table and gathered their empty dishes. "I'll go see what is taking that sandwich so long."

"Louisa," John said as she walked away. He sighed and shook his head.

"Trouble wit' th' missus?" Alfie asked as he sat down again.

"She's not my missus," John muttered. Rose brought out the sandwich and placed it in front of Alfie.

He winked at her. "Ta, luv."

John leaned his arms on the table. "So there's a boxing mill here?" He made a conscious effort to regulate his language. She was wrong, he didn't hide his intelligence.

Alfie glanced at him around his sandwich. "Aye. Retirement not treatin' ye well?"

"It's fine. The mill will bring business."

"There's exhibitions next week, leadin' up to th' main event. Purse fights. I kin get ye one, if ye want."

"Thanks, but I'm not interested."

"Think abou' it. There's a bloke lookin' to make a name fer hisself. He's not that bad. Ye've got at least a head on 'im and more'n two stone, I figure. Ye'd take 'im down wit'out breakin' a sweat."

John cocked an eyebrow at him. "Doesn't sound like much of a challenge."

Alfie laughed, bits of food flying out of his mouth. "That's th' point, Johnny. We'll split the purse."

He glared at his former manager. "Did ye come 'ere jes to get me to fleece th' bloke wit' ye?" He heard his words and forced himself to speak as he would to Louisa. "I wouldn't do it for you before, I'm not going to do it now. I'm a respectable businessman now."

Alfie raised a placating hand. "I'm not suggestin' anythin', John. Tell ye wot, you keep th' purse an' I'll make th' rounds wit' th' side bets."

"It doesn't matter," John said, sitting back. "I'm not interested."

Alfie looked at him for a long moment before a slow smile crossed his face. "She is yer missus, ain't she? Well done, mate."

"What?" John shook his head. "I tol' ye—told you she's not. And she has nothing to do with this."

Alfie shook his head. "I've seen it happen time an' again. A fighter meets a skirt, gets caught up in 'em and it all changes. It happened wit' ye an' Amanda for a bit, but ye got out of it."

John rubbed his head. He knew it was useless to talk to Alfie; he would only hear and see what he wanted to.

Was he right? John knew his feelings were getting more involved with Louisa every day, but he didn't see that as a negative thing. He certainly didn't see it as changing him. He simply didn't want to fight. It didn't matter that he knew Louisa wouldn't like it; she had vocalized her objections to pugilism several times.

"Don't you miss it?" Alfie asked him.

Miss it? John looked down at his hands, folded in front of him. His large hands, ones that provided him with more money than he had expected to ever earn in his lifetime. What he had said to Louisa wasn't wrong; the inn hadn't been flourishing before she came. He had been floundering, thinking every day about what a mistake he had made. He enjoyed serving drinks, but she did all the hard work to make this place run. He had been in over his head and he knew it now.

In the ring, he had been a champion. In control of his opponent, himself, the fight. He would see the man in the minutes before they began and know exactly what he needed to do to defeat him. And he would do it. Play with his opponent for a few rounds sometimes—the crowds liked longer fights—but the end was always inevitable to him.

It had grown wearying, however. Not the fights or the winning, but the constant talk of the sport, surrounded by men like Alfie. He had begun to want more from life and thought buying the inn would give him what he was looking for. Only it had been falling apart around him until Louisa came. And now that was falling apart too, with her equating marriage to him with slavery and wanting to hide their relationship.

Things were getting out of control again and he didn't like it.

John focused on his former manager. "Fifty pounds?"

"Aye."

With fifty pounds he could take Louisa to Bath and work on convincing her to not be afraid to let people know about their relationship. Get things under control again. "Tell ye what, Alfie. Get me in that ring and I'll show ye jes' how much I miss it."

# CHAPTER FIFTEEN

Something was off, she knew it. People—John—had been acting strangely the last few days. He had been eating odd things like raw eggs and spending more time in the stable once the pub was closed. He would come to bed sweaty and sore. Louisa knew he was working with his training bag, but why he was working so long and hard she didn't know.

There was subterfuge happening as well. Whispered conversations with Rose, conversations that ended as soon as she approached, denials that they were speaking of anything. Thankfully, Alfie Spike hadn't reappeared since that horrible encounter. She had thought he would have stayed, but she did not make it habit to look gift horses in the mouth.

An illogical part of her mind kept delving into foolish territory. Thoughts of John and Rose kept bubbling up, little images of them in the stable together. She knew it was wrong, knew that John would not do that to her. If she knew anything about him, it was that he was honest. If he was tired of her, he would tell her and vice versa.

She just didn't think the thought of him growing tired of her would make her feel so . . . hurt. Angry. Depressed.

It was good that he wasn't tired of her, then.

But still, something was off and for once he wasn't talking with her about what was going on in his head. His feelings. She had grown to expect those conversations, was beginning to not want to avoid them, but he wasn't trying to talk about those things.

People were beginning to arrive for the boxing mill. The main event wasn't for a few more days, but she had heard of exhibitions that were to take place beforehand. She hadn't heard who the fighters were, frankly didn't care so long as their inn and pub received more business. Thanks to the event, things were already picking up to the point where Louisa had to help out serving in the pub every night; business had gotten too hectic for Rose and Fanny to handle serving on their own along with maintaining the rooms and seeing to those customers. Louisa had already made notes to hire additional staff when special events came to town.

She bustled around the tables, dropping off food, clearing tables, taking orders. John and Mr. Packard were kept busy behind the bar serving drinks. Glancing over there now, she saw that it was just Packard seeing to the drinking patrons; John was nowhere in sight. Where would he have gone on such a busy evening? With an uneasy weight in her chest, Louisa made her way over to the bar.

"Three pints, Mr. Packard," she said, wiping some spilled ale off the counter. "Where is Mr. Taylor?"

Packard jerked his head in the direction of the corridor. "He went to the cask room. Said he needed to tap a couple more to get us through the mill fine."

"Oh." Didn't she see Rose go the same way a few minutes before as well? The uneasy weight grew. Pressing her lips together, Louisa marched to the corridor, even though her logical mind was screaming at her to not go there. But logic also dictated that it would be best to have everything out in the open, to know for sure what was going on.

She rounded the corner into the corridor to see John and Rose standing at the end. He was speaking to her in hushed tones: ". . . not to worry. I will be there."

"Where will you be?" Louisa's voice rang out in the corridor angrily.

Both looked at her guiltily. "Nowhere," John said. "Just . . . behind the bar."

She pierced Rose with a sharp look. "There's work to be done, Rose." Her voice was tight and hard. The maid quickly left the corridor to resume her duties, glancing at John over her shoulder as she left.

"Is something the matter, Louisa?" he asked.

"You tell me. What were you talking about with Rose?"

"Nothing important."

She scoffed. "Then why couldn't you have the conversation out in the pub where everyone can see? Why did you have to hide back here?"

"We weren't hiding. It was quieter back here." He walked toward her.

"Yes, quiet enough to have an intimate conversation."

"Intimate conversation?" John stopped and placed his hands on his hips. "What do you think is going on between me and Rose?"

She pressed her lips together and raised her chin. "I don't

think anything is happening. All I know is that we have a busy pub out there and two of my people were back here instead of working."

He scrutinized her. "Good," he said slowly. "Because you have nothing to worry about, kitten."

"Usually when men say that, woman have cause to worry."

"Not with me you don't."

"Seems to me another thing a man would say." She spun on her heel and marched back to the pub. "We have a full pub, John. I suggest you return to work."

Louisa studiously ignored him for the rest of the evening. She may not have caught him doing something illicit with Rose, but that did not mean he was innocent. She could feel his eyes on her several times and would not give him the satisfaction of knowing she was aware of him. It helped that she was nearly run off her feet. Men had arrived in droves in the last little while, all chatting about women, horses and boxing. Money had been exchanging hands in some pre-fight betting. She did not like to see that, did not like to have the reminder of how gambling had affected her life, but so long as the men continued to buy food and drink she would tolerate it.

The pub finally began to clear. They would not close, for all the customers were going to one of the exhibition bouts and would likely come back after for celebrating their wins and mourning their losses. But the respite would be appreciated, as it would give them time to clean and prepare and perhaps even rest a few moments and eat a few mouthfuls.

"Maisie, set out some nibbles for the staff," Louisa instructed. "We'll take the opportunity to refresh ourselves during this lull."

"Aye, ma'am."

"I'll have Mr. Taylor and Mr. Packard send back some ale as well."

"Very good, ma'am."

Louisa went back into the pub, mentally preparing herself for speaking to John, even if it was just about ale for the staff. He wouldn't begrudge it, she knew, would likely agree, but she did not want to look at or speak with him after what she saw in the corridor.

She was in luck, though. It was just Mr. Packard behind the bar, wiping glasses. "Mr. Packard, please pull some half pints for the staff and bring them back to the kitchen. We'll have a few moments to ourselves back there."

"Aye, Mrs. Brock."

Louisa glanced around, not seeing John anywhere. Or Rose. Had they disappeared together again? There were still several customers nursing their drinks. She swallowed, hating herself for what she was about to ask. "Where is Mr. Taylor?"

Packard looked a little scared. "I, uh, I think he went to the bout, ma'am."

"With Rose?"

The portly man shook his head. "I dunno. Don't think so. Saw her go upstairs a few minutes ago."

Relief eased through her. They weren't together. He had gone to watch the exhibition match. She nodded, understanding the pull of the sport he had been a champion of for so many years. She could allow him that. But why would he go without telling her? That seemed odd.

Brushing the thought aside, she turned her attention to the remaining customers. Fanny was clearing some of the empty tables, so Louisa made her way over to the occupied ones.

"Need anything else, gents?" she asked.

The young Corinthians looked up. "No. We're about on our way."

"Going to the bout?"

"Yes. Should be a good one."

She shook her head. "I know nothing of pugilism and that is as much as I want to know. But enjoy the fight. Be sure to come back here. We will still be open and serving pints to winners and losers."

"I disagree that it will be a good fight," another one said. "I think it will be quite lopsided. Doesn't make sense to me to pit a champion against an unseasoned fighter."

"But he's been in retirement," the first one argued. "The champion is not in champion shape anymore."

A frisson of apprehension spiraled down her spine. "The bout is between a retired champion and a new fighter?"

The first Corinthian looked at her. "Yes. I thought you knew."

She shook her head. "Knew what?"

He looked at her, confused. "But don't you work here with him? John Taylor, I mean?"

Her breath seized in her body. "John Taylor is fighting tonight?" she squeaked out.

"Yes." He checked his timepiece. "In fact, the bout has already started. Bottoms up, Drake. His fights don't normally last more than four rounds."

"He might draw this one out, seeing as how it's an exhibition," Drake pointed out as they left the premises.

Louisa walked back through the kitchen and into the office in a daze. She waved permission to Maisie to begin serving the staff, but did not speak. In the office, she sat down slowly on the newly made chair, one she had had custom made to accommodate Giant Johnny.

He was fighting. He hadn't said anything to her about it, but he was fighting. Tonight. Right now, in fact. No wonder he had been spending so much time in the stable this past week; he had been training. And hadn't told her. Was that what all those secret conversations with Rose had been about?

Why was she even focusing on Rose when at this very moment his face was being pummeled by another fighter? Good Lord, he could get seriously injured! What if he were to be knocked unconscious? What would she do then? It was bad enough to think of his bones breaking, but unconsciousness? She had heard of pugilists being beaten so hard they didn't wake up. What would happen to her if John didn't wake up? Their contract would not likely stand up in a court of law, so she would lose the inn, lose her stability and independence.

More importantly, she would lose John.

Louisa stood abruptly. She had to stop it, had to stop the fight. She didn't know how she would do it, but she had to. She had to save John.

Grabbing her cloak, she dashed out of the office and into the pub. "Packard, where is the fight?" she asked.

"The old church stable, ma'am," he replied. "The boxing mill is there too. It was the only place big enough for the crowds." His voice faded as she stalked out of the pub and into the night.

Louisa scurried out of the inn yard, heading in the direction of the match. Stragglers were with her and she brushed by them impatiently, intent on her mission. She had to get to John before something serious happened to him.

She rounded the corner and the old stable came into sight. She could hear the shouting and cheering though she was still quite a distance away; the crowd must be large and enjoying the fight. That must be a good sign. If something bad had occurred, surely they would not be cheering as such. She did not slow her pace, but hurried on. The noise grew in volume as she approached the building.

Slipping inside, her senses were bombarded. Lanterns hung from the rafters and beams, casting light throughout the entire scene. Men and women of all types were there, shouting and cheering on their fighters. More shouts for bets added to the confusion and money was changing hands at a furious pace. And the stench—oh, the stench—of a plethora of sweaty, drunk humans in a confined space filled her nostrils, making her eyes water. Louisa swallowed, her throat becoming thick with bile. She didn't know if it was from the disgusting smell or from the pure delight all these people were displaying at watching two men beat each other up.

Louisa pushed through the crowd, determined to get to the fight and stop it. She gritted her teeth as she fought through the crowd, using her elbows to get around people. Many dirty looks were sent her way and several unpleasant comments tossed, but she pressed on. As she drew closer to the center of the stable, the sound of fists landing on flesh joined the cacophony and spurred her on.

She had to stop when she reached a rope, keeping the

spectators from the fighters. It was set up in a square about ten square feet. But she hardly noticed, her eyes riveted on John in the middle of the ring fighting his opponent.

Just as the time she had seen him in the inn's stable, he was shirtless, trousers and boots being the only items he wore. His skin was sweaty, glistening in the light from the lanterns; already one eye was swelling shut and a bruise was growing on one of his sides. But he danced—or looked like he was dancing—moving toward his opponent and away, his hands always up in front of his face. Louisa watched the play of his muscles as he fought, the way they coiled and released with precision.

He towered over the other fighter. His reach was longer. His body stronger. His opponent bobbed and weaved around the punches, taking the opportunities to get closer to land some decent hits. The men around her pushed into her, shouting at their chosen fighters. From the sound of things, John was the heavily favored one, and looking at the fight, it was not hard to see why. He was dominating the bout, but also seemed to be drawing it out. Seeing him fight, seeing him in this element where his success was unsurpassed, was novel and a part of her wanted to just stand and watch him win.

The fighters drew closer to where she was standing. Louisa had to think fast. How could she stop the fight? What would happen if she were to climb into the ring? She did not want to risk getting hit herself. What if she reached out and grabbed John when he was close enough, or tapped him on the shoulder? But that was dependent upon him coming within her reach and she did not want to distract him to the point of him getting hurt because he wasn't paying attention.

Scenarios flew through her mind, all the while with her eyes on the fight. John landed hit after hit, enough to make his opponent stagger and shake his head, but not enough to send him off his feet. Even though she had never seen a prize-fight before, had never seen John use his full strength, she knew he was holding back.

The fighters were making their way back in her direction. She had missed her opportunity the last time, she could not afford to do so again. She focused on John, intent on stopping the fight.

They were closer, but not close enough yet. Louisa still did not know what she was going to do, but she knew they had to be closer. John swung and missed, a rare event from the looks of things. His opponent saw the opening and took advantage, stepping closer with quick movements and aiming his fist for John's head.

Fist collided with face. The crack was heard by the front spectators and John's head whipped to the side. He staggered back, one hand to his head, his body hunching over. This gave the younger fighter another opportunity. The same hit, this time with more force as John was not holding himself up or protecting himself with his hands. Another crack, another whip of his head.

Blood flew through the air. Louisa saw it in a surreal moment, saw it flying off John's face and in her direction. The blood arched and began its descent, landing across her face and on her clothing. She couldn't help it.

Louisa shrieked. Loudly. And high-pitched. Enough to stop the fight and silence the stable. She shrieked out of shock and surprise. Why she had never considered what proximity to the fight might bring was beyond her. Now she stood with a large streak of John's blood on her. She could feel where it had landed on her face, warm and oozy and beginning to slide down, thanks to gravity.

Even the fighters had stopped. John's eyes widened when he saw who it was and what had happened. He took a step toward her, one hand outstretched, concern in his one good eye. Blood was dripping out of the fresh wound on his face, but he paid it no heed.

"Louisa?" he asked. "Are you hurt?"

Seeing his face, seeing what his opponent had done to him, was what spurred her on. Looking him dead in the eye, she lifted her chin and shouted, "Two pounds on Johnny Taylor!"

"**O**uch!" John winced and jerked away from the cold compress Louisa pressed unceremoniously against his face. "That hurt."

She gave him a disbelieving look. "You just had a man intentionally hit you in the face more times than I counted and you are complaining that this hurts?"

"I am sensitive," he said, giving her a sheepish shrug.

"What you are is a big baby." She pressed the compress back to his face. "Hold this." He dutifully held the compress while she wiped more blood off the rest of his face. "How you have managed to keep all your teeth and not damaged any facial feature besides your nose is beyond me. That was the most brutal thing I have ever seen."

He tried to smile at her, but groaned and returned the compress to his face. "But you liked it, didn't you?"

"Liked seeing a man pummel you with his fists? Liked

seeing your blood on his hands and skin? Liked seeing you beat a man—a man who most likely has a mother, a sister, a wife, concerned just like me—beat a man to a near pulp? And all this for a purse of what, ten pounds?"

"Fifty. You were concerned about me?"

"Fifty pounds to beat a man up?"

"Yes."

"And you won it?"

He grinned, despite the pain. "You saw me get this." He waved the purse in front of her. She batted his hand away and he tossed it on the bed. He took a long sip from the Scotch sitting on the nightstand.

She fingered the cut on his cheek. "You need stitches. Let me get my needle and thread."

"Whoa, whoa, wait." He grabbed her wrist. "You have a needle and thread? I don't think I trust you with that."

"What, are you afraid of needles too, you big baby?"

"When they're in your hand, it's probably best I am."

"Be quiet, you big galoot."

"Mm, you're talking dirty again."

"And you must be punch-drunk." She rummaged through her sewing bag and retrieved her needle and some thread.

"Just drunk on how beautiful you look today."

"I look beautiful every day." She said this matter-of-factly as she threaded the needle and swirled it around in his Scotch. "Hold still." She stood between his legs and dabbed his wound clean, beginning to stitch it shut.

"Have you done this before?" he asked, watching her intently, trying to remain still despite the painful pull of needle through skin.

"No, but I've seen doctors do it many times. I was a governess, remember."

His hands settled on the back of her thighs, his thumbs caressing the cheeks of her bottom. "You were concerned about me?" he asked again.

"Was fifty pounds really worth this?" She avoided his question. "What are you going to do with that money anyway?"

"Can't a man have some secrets?"

"Not when it involves getting your face bloodied and bruised like this. Tell me what was so important that you had to do this."

"Well, Christmas is coming up and a man likes to spoil his woman, give her something nice to mark the occasion. I was thinking we could go to Bath for a few days, stay in a nice hotel, eat some Sally buns, perhaps get you a nice dress."

Her needle stilled and she looked at him for a long moment. He looked disgruntled at having to tell her, but also eager to see her reaction. "I don't need any of those things." She fought the warmth spreading in her chest at his thoughtfulness.

"It's not about what you need, but what I want to give you."

"Give me a private dining room, John. I don't want to go to Bath." She broke off the rest of the thread and dabbed at the stitched wound again.

He moved his face away from her touch. "It's always about the inn, isn't it? I bet you were concerned for me because of how my being hurt would affect business, right?"

"And don't call me your woman," she snipped. She began to wash the needle in the basin on his vanity.

"Yea gods, Louisa, a man can't do anything right with you, can he?"

"And I was concerned because I didn't want to have to see your broken face in bed with me," she growled.

"What?" he snapped.

"I happen to like the way your face looks, you big galoot, and I don't like thinking of it being hurt."

He grabbed her and pulled her close to him. "My face isn't hurt."

"Says the man with eight stitches in his cheek, a fat lip and a black eye."

John shook his head. "I'm too tall for anyone to land decent hits. My face won't ever be broken."

She framed his face with her hands. "This looks broken to me and I don't like it. I thought you were retired."

"I was a boxer for a decade, kitten. It's not like I can just turn it off like it was an ale cask."

She traced his eyebrows. "Do you miss it? Is that why you did this?"

"Do I miss it?" He shrugged. "Like I said, it was ten years of my life and I was good at it, pretty much all I've been good at my whole life. And you know why I did it. For you, kitten."

She took a deep breath through her nose. "I really don't want to go to Bath, John."

"Then we'll figure something else out to do with the money. Just nothing to do with the inn, agreed?"

She nodded. "I can do that."

"Can we seal this bargain with a kiss?" He grinned at her hopefully.

Louisa grimaced. "I don't think you understand how your face looks right now when you smile."

"Kiss me anyway? Make my pain go away, kitten."

"You truly are a big galoot, Johnny Taylor." She kissed him anyway.

# CHAPTER SIXTEEN

The boxing mill was stupendous for business. Men, young and old, had been arriving since yesterday in anticipation, watching more of the exhibitions that led up to the main fight. The inn was near capacity, all but a few rooms taken. Those rooms Louisa was certain would fill as well, even if not with sportsmen in town for the event. There was a winter storm brewing and stranded travelers would need a place to stay. It was music to her ears, the sound of coins exchanging hands.

Louisa weaved through the tables, carrying two servings of pie to a table, followed by Rose with just as many. They placed them in front of the men who ordered them, who were laughing raucously.

One of them grabbed Louisa's wrist. "Wait a moment, luv, I've a question for you."

She wrenched herself away from the man, glancing over her shoulder at John behind the bar, pouring drinks. He wasn't looking her way. "What is it?" she asked, trying to remain civil. The man was a paying customer.

He glanced at his friends with a grin. "What is your opinion of premarital relations?"

"With you? Not a very good one, I am afraid."

His friends guffawed at that. His face flickered, but he persevered. Rose moved away as she saw to other tables. "What I mean is, luv, we've been having a conversation here. Do you think a man, a healthy man, has to marry a girl he's been sleeping with?"

She frowned. "Does the girl have expectations?"

"Perhaps." The man shifted uncomfortably. "But in this day and age, a girl should know that a man's not going to buy the cow when he's getting the milk for free. Don't you agree?"

His friends laughed again, pounding the table with their fists and tankards. Their noise added to that already filling the pub. The man looked at her with an expectant smirk.

Louisa shifted her weight to one hip, looking at the man through narrowed eyes. This clearly was the kind of man who preyed on innocents, luring them into a sense of security before ruining them. It left a sour taste in her mouth that men like him existed, even more so that he and his drunken friends had been allowed in her inn. At some point the value of a shilling was not worth the sacrifice.

"Well, luv, what do you say?"

"I agree," she declared.

He blinked, clearly not expecting that response from her. "I beg your pardon?"

"I agree with premarital relations. After all, a woman should be assured the entire pig is worth it when all she can expect is such a small sausage."

The table was silent as her words sank in. The man's face

reddened as his friends broke out into more laughter. He opened his mouth to say something when one of the others clapped him on the back. "Don't be sore, Preston, not when you goaded her."

Louisa pasted a polite smile on her face. "Enjoy your pies, gentlemen. If you need anything else, Mr. Packard or Mr. Taylor behind the bar will see to it." As she walked away, she made a mental note to tell Rose and Fanny to avoid that man for the rest of his stay.

"Louisa." John forestalled her retreat into the kitchen and gestured for her to come to the bar. "Are you all right?" His eyes were on the table she had just served.

"Yes, it was just some men who thought alcohol made them humorous."

The door banged open and they both looked at a young lady with two blond children. She looked around and saw John and Louisa watching them. She took the children by the hand and approached the bar, ensuring she kept the girls from the more rowdy tables.

"Are you the proprietor?" The young brunette asked as the small group stopped at the bar. She spoke in the cultured tones of the nobility. "Please tell me you have a room. The last two my husband and I stopped at were full and the snow is getting worse."

John nodded. "I am Mr. Taylor and this is Mrs. Brock. We are the owners."

"We do have a room available," Louisa said. "It is large enough to accommodate your family. Two large beds."

Relief washed over the young lady's face. "Thank goodness. My husband is just seeing to the coach and horses."

"Why don't you have a seat here while you wait?" Louisa gestured to a nearby empty table. "I will have one of our maids ensure the room is ready and have a tea tray sent up for you. You and your daughters must be cold and tired from your traveling."

"Mama," the eldest girl whispered not-so-quietly, "she looks like the lady in the portrait. Like Grandmama."

The young lady smiled sheepishly at Louisa. "I apologize. You do bear a resemblance to my late mother-in-law."

"Think nothing of it," Louisa assured her. She smiled at the girl. "I am sure I would know if I were related to such lovely young girls." Her comment made them both turn shyly into their mother's skirts. "I will just see to your room and tea tray."

"Is there perchance a private dining room available?" the lady asked. She cast a wary glance around at the men well on their way to drunkenness.

Louisa shot A Look at John, who said, "Not yet, but none will bother you here. I will see to it."

"Thank you," she said, the conversation drifting away as Louisa headed into the kitchen.

"Maisie, we need a tea tray," Louisa said. The cook was already putting together several more pies and looked flustered.

"We're running out of dinner pies, Mrs. Brock," she said. "We've enough for twenty more, but that's it."

"That's a good thing," Louisa smiled. "If you can, save one for Mr. Taylor and me. But we can eat something else later. Timothy, how about that tea tray? Four settings, please. I'm going to check on the rooms." She went up the back stairs and let herself into the room she promised to the new arrivals.

Her practiced eye scanned the room, taking note of how prepared it was. It was set up for two, recently cleaned and dusted, new linens on the beds, pillows neatly plumped, washstand ready for fresh water and use. She grabbed the pitcher and hurried downstairs, filled it with the pot of warmed water from the back hob and returned it to the room. She stepped back into the corridor and headed for the linen closet, fetching several more towels; the additional young guests would likely need them.

She closed the linen closet and headed back to the room, her arms full of towels. Just as she was passing another door, it opened and someone stepped out, crashing into her and sending her towels scattering on the floor. A firm hand grasped her elbow when she was teetering, steadying her.

She opened her eyes and looked into the bluest, coldest eyes she had ever seen. Blond hair fell across his forehead, but the boyish look did nothing to reduce the effect of his eyes. She unconsciously fought to suppress a shiver.

"My apologies," he spoke in a deep, cultured voice. "I did not mean to step into you, Miss—"

"Brock. Mrs. Brock," Louisa said. She bent down to retrieve the towels, refolding them to stack neatly.

He bent down with her, one hand holding on to a black cane with a golden wolf's head. The creature was in a frozen snarl, making her wonder about the man who held it. "Our proprietress, from what I understand. Mr. Taylor informed us you were around somewhere."

"Yes, I oversee the maids and the kitchen. The boxing mill and weather are stretching our staff thin, so I am helping where I can." She took a towel from his offered hand and folded it, adding it to the stack.

"An employer who does not mind getting her hands dirty. Most admirable." He straightened with her, offering his hand to assist her up, which she did not take.

"Are you here with your wife, Mr.—"

"Grant. And no, I am betrothed but not yet married. I travel with two companions who are waiting for me below stairs to dine. It has been a long day and the kitchen smells promising."

Louisa smiled politely. "You will not be disappointed, Mr. Grant. Our cook lives up to the smells."

"That is reassuring."

"If you will excuse me, sir, I must see to this room." She nodded and turned on her heel, delivering the towels to the room. One last review of the room and she left, taking the back stairs back down to the kitchen.

Timothy was just finishing up preparing the tea tray. Louisa measured out the leaves into the teapot and added water from the kettle they always kept boiling for just this reason. She closed the teapot and put a cover on it. Once more up the back stairs and she put the tray in the room, locking it behind her.

When she returned to the pub, the crowd had grown; she could not see across the room and the noise had increased. She glanced at the bar, where John was still busy with the drinks. The young lady and her two daughters were sitting at a table, her gaze wary and nervous. A man sat with them, his back to Louisa, a reassuring hand holding the young lady's. The man must be her husband.

Louisa pushed her way to the bar. She leaned over the end. "John, the family's room is ready. I put the tea tray in it to get the children out of the noisy pub. Where is the book?"

He pushed it toward her. "They're signed in."

"I just want to check the name so I can address them properly. She's obviously nobility; I assume her husband is too."

"Yes, a baron."

Louisa flipped to the relevant page and trailed her finger down to find the right entry. When she saw one for two adults and two children, she looked over at the name.

And froze. Her heart even stopped for a moment.

*Baron Brockhurst and family.*

Dear God, he had caught up to her. A coincidence, it had to be. There was no possible reason he should expect her to be here. The young lady had no idea who she was and had given no indication that she was expecting to find anyone here.

"Louisa?"

She glanced up at John to see him giving her an odd look.

"I called your name about three times. That family looks ready to go up." He gestured to their table.

Louisa followed his finger with her eyes to see the man standing at his table, his hand loosely holding his wife's in the air. Baroness Brockhurst was looking between the two of them, confused. The baron was staring at her, his hazel eyes wide. His blond hair was tamed into neat waves, different from the young shag she had last seen on him. His clothing was finely tailored, understated in its elegance, the grays and greens complementing his coloring.

"Matthew?" The baroness said. "You look like you've seen a ghost." She glanced at Louisa again.

"Anna-Louise?"

Louisa looked at John, who was still watching her. "I have to go," she whispered.

"Go? Go where?"

"I just—" She spun on her heel and began to push her way through the crowd.

"Anna-Louise!"

She tried to pick up her pace, but the crowd made it difficult.

"Anna-Louise, wait!"

She grimaced as she pushed her way through the bodies filling the pub. Her heart was pounding in her ears; all she could think about was getting away from her brother. If he caught her, everything would fall to pieces. "Move," she whispered, but she doubted whoever was in front of her heard. Her panic propelled her forward. She wasn't looking where she was going and ran straight into a hard chest.

"Excuse me," a deep voice said.

"Get out of my way." She tried to move around whoever it was.

"Louisa?"

She looked up and saw the familiar face of her friend's husband, Jacob Knightly. She had lived with him, Claire and Sara for the better part of a year. What was he doing here? Oh God, he was here for her, wasn't he? A glance over his arm showed her Stephen Montgomery standing beside the table and the man with the wolf's-head cane sitting, looking confused.

She tried to move around him, but Jacob grabbed her arms. "Wait, where are you going? It's me, Jacob."

Louisa struggled against his grasp, but it wouldn't loosen. "Let me go!" she shouted. She tried to kick him.

"Anna-Louise?"

"Louisa, calm down. What has gotten into you?"

"Get your hands off her!" The roar carried over the noise of the pub, silencing everyone and everything. John barreled through the crowd, his face intent and angry, his purpose clear. Jacob released his grip on Louisa—was it out of fear? Shock? Did it matter?—and John immediately brought Louisa close to him, protecting her.

He looked at her, his eyes scanning her face. "Are you all right? Did he hurt you?"

"No, John, it's not—"

Jacob interrupted. "I don't know what you're getting at, mate, but I didn't even touch her long enough to hurt her."

"You"—John pointed his finger in Jacob's face—"you need to stay away from her."

Recognition dawned on Jacob's face. "You're John Taylor, the Five Hit Wonder."

John's face remained angry. "Yes, and it appears you know exactly what I can do, so step back."

Matthew Brockhurst joined the fray. "What exactly are you doing with my sister?"

John and Jacob turned to look at the smaller man. "Who?"

His finger waved between the two of them. "Both of you. How do you know my sister and what gives you the idea that either of you can even touch the sister of a baron?"

"Sister of a baron? Louisa Hurst?"

"What are you talking about? This is Louisa Brock."

John and Jacob spoke at the same time, both looking at each other when they said Louisa's name.

Baron Brockhurst frowned. "No, that is Miss Anna-Louise Brockhurst. My sister. Who I have been searching for the past six years."

"What?" John looked at her, still in his embrace. "What is he talking about?"

She begged him with her eyes to let it go, let her go.

"Six years?" Jacob said. "We've been searching for five months, after she disappeared from home without a trace."

"Home? What home?"

"Disappeared?" John was still looking at her. "What is going on, Louisa?"

"Her name is Anna-Louise, Miss Brockhurst to you," Baron Brockhurst said hotly. "And where were you living all these years?"

John now pointed at the baron. "I suggest you stop talking, milord, and let her speak." He turned back to her. "Tell me what's going on, kitten."

"Kitten?" Brockhurst demanded. "Who is this man to you, Anna-Louise?"

"John," Louisa whispered, "I need to get out of here."

"Right." He held her to him with one arm, using the other to make a path through the pub crowd, all watching the farce unfold. He led her back toward the kitchen, where it would be quieter.

"Wait, where are you going?" Matthew called out.

"Come back here!" Jacob shouted. "Let's go," he said to his friends. All four men followed in John's wake.

"Victoria, this will all be sorted soon," Matthew assured his wife. "Take my family to our room," he ordered Rose without missing a step.

In the kitchen, John was trying to get Louisa to tell him what was happening. "Kitten, who are these men? What do they want with you?"

Everyone was talking at once.

"Where you have been, Anna-Louise?"

"What were you thinking, disappearing like that?"

"Do you have any idea what we've been going through?"

"What is going on? Just talk to me."

"Where have you been living? How did you end up working at an inn?"

"She's the proprietress, not working here."

"You *own* the inn? When the hell did that happen?"

"Have you been well?"

"I had almost given up hope."

"Enough!" John roared. Louisa had her hands over her ears. He glared at the other men in the room. "I can fight all of you at once, have no doubt about that. I am in charge here and I say you all stay quiet." His glare transferred to the kitchen workers and Maisie. "Give us the room."

When it was just the six of them, he turned his attention to Louisa, rubbing her arms reassuringly. "Kitten—"

"Wh—" The baron tried to interrupt but John's glare cut him off.

He tried again. "Kitten, we're all a little confused and frustrated here. An explanation would be helpful."

Louisa looked at him imploringly, shaking her head.

"Please," he said.

She looked at all the men in the room, all watching her with varying degrees of emotion on their faces. Jacob had his arms crossed, Stephen was leaning against a counter, Nathan was studying his cane, and Matthew had his hands on his hips; it was clear they were all waiting for answers.

Louisa brought her eyes back to John. "John, I really—I'm sorry, I really am."

"For what?"

Her voice was a whisper. "My name is Anna-Louise Brockhurst. I am who he says I am. I am his sister."

"What?"

"You heard her," Brockhurst said.

"I told you to be quiet," John snapped.

"Who are you to speak to me like this?"

"He's my husband!"

Her declaration rang in the kitchen. She glared at her brother. "He's my husband," she repeated.

"That was fast," Jacob muttered, shifting on his feet.

"What are you implying?" John growled. Jacob raised his hands in apology. John focused on Louisa again. "What is your brother talking about?"

She took a deep breath. "I left Willowcrest, one of his estates, six years ago."

"I've been searching for you ever since, Anna-Louise." When John moved to rebuke him again, Brockhurst snapped, "I am allowed to speak to my sister."

"It's fine, John," Louisa said. John nodded reluctantly.

"Thank you," he said. He looked at her, his eyes bright. "I haven't stopped, not since finding you gone."

"Is this a habit of yours, Louisa?" Jacob asked angrily.

"It is my turn to speak," Brockhurst said hotly. He returned his attention to his sister. "Obviously there were some distractions. Victoria, my wife, we've been married for four years. Our daughters, Hannah and Maria, they would love to get to know their aunt. Your portrait, the one with you and me and the dog, still hangs in the entry of Riverwood. I've never given up hope of finding you. To think it is a winter storm that finally reunites us."

"Is it my turn now?" Jacob asked with sarcasm in his voice. When Louisa nodded, he continued, more calmly, addressing John and Brockhurst. "I don't know anything about her before eighteen months ago, but I met her as Louisa Hurst. She was a governess and a friend of our wives. Sixteen months ago she moved into the estate Ridgestone with her friends to start a private school. She disappeared this last June just as Sara was getting married. No note, no clues, nothing; she just disappeared. Our wives, being the good friends they are who care about her, have since sent us all over in search of her. Home for a week, search for a week or two, depending on the distance. We were on our way to Bath to see what we could uncover when the storm diverted us. Fortunately for our search."

"Louisa?" John asked softly. She stared at his chest, unable to look up until he cupped her face and tilted her head up to look her in the eye. His were a mixture of confusion and compassion. "Is all this true?"

She nodded, not speaking.

He swallowed, nodding slowly. He thought for several moments, swallowed again. "Do you need some time?"

She nodded. "Please," she whispered.

He took a deep breath and turned to their audience. "I suggest we take a break and go to our respective rooms. We will discuss this more in the morning."

Brockhurst spoke up. "No, I want—"

"This isn't about you, milord," John said firmly. "Can't you see how overwhelmed she is? This is my inn, my wife. This will keep until the morning." When none of them moved, he added, "Tell Packard behind the bar that your drinks are on me this evening. Go."

He didn't wait for them to leave before escorting her back to the office and into his room. He closed the door, releasing her arm. She immediately moved to the wardrobe and began taking her things out.

John rubbed his head before putting his hands on his hips. "I am your husband?"

"I couldn't think of anything else to get them to listen to you."

"So you lied?"

"It worked, didn't it?" There was a growing pile of clothes on the bed. "I need to go to the cottage. The rest of my belongings are there."

"Why do you need your belongings? Where are you going?"

"I have to leave, John. I know it's busy and I'm sorry to leave you in a lurch, but I have to go."

"Wait, go? You're leaving again? Was that man right—this is a habit for you? Just like lying, apparently."

She shot him a glare. "Don't you dare judge me. You know nothing about it."

"So tell me. Don't run away."

"I'm not running away."

"Sure looks like it to me."

Another glare. She gathered her things. "I'm going to the cottage, get out of my way."

He shook his head. "No. I'm not letting you do this." He took what he could from her arms and threw it back on the bed.

"Don't try to stop me, John." She gathered her things off the bed. He took them from her again and threw them back down.

"Those men out there have been searching for you, Louisa, your brother for six years. Have the strength to face them and give them an explanation."

"I can't, I truly can't."

"Yes, you can." He stepped close to her and held her arms. "I will be here to help you. You won't be alone."

Louisa stared at him for a long time. He didn't understand. No one did. She could not explain to anyone about what happened with Lord Darleigh, not without risking prosecution. The only thing that had kept her alive and free these last years was her ingenuity with her deceptions. It had all been working so well until today, but who could have predicted her brother and her friends' husbands would all show up at the Beefy Buzzard? And on the same day.

But looking at John standing in front of the door, blocking her way, keeping her from her freedom, she knew that her deceptions weren't over. The idea of ending them was tempting, but her sense of self-preservation was too strong. She had to lie again, no matter how much she didn't want to, no matter how hard it would be this time. She couldn't deny that she had come to care for him, but it made little difference to her decision. She had come to care for her friends and that hadn't stopped her either. It hadn't been easy to leave Willowcrest or Ridgestone, but she had been strong enough to do what was necessary then and she was strong enough now. Her affection for others did not outweigh her need to stay alive and free.

That was one thing John had gotten right: She could do

this. It wouldn't be hard; he seemed to genuinely want to help her. And all men needed was the hint of a vulnerable woman for their protective instincts to rise up. He would be so focused on protecting her that he would not consider any other scenario.

She slipped into the new deceit. "You will be here to help me?" she asked, making her voice quiet with a hint of pleading.

John nodded. "You are not alone, kitten. Never again will you be alone."

She took a deep breath. "What happens now?"

He glanced at the door. "I need to check on Packard. The pub is full. But you can stay here and relax. Lie down, read, think, do whatever you want. Just relax."

"I don't want to be alone, John."

He kissed her forehead. "I will come back when I can. You're not alone. I'm not going anywhere. We will sort this all out tomorrow."

She nodded. "All right. Tomorrow."

John smiled at her, kissing her lips softly. "I will be back. I promise."

Louisa watched him leave the room, closing the door behind him. She would have to wait a while longer, wait until there was little risk of being followed. Then she would make her move.

## CHAPTER SEVENTEEN

John woke from a fitful sleep, still fully clothed, to find himself alone in the bed. He had fallen asleep before Louisa had. He sat up, straining to hear any sounds, but the inn was silent. She could have gone to the privy, but he didn't really believe that. He lit a candle, the flame revealing that even the indentation on her side of the bed had disappeared.

How long had she been gone? Too long, by the look of things. Could she have simply wanted to return to the cottage? He knew she liked to be alone after a crisis and this evening definitely qualified as such. Needing to assure himself of her whereabouts, he left his room and headed for the back door leading to the cottage.

The storm had stopped, the sky now crystal clear with a full moon shining down, illuminating the fallen snow with a haunting quality. Small footprints led from the inn toward the cottage, confirming his suspicions. It had been after the snow stopped, as the tracks were not filled in at all. His unease prodded him toward the cottage.

Halfway there another trail of footprints veered off, this

time heading away from the small building toward the stable, footprints exactly the same as the ones he was currently following. Louisa had gone to the cottage after all, but then left. His unease graduated into a fully ominous feeling. John followed the second trail, stopping when the footprints passed the stable and headed out onto the public road.

She had left. Without a word, in the middle of the night with the weather as dismal as it was. John cursed himself for ever falling asleep when she had clearly been in a state of nerves. Knowing now what he did of her, thanks to all the revelations of the evening, he supposed he shouldn't be surprised, but it still hurt.

There was only one thing to do. He couldn't very well leave the woman he loved out in the cold, facing who knew what kind of danger. Striding into the stable, he roused a groom to hitch a horse to the cart. When the young man protested about the weather, the vicious snarl John gave him sent him fleeing to the task.

John stalked back to the inn. Once there, he stripped his bed of the heavy blankets, wrapping them up in a ball under his arm. Shrugging into a long coat and jamming a wool cap onto his head, he returned to the kitchen, stuffing bread, cheese and apples into a small leather satchel. Leaving the items for a moment, he went into the cellar and retrieved a bottle of brandy. Adding it to the satchel, he returned to the stable to find the cart waiting, the groom holding the horse's head.

He put everything into the cart and located several lamps, lighting one to hang off the cart bench and adding the rest to the pile from the bed. He did not know how long it would

take to find her and he did not want to have to return due
to lack of supplies. He judged there were still several hours
before sunrise and he wanted to have as much access to light
as he possibly could in the meantime.

Swinging up on the cart, he gave a curt nod to the groom
and flicked the reins. The horse protested at first, but another
flick had the animal moving out into the moonlight. John
guided the cart, ensuring Louisa's tracks stayed. As long as
she had stayed on the road, he would be fine; he didn't know
what he would do if she ventured off into the hills and woods.

Leaving the town behind, the cold beginning to seep
through his coat, he fought to keep his worries at bay. It
would help no one to imagine her hurt somewhere he couldn't
find her, freezing to death. Or beset upon those who would
do harm to a woman. The moon was his friend tonight, keeping the lane and her footprints visible.

Reaching into the satchel, he pulled out the bottle of
brandy and uncorked it with his teeth to take a swig, a part of
him noticing he had grabbed one of the better bottles. Under
normal circumstances he would take the time to savor it; tonight he was glad for the warmth it brought. He wrapped his
coat around him more closely to help fend off the chill.

He thought of all that had been revealed in the evening,
of how little he actually knew her. Those gentlemen had been
looking for her for nearly six months, her brother for over
six years. How had she managed to stay hidden for so long?
What happened to her to even send her on the run in the first
place?

And she hadn't been married. He didn't know what hurt
more: her disappearance or her distrust. After all this time

together, working so closely—*sharing his bed, damnit*—she still didn't trust him. It was so obvious now and a part of him didn't know why he was bothering to find her. Why would he be so intent on helping the woman when she wanted nothing to do with him, thought so little of him that she didn't even think he was worthy of her trust? He didn't even know for certain what he would do when he caught up to her.

In the lonely silence, following her trail, John gave in to his impulse, born out of fear, hurt and anger. "Jesus fucking Christ!" he yelled.

It felt good to shatter the night with that. A small surge of satisfaction went through his blood, but it was short lived. , he had been driving for near an hour and still no sign of Louisa beyond her footprints. She must have left hours ago in order to make it this far.

John squinted. There was a small figure stumbling up on the road ahead. He slowed the cart to a plod, relief washing over him when the figure glanced back and the light reflected in Louisa's eyes. They widened when she saw him, but she pressed her lips together and lifted her chin, turning her face to continue walking. Her cloth portmanteau was slung over her shoulder.

He pulled up beside her, unable to speak at the relief of knowing she was unharmed.

"What are you doing here?" she snapped.

He cleared his throat. "I would think that is obvious."

"I didn't ask for you to come after me."

"That was pretty obvious as well, considering you left without saying anything. Did you even think of letting me know what was going on in that head of yours?"

"That would have defeated the purpose of leaving."

"Of sneaking off. Running away." She didn't respond to that. "Get in the cart, Louisa."

She gave a snort. "No."

"Your feet must be cold."

"That's not the point."

His frustration level was rising. "It never is with you, is it? You can't ever say or take anything at face value. It all has to be so fucking complicated with you. Heaven forbid you should just get in the damn cart and warm up your feet, not when your goddamned pride is at stake."

"There's your prize-ring language coming through again."

"Aye, the bloke from the trenches, 'e must be reachin' above 'imself, thinkin' the lass from Mayfair might stoop to talk to 'im."

"Don't do that, don't talk down about yourself."

"It's just what you're thinking, isn't it?"

"I have never thought that of you."

"You don't have to think it, but it's the way you treat me. Good for nothing but a warm bed and a roof over your head. No wonder you didn't want to marry me. You can't even tell me who you are, why should you ever consider spending your life with me?"

"Why would you consider spending your life with me if you don't know who I am?"

"Because I fucking well love you."

She stopped in her tracks, her fingers flexing around the strap of her portmanteau. "You don't sound too happy about that." Her voice was quiet, grudging.

He reined to a halt. "Well, I'm not too happy about much

right now." He took a deep breath. "And I certainly didn't intend telling you like that."

"It doesn't change anything."

He looped the reins on the cart and jumped down. "I didn't tell you for it to change things, I told you because it's the truth." Now that they were stopped and he was facing her, John could see her cold skin and the shivers that were threatening to rack her body.

She dropped her portmanteau on the ground and crossed her arms, putting her hands under her armpits. "And just what do you think you're going to do with this love?"

"Love you, damnit. That's what people do with love."

"Bollocks!" A flicker of shock flashed over her face. A small, breathy laugh escaped her and she quirked a smile. "Bollocks." Her smile grew and her voice rose. "Bloody hell. Damnit." She looked at him, her eyes bright, shaking her hands in front of her. "More. Give me more."

He crossed his arms. "Crikey."

"Crikey?" She raised her brows and he nodded. "Crikey!"

"Sod it."

"Sod it!"

"Fuck."

"Fuck!"

"Jesus Christ."

"Jesus Christ! Fucking Jesus bloody Christ's bollocks, damnit. Sod it."

Her eyes were bright, her smile wide, breathing heavy from her shouting. He lifted his brows. "Are you finished?"

"Crikey," she said quietly.

"Feel better?" When she didn't say anything, he moved to

brush some hair out of her face, but thought better of it and dropped his hand. "Yea gods, Louisa. Your lips are blue. Can you just get into the cart?"

She shook her head. "You'll just take me back to the inn."

"Jesus, I'll take you wherever you want. I just want to help you."

"I don't need your help."

"As if I didn't know that already."

"I can take care of myself."

"Yes, you're this sentient, logical human being. Why don't you put some of that sentience and logic into action and get yourself into the damn cart? You won't be able to take care of yourself when your feet fall off from frostbite."

Louisa clamped her mouth shut and pressed her lips together. She glared at him, but John just shrugged, not breaking eye contact. Long moments passed in which she could feel the cold burrowing deeper and deeper, her boots long since wet and her stockings soaked. She couldn't fight the shivering anymore and it began to overtake her body.

His face and voice turned pleading. "Please, Louisa, give me this. Allow me this."

There. That was what she was waiting for. She could make the decision and not lose face. She turned and tried to climb into the cart, but her feet and hands were too numb. Familiar large hands circled her waist and John lifted her with ease and she settled on the bench, thankful to have her feet out of the snow.

He tossed her portmanteau on the bed of the cart and climbed up beside her. Reaching around, he brought forward a blanket and wrapped it around her, tucking it close. He settled another blanket around her legs. "Comfortable?" he asked quietly.

She nodded.

From underneath the bench he pulled out a bottle. "Brandy," he said, offering it to her. "It will help warm you."

She took a swig, her frozen lips wrapping around the bottle, and coughed at the fire that blazed down her throat. "Crikey," she croaked.

He didn't chuckle or smile. "Are you hungry? I have bread, cheese, apples."

She shook her head and took another drink. "This brandy is warming me up."

"Don't go too fast with that," he cautioned. "Especially if you're not eating." He picked up the reins. "Where do you want me to take you?"

Louisa held the bottle in her lap, staring at it. "I don't know." Her voice was a whisper.

"I didn't hear you."

"I don't know where I want to go," she said more loudly.

He heaved a sigh. "Where were you going on foot?"

"I don't know, I was just walking."

"Just walking? At this time of night and in ankle-deep snow?"

She snapped at him. "Do you think I want to be like this? Do you think I enjoy not knowing what to do? This is how I've lived for the last six years, John, constantly looking over my shoulder and holding my breath that someone might recognize me and I would have to run again."

"But what are you running from?" he demanded. "What is so serious that you can't face it? You've obviously had people who cared for you, so why leave? Just tell me. It can't be that bad."

"I murdered a man!"

Her shouted confession rang through the cold air. Good Lord, that was the first time she had said it out loud and she didn't know how to feel. Relieved? Scared? She didn't know how to define whatever was rushing through her veins right now.

John was staring at the reins in his hands. He wasn't speaking, which was odd for him. He always spoke. Made her speak too. Which is why she was now shouting her secrets out into the open air and he was staring at the reins in silence.

"John?" Her voice was tentative.

He inhaled deeply through his nose and let it out, his large body deflating as he exhaled. He took the brandy from her and took a long pull. "I don't think I heard that correctly. Could you repeat it, please?"

"I murdered a man." Her repetition was less vehement than before.

Another deep inhalation and exhalation, another swig of brandy. "I assume there is an explanation. You don't strike me as the kind of person to kill in cold blood."

She took the brandy back. "I need more of this if I'm going to tell you." Her grimace wasn't as pronounced this time. She must be getting used to the spirits. "It's a long story."

"Are you expecting a witty quip? Because I'm not in the mood for it right now. I'm bloody cold and the woman I love just told me she killed a man."

"Right. It was six years ago."

When she stopped speaking, he bowed his head. "That part was simple to deduce. Just tell me."

Louisa took a deep breath. "His name was Lord Blaine Darleigh. A friend of my brother's from Oxford. Last night Matthew was apologizing for the way he had been. Darleigh was part of that set. The drinking, the gambling, I assume the whoring as well. I was seventeen, so he was still my guardian, but Matthew was more drunk than sober in those years. Once, when he was still suffering from his previous night's revelries, I talked him into letting me live at Willowcrest, a small estate that was part of my mother's dowry. I just wanted to get away from him and his drunkenness.

"What I didn't count on was Matthew using the estate as a gambling stake the week after I moved. And he lost it. To Darleigh. He showed up the next day, without warning, with the deed, stating that the bet was for the estate and all of its contents. Contents he . . . took to . . . include . . . me."

John drew himself up, but didn't speak.

She felt the familiar cloak of detachment fall over her shoulders. She had been wearing it for so many years to avoid emotional entanglements and it would serve her well as she told this story. She heard the impassiveness in her voice. "I fought him. Truly fought him. I hadn't ever physically fought anyone in my life before then; I didn't even know I had it in me. But I did fight. We were in the drawing room, later the library, when I tried to run away. I thought there might be something in there I could use as a weapon.

"It turned out the only weapon I needed was myself. We were by the hearth when I pushed him away again. He stumbled, tripped over my embroidery basket, I think, and hit his head against the mantle. The blood just . . . gushed out of his head. I stared at it, at the puddle that was growing on the floor, and couldn't think. I just looked at it. It was so red—not as bright as one would think, but darker, almost like—I can't even think of what to compare it to. A dress? I've never seen a sunset that color before. It just was . . . red.

"It was thinking about how difficult it would be to clean up that spurred me into action. I knew if I was found with a dead body in my library, the body of a peer, I would be charged. My brother wouldn't be able to help me. My servants wouldn't be in a position to help me. There was no one. No one. The only thing I could think of to do was to leave. Run. Become someone new. Before yesterday, I hadn't even heard my full name in six years. Anna-Louise Brockhurst.

"Cumberland was the first place I went. I was a companion, but that only lasted a couple of months. Then I was a governess. I kept bouncing from family to family, always choosing families that were merchants looking to break into the nobility somehow, but people who wouldn't know me. But two years ago, I was in a town where I met three other governesses. We became friends and I convinced them to pool our resources to create our own private school."

She smiled sadly. "Complete independence. I wouldn't be subjected to the whims of employers, wouldn't have to defend myself against any man, complete financial and personal independence. That is where Jacob Knightly and Stephen Montgomery come in. Claire and Bonnie married them, and Sara was marrying the vicar, Charles Pomeroy; I don't know the connection to the man with the cane. But with each marriage, the Governess Club fell more and more apart. As much as it isn't for me, their marriages are important to them and I couldn't ask them to sacrifice that for me.

And there would come a point when they wouldn't have time for the club at all.

"So I left. Again. And that's how I ended up at the Beefy Buzzard. And now here we are."

Silence settled around them, her story told. The forgotten cold made itself known again and Louisa sipped more of the brandy, her eyes not leaving John. He was hunched over, rubbing his head, an action that showed his distress.

It was odd, speaking her story out loud. She still couldn't define how she felt. But something else was creeping up on her and it felt suspiciously like—worry. Worry about what John was thinking, what he was feeling about her revelation, how he was not speaking. So unlike him.

She swallowed. Had hearing the truth about her killed his love for her? She didn't want to admit how much that thought scared her, how much she wanted him to continue to love her.

Louisa reached out tentatively, her fingers brushing his sleeve before pulling back. "John?"

"You were never married?"

She shook her head. "No. It was easier for me to travel alone if I posed as a widow."

He took the brandy from her and took a long swallow. "We need to get moving," he finally said. "The horse must be cold." He flicked the reins and the cart jolted into motion, turning back in the direction they had come.

"We're going back ho—to the Beefy Buzzard?" she asked.

He nodded. "You said you didn't like who you were, how you keep running. I figure the only way to change that is to stop running."

Panic bubbled up in her and she struggled to tamp it

down. "But, Darleigh—Matthew—I will be arrested if I'm found."

"That is a possibility," he conceded. "But it was self-defense. The courts should recognize that."

"What?"

"As for being a fugitive, well, we'll find you a good lawyer. Your brother must know someone."

"But—"

John finally looked at her and took her hand. "I know you can look after yourself. I know you are strong enough to do many things without me. But you don't have to anymore. You don't have to be alone; you can make the choice to allow me to do this with you. For whatever you need, I will be here. That is what I am going to do with my love for you. Love you with it."

He gave her a small smile and squeezed her hand. "So yes, we're going home."

## CHAPTER EIGHTEEN

John sipped his tea from the large pewter mug, his dirty breakfast plate beside him on the bar. It was early yet, the closed sign still hanging in the window. He had debated opening as usual, but decided against it. The staff would tend to their current customers, but all others would be turned away. He would not give Louisa any means of distraction, not today.

His gaze roved over the other occupants in the room. Rose was doing a fine job of seeing to Louisa's brother and family and the three gentlemen who had come in search of her. The two blond-haired children sat with their parents, the elder daughter chattering away and the younger one continually staring at him. Her brother kept casting glances in his direction, ones that he could not quite interpret but still recognized the challenge in them; John didn't bother returning any of them. One of the three gentlemen—the Scottish one—was studiously reading a week-old newspaper, his face hidden. The other two were having a murmured conversation as they ate.

He had not slept again once they had returned to the inn. John had spent the remaining hours of the night with Louisa tucked into his side, her shivering finally abating as her body warmed. She had fallen into an exhausted sleep, one she had yet to wake from, and he was loath to disturb her. It had been a trying few days for her—a trying *six years* for her.

So he had lain there, feeling the warmth of the blankets and her body. He couldn't stop wondering how this would all develop. He didn't want to contemplate her locked in a place like Newgate or whatever passed as the local constable's cell, but the reality kept threatening to move beyond the periphery, leaving him chilled.

Movement captured his attention from his tea. Matthew Brockhurst was standing by his table, his wife holding on to his arm. The man leaned down and said something that put a resigned look on her face and caused her hand to drop. She pasted a smile on and turned her attention to her daughters, encouraging them in their meal.

Baron Brockhurst—*yea gods*, John thought, *how stupid am I to ignore the signs she is nobility?*—straightened his coat, his eyes fastened on John as he tried to affect a casual demeanor. The conversation at the other table paused and the newspaper lowered enough to be seen over. The air in the room condensed as the baron moved closer to John, the tension hanging palpably. All eyes were on them.

The man came to a stop a few feet away, shoving his hands into his pockets. "Good morning, Taylor," he greeted in his cultured voice.

John straightened, keeping his hands on the bar, bobbing his head in what passed as a bow. "Milord."

Brockhurst gave him a small smile. "Shall we dispense with the formalities? We are brothers by marriage, after all. It would be awkward for you to 'milord' me over Christmas dinner."

"If you insist."

He glanced over his shoulder at the rest of the room. "You know, I saw you fight a few years ago. In St. Albans."

John searched his brain for a moment. "Against Black-Eyed Stan? If I recall, I felled him in one round."

"Yes. Sadly, I bet against you."

John pressed his lips together. "I understand your betting history is not the most successful."

His brows knit together in confusion. "I've had my losses, as has every gentleman."

John chose not to respond to that, taking another sip of tea.

Brockhurst cleared his throat and glanced around John. "Is Anna-Louise still sleeping?"

"Yes."

"Does she—uh—does she normally sleep this late?"

"No."

Brockhurst gestured to the kitchen door. "Can you go wake her? I would like to speak with her."

"No."

"Excuse me?"

John drank more tea, setting his cutlery on his dirty plate. "I will rephrase. I can go wake her, I do have that ability, but I will not."

Brockhurst started to scowl. "I don't quite follow."

John looked him clear in the eye. "She had a trying day

yesterday, followed by a similar night. She needs her rest and I intend for her to get it."

"She is my sister."

"I am aware of that. She also announced to you yesterday that she is my wife."

"I can go back and do it myself."

"I see a few issues with that. First, you don't know where she is sleeping and I don't like the idea of you wandering about my inn disturbing my other guests. Second, you would disrupt my staff at work, another thing I would not appreciate. Third, you would have to get through me first and I don't actually see you being successful at that. One round, remember?"

Brockhurst's scowl deepened. "Did you just threaten a peer of the realm?"

John shook his head. "I stated my intention of protecting those who are close to me."

The scrape of a chair ripped through the tension. Both men looked back at one of three gentlemen rising and making his way over. Yea gods, another one to come lay claim on Louisa?

The newcomer stuck out his hand to Brockhurst. "Don't think we've met. Jacob Knightly."

Brockhurst eyed the hand with disdain. "Mr. Knightly?" He turned his head away.

A knowing grin crossed Knightly's face and he glanced at John as if to say *Watch this*. "Yes. Mr. Jacob Knightly. Formerly the Earl of Rimmel, before my sister-in-law, the Marchioness of Maberly, experienced the joyful event of providing my brother, the Marquess of Maberly—yes, the eldest son of the Duke of—with his heir, thus reducing me to the spare's spare, sans title."

Brockhurst's face flushed during that little speech, something that brought John a small degree of satisfaction. To his credit, he recovered well and offered his hand. "Matthew Brockhurst, Baron of. Anna-Louise is my sister."

"Yes, that came up last night." Jacob continued to smile. "It seems to me that whatever you want with our Louisa, you have to go through this man. Even if I were on your side, I don't think you would be on the winning side of that bet. Too bad I'm on his. They are too." He gestured to his friends, the blond one fingering his wolf's-head cane and the Scottish one with his newspaper folded in front of him.

"Jesus, I just want to talk to my sister," the man muttered. "It's been six years. I had all but given her up for dead and now I find her here."

John looked at him, compassion softening his approach. "I'm not saying no, I'm just saying be patient. Let her sleep."

"For how long?"

He shrugged. "As long as she needs. You have a wife, you know how it works."

A commiserating smile tugged at his lips. "Indeed. When she wakes, keep her here." He nodded and turned on his heel to return to his family. He spoke with them quietly and gathered them up to return to their room.

John shared a look with Knightly. "Can I get you anything?"

Knightly cocked an eyebrow. "Is it too early for Scotch?"

"Not if you don't want it to be."

A full-fledged grin broke out on his face. "Oh, we are going to get along well. Just make sure it's the good stuff."

"When you only deserve pig swill?" John returned his grin. "I'll see what I can find."

Louisa stepped into the kitchen to see Timothy and Alan putting away dishes Maisie was washing. "Why aren't you working?" she asked, her brow knitted. "I thought you were making steak-and-kidney pies today?"

Maisie looked up. "Mr. Taylor closed the pub today. Not much to do."

"What? He closed the pub? Why would he do that?"

Maisie shrugged. "He just said we only had to see to the ones already here."

Louisa straightened, grateful to have something to focus on instead of her impending crisis. "Where is he?"

"Out in the pub."

She spun on her heel and marched out, all business. He should not have made such a decision without consulting her. Did he understand how much revenue they would lose? The boxing mill was still on and people needed to eat. And drink. She pulled open the door to the pub and stepped into the room, freezing immediately.

John was sitting at a table with Jacob, Stephen and Nathan, glasses in front of them and a half-empty bottle of Scotch. They were laughing at something while her brother sat across the room, watching them with his own glass of Scotch, a short, portly man at his table.

Good Lord, was that the magistrate with him? The constable? For the first time, Louisa regretted not venturing out into the town more, not learning who lived here. She had left that to John. And now here he was, getting thoroughly foxed from the looks of things, with the magistrate waiting to arrest her. Was this how things were going to happen, her getting arrested while John drank himself under the table?

Some love he showed.

He spied her standing at the door. "Louisa!" he bellowed. All the men stood quickly. "We've been waiting for you."

She motioned him over, grateful he complied without making a bigger scene. When he was near, she crossed her arms. "What do you think you are doing?" she said. "You closed the pub without speaking to me about it."

"You were sleeping. I didn't want to disturb you."

"But why close it in the first place? This boxing mill is a chance for us to make a larger profit than we have in the past."

He leaned in, concern on his face. "I thought we would need privacy to deal with the situation of your brother and friends."

She blinked. "Oh." It was actually sweet of him, when she thought about it. "You still should have consulted me. And this wouldn't have been an issue if we had a private dining room."

John shook his head at her, a small smile tugging at his lips. "Can't you ever just say 'thank you'?"

She huffed. "Thank you." She eyed the portly man with her brother. "Who is that?" she whispered. "Is he the magistrate?"

He followed her gaze. "I don't know. Never seen him before."

She glared at him again. "And you thought drinking was the best way to handle this situation?"

He shrugged, the smile still on his face. "Didn't seem it would hurt."

Her brother walking toward them caught her attention. His steps were tentative, his gaze unwavering. "John," she whispered, her eyes wide.

He grasped her hand. "Just breathe, kitten. His sister has returned from the dead. Give him a chance."

She clutched his hand, her grip tight as she watched Baron Brockhurst approach. "Anna-Louise," he said. "How— you are well?"

She pressed her lips together and lifted her chin, her fingers digging into John's hand. "I go by Louisa now and yes, I am well."

"Right. Louisa. You met Victoria last night, and my girls."

"They seemed nice."

"They are looking forward to getting to know their aunt. They are already planning what room will be yours." He smiled the smile of a proud, indulgent father. "Victoria's family lives in Cornwall and she has always encouraged me to continue searching for you. Not that I was giving up," he added quickly. "But she kept my spirits up."

"She sounds lovely." Louisa paused for a moment. "Wait, what? Room? What are you talking about?" She looked at John, who looked just as confused as she did.

Brockhurst took a deep breath. "An—Louisa, this is Mr. Coates, a solicitor. Not mine, but one from here that I found on short notice."

"Is this about Darleigh?" she asked. "Do I need a solicitor already?"

Her brother looked confused. "Darleigh? What does he have to do with this?"

"Isn't that why you've been looking for me? I have to admit, I am surprised the authorities haven't found me after all these years."

"What are you talking about?"

Louisa took a deep breath and looked at John for encouragement. He nodded and squeezed her hand. "I am the one who killed Blaine Darleigh," she told Brockhurst.

"Anna-Louise," he said slowly, "Darleigh is not dead."

"What?" Surely she misheard him. She felt the blood drain from her face. John guided her over to where he had been sitting. Her friends, who continued to remain silent, pulled up more chairs to accommodate the entire group. John took the chair on one side of her, her brother on the other.

"Anna-Louise, I need to explain what happened."

"She said to call her Louisa," John said, shooting him a quick glare.

Brockhurst glanced at his table companions. "Perhaps we should discuss this in private. Is there another room we can use?"

"Louisa, do you want to speak in private?" John asked her when she didn't respond. She met his eyes briefly and shook her head. He addressed the baron. "I believe the other gentlemen will understand the need for discretion and silence in this matter."

Jacob nodded. "Our lips are sealed." Stephen murmured his agreement and Nathan looked at her brother, his blue eyes ice cold.

"Louisa," Brockhurst tried again, "Darleigh isn't dead. I

went to Willowcrest two days after I lost it to him. I know," he said, forestalling whatever she might have said, "I shouldn't have staked it in the first place, but you have to understand. I was young, drunk more often than not. I was wholly unprepared for our father's death and the responsibilities of the title. God, I was twenty years old."

She found her voice again and it was cold, even to her ears. "I was seventeen when Darleigh tried to rape me, Matthew, three years your junior. He said he had won my home from you, and all its contents. I was one of the contents, in his opinion."

He had the grace to flush and nodded. "That is what I deduced when I arrived the day after he had. The servants had found him in the library and patched him up as best they could. They hadn't contacted any doctor or authority, so it was contained within the estate. But he didn't die. When he woke up, though, he wasn't the same. I took him back to his estate and told everyone he took a fall from his horse and hit his head. He has a round-the-clock nurse now, can hardly do anything for himself. Can barely talk."

He offered her a tentative smile and put his hand on hers. "So you're safe. I took care of it and Darleigh can't ever say different. I behaved like your brother for the first time in my life when you needed it the most but weren't around to see it."

Silence settled in the pub. Louisa could feel all of their eyes on her, but all she could do was stare at the glass in front of her. She hadn't killed Darleigh. It was a relief, on some level, but all those years spent running from something that didn't actually happen. What did that make her? She hadn't even had the courage to stay and face the consequences. And she hadn't ever since. Every time something happened to threaten her, she ran.

Until last night. Until John, her big galoot, had taken her hand and brought her back to the inn. He didn't force her, didn't impose himself on her, but saw her for who she really was and stood beside her anyway. He loved her and she loved him in return.

Good Lord, why was she thinking of this now? Louisa pushed the thought away and looked at her brother. He looked so earnest, so sincere. But she couldn't forget so easily. "You—" She stopped and composed herself. "Darleigh is not dead?"

Matthew shook his head. "No."

"But you, you have never been there for me, Matthew. You are the reason Darleigh could attack me in the first place and why I ran. It all comes back to you."

He nodded and bowed his head for a moment. "I know. I know that and acknowledge it. All I can do is say that I am different and will be a better brother from now on. I spent six years looking for you, An—Louisa, that must count for something."

She glanced around the circle. John was rubbing his head, Jacob was studying his hands, Stephen and Nathan just looked awkward. But not as awkward as the solicitor hovering on the periphery, not quite part of the circle.

She frowned. "Why the need for a solicitor?"

Her brother sat up. "Ah. That. I want you to come home with me, Victoria and the girls. I am your family and I will care for you from now on."

*That* was a surprise. Louisa shook her head. "No." She

saw John stop rubbing his head, his hand dropping to his lap. "No," she repeated.

Matthew looked awkward. "You know I am your guardian until you are twenty-five years of age. That is still two years away."

*Why isn't John saying anything?* He was just sitting there, so she latched on to the first thing she could think of. "I told you yesterday that John and I were married."

"Hence the solicitor." Matthew gestured to the portly man.

Louisa stood up, moving away from the table to pace, her arms crossing and uncrossing as she did. "You are going to have it declared invalid because we didn't have my guardian's permission? That is archaic, even for you. You haven't ever been much of a guardian and if you think I need one now, then you are sadly mistaken." Her skin began to itch and she unconsciously rubbed her arms to lessen the sensation.

"There's the Louisa I know," Jacob muttered under his breath. He raised his hands up in defense against her glare and made the motions of locking his mouth shut.

"Not based on consent, but Taylor didn't know your real name until last night. Anna-Louise Brockhurst."

"I don't understand."

Mr. Coates cleared his throat. "If you married Mr. Taylor," he nodded at John, his eyes wary, "but gave a false name, then the marriage is fraudulent."

"Fraudulent?"

"You did not use your legal name, nor did you sign it, thus making it null and void, just as with any other legal contract. As that appears to be the case, Lord Brockhurst is still your legal guardian."

Louisa stared at the small, portly man for so long the solicitor started to squirm in his shoes. "Uh, you do understand what I am saying, correct?" he ventured.

When her brow lowered and her eyes turned into a ferocious glare, her stance clearly preparing to attack the man, John stood up and took her arms. "Louisa," he said quietly, repeating her name until she looked him in the eyes. "Perhaps it's time to cut the line, tell them the truth."

"But he just said that we're not married," she whispered angrily.

"We're not." John rubbed her arms before cupping her face, reiterating the truth with a disbelieving shake of his head. "Are you listening to yourself? You are getting upset over being told a fake marriage is in fact fake."

She blinked at him. "Why aren't you more upset at this?" she demanded. "Matthew is destroying what we have here."

"What do we have, kitten? Tell me that."

Louisa stared, her throat closing. He wasn't truly serious, was he? Was this the same man who followed her last night and declared his love for her in the most objectionable manner? Had she truly been contemplating loving him back just moments ago?

He kept speaking, his eyes kind and gentle. "I have made my position with you clear. I am not going anywhere and not changing my mind at all. What we have is up to you. You are the one who has to decide." He smiled at her, a touch of sadness in it. "I fucking well love you, Louisa. No matter what you do or where you go, I will be here, loving you. You just have to decide what you want."

She couldn't stop staring at him. Was he speaking a foreign language? She couldn't quite comprehend what he was saying. "Wh-what?" she stammered.

"It's your choice," he repeated.

"My choice?"

He nodded.

She glared at him, his words unsettling her. She shoved at his chest, not moving him an inch. "Aren't you going to tell me to stay?" Isn't that what men in love wanted, for the woman they loved to stay with them?

His thumb traced her cheekbone. "No. This is your decision. You have to want to stay if you are going to be happy here."

"Excuse me." Brockhurst's voice interrupted them. "This tête-à-tête has gone on long enough. You need to stay away from my sister, Taylor."

John's hand dropped from her cheek and a chill immediately took its place on her skin. She looked at him, at the flare of anger in his eyes. He took a deep breath and stepped away from her. "Of course, milord. For now," he added that part in a low voice, his gaze steady on the man.

Brockhurst skirted around John, his eyes wary. "Anna-Louise, think of it. A prizefighter, that's all he is. You don't truly want to be tied to that for the rest of your life, do you? Living in an inn? You deserve better. Come home with me to Riverwood. Come home to your family. There will be dresses and London seasons waiting for you. Come and let me give you the life you were raised to have, the life you deserve. The life he can't give you."

Louisa's eyes narrowed at his insulting words toward John. She opened her mouth to rebuke her brother, but was interrupted.

"Hold on just a moment." Their heads swiveled to see Jacob standing and approaching. "If you two get a chance to make your case to her, then we do as well. Our wives have been beside themselves this whole time and Montgomery even left his newborn daughter to continue this search."

The five of them stared at Jacob. He looked back and shrugged. "It only seems fair."

"Very well," Brockhurst said. "What have you to add? What can you offer my sister that I can't?"

"Well, uh," Jacob said, looking back at his friends for help. "I don't actually have anything. I didn't think that far ahead."

With a sigh, Stephen slapped the newspaper down on the table and stood. "Miss Hur—um, Brock—hurst—shall I just call you Louisa, for clarity's sake?"

"Please."

"Louisa, your friends are concerned for you. You disappeared without a word and they had visions of your demise for months."

"Oh, for God's sake!" Nathan joined the group, his cane tapping on the floor, and shook his head in disgust at his companions. "Both of you are hopeless." He turned his attention to Louisa. "Miss Brockhurst, I don't know you, you don't know me. The only reason why I am here is because you are important to Sara, who is important to me. I have no personal stake in your return to Ridgestone besides assurances of your health and well-being."

"And you think I am hopeless at this?" Jacob muttered.

Nathan shot him a glare before turning back to Louisa. "It occurs to me that you have the worst possible dilemma ahead of you—the choice between people who obviously care for you. It is like asking a well-loved child who their favorite parent is. Our ladies at Ridgestone have truly been beside themselves with worry; of that I have no doubt. Your brother has spent the last six years searching for you, castigating himself for his role in your disappearance. And Mr. Taylor here has done little to conceal his feelings toward you; a larger bulldog you could not find.

"When you make your choice, know that the other parties will be content so long as you are. Choosing one over the others does not eliminate them entirely. Well-sprung coaches and the postal system exist for a reason. Just know that you have eleven people who are proud to know you; you will never truly be alone again, for whatever comfort or distress that might bring you."

Louisa was grateful for his words, oddly delivered as they may be. It struck her that he was right. She did have people that cared for her. She had spent the last few years so focused on looking for those who wished her harm that she had overlooked those who wished her well.

"What is this about her making a choice?" her brother said angrily. "I am her guardian. The choice is mine. Pack your things, Anna-Louise. I'm taking you out of this hole and back where you belong."

"How about we let her decide?" John said, his voice tinged with anger.

He wasn't alone. Louisa glared at her brother. "How dare you? You waltz in here, take one look at the place and deem it a hole? We have worked hard to improve it, to make it into the most successful inn on this road. It may not be Mayfair, but it is no less valuable to me or to John. And who do you think you are? You don't see me for six years and you think you can commandeer my life?"

"I am your brother and your guardian," he protested.

"That means very little to me at this moment in time," she relied hotly. "The only family I have recently known are my friends at Ridgestone and—and John Taylor. He may be a retired prizefighter, Matthew, but he is an honorable man with more integrity and compassion than I have ever seen in you before."

"You haven't seen me in so long, Anna-Louise. I have changed from that man I used to be. You don't know me anymore."

"That's my point, Matthew." Louisa took a deep breath to calm herself and moderated her voice. "You don't know me anymore either. I have changed from that young girl I was. I have seen and done things I never imagined I would have as a baron's sister. I have been my own guardian for six years; I don't need you or anyone to make decisions for me. John and my friends know that much about me and I ask that you respect me enough to allow me to do so."

"Anna-Louise—"

"Good Lord, that's exactly what I am talking about!" Louisa threw up her hands in frustration before taking a deep breath to calm herself. She pressed her lips together and lifted her chin. "I am no longer Anna-Louise, Matthew. That girl died that day in the library. I have been Louisa for six years and I intend to be her for the rest of my life because she is not a weak entity, dependent upon those who would make her so. You can't even acknowledge that."

"Matthew?" A low, contralto voice came from the stairs.

Victoria Brockhurst was standing at the bottom, watching the byplay. "We could hear you upstairs. The girls are worried."

"Everything is fine," Brockhurst assured his wife. "We are just discussing An—Louisa's options."

Victoria gave Louisa a tentative smile. "I do hope that you will choose to make us a part of your life. It would be lovely to have more people around the table at Christmas. I come from a large family and can find holidays at Riverwood more quiet than I would like."

Louisa smiled back, surprised and grateful at the effort this stranger was making on her behalf. "Thank you. I will be sure to make myself known to you. After all, well-sprung coaches and the postal system exist for a reason, correct?"

There was muffled coughing at the table and more Scotch was poured. Victoria's smile grew. "Indeed. Shall I bring the girls down?"

"In a few minutes, my love," her husband said. "We are not quite done here yet." With another smile at Louisa, the blond woman disappeared up the stairs.

When her brother looked like he was going to begin another guardian rant, Louisa spoke. "Matthew, please understand. This is my life, not yours. This choice is mine. That is the way you can be a good guardian to me."

Matthew looked at her silently for several heartbeats. He took a deep breath and rubbed his chin, looking at John, who just shrugged. His gaze shifted back to Louisa. "This is what you truly want?"

"Yes. I need to decide my own life."

The smile he gave her was sad. "Well-sprung coaches and

the postal system, right? Just promise me you won't disappear again. Come to me if you need help."

Louisa gave him a smile she didn't quite feel. "I will do my best, but I have relied on myself for so long, it may take some doing."

His smile remained sad. "I understand. And I apologize for how my past actions have harmed you. Truth be told, it was losing you that made me cast off that immaturity and recklessness. It was hard, but once I met Victoria, she helped me achieve the stability you now see. If you will excuse me, I will go inform her of what has transpired. I shall see you later." He gave her an awkward kiss on the cheek and left.

Well, that was one down. Louisa took a deep breath and glanced between John and the men at the table. Jacob stood and approached her and John, his eyes never leaving hers. When he stopped in front of her, he shoved his hands in his pockets, his lips pressed together and his brow furrowed.

He spoke. "Louisa, did you ever stop to consider how your disappearance would affect Claire and the others? Stephen wasn't mistaken. They have been worried sick, imagining all sorts of things happening to you. They have barely let us rest since Sara jilted the vicar."

"What?" Louisa was incredulous. "You mean she actually went through with it? I left as it was happening, but thought she would come to her senses."

Jacob made an impatient sound. "The point of the matter being that your disappearance created a turmoil in the house."

She lifted her chin. "I knew they would be fine. They all had their husbands. They don't need me."

"If you think that is true," Jacob scoffed in reply, "then we have just wasted the last five months searching tirelessly for you. Yes, Claire has me, Bonnie Stephen, and now Sara has Nathan, but none of us is you. For God's sake, you have known them for years. Do you honestly have no concept how much your friendship means to them? You are not dispensable to them; you are their friend and they have been worried sick about you. Not even a quick note explaining yourself or indicating that you are well? Shame on you, Louisa, whoever you are. Shame."

"You don't understand," she said.

He hunched his shoulders in exasperation. "Of course I don't understand. I have no insight into what goes on in that head of yours. None of us do. I've known you for more than a year—Claire and the others for longer—and your first instinct was to run away, not talk about it with the friends you had been living with. I don't know what hurt Claire more—your disappearance or the fact that you didn't trust her enough to tell her something was bothering you."

"Are you trying to guilt me into returning with you? That is quite the strategy. Is that how you managed to convince Claire to marry you?"

"Louisa," John admonished in a low voice. She pressed her lips together, refusing to apologize.

"No." Jacob shook his head. "I'm not trying to guilt you. I'm trying to understand. And I do believe you owe your friends an explanation, at the very least."

Louisa turned away, moving to stare out the window. Jacob's words surrounded her, suffocating her. How could he say such things? To hear him voice such things was odd. She never would have expected him to have any sort of insight—on anything. It occurred to her that she had always sold her friend's husband short, never believed he would be able to contribute any sort of substance to Claire's life. It was a shock to think he was more than what she expected.

That thought sent a jolt through her. She stared at her reflection in the glass. Good Lord, who had she become? She could see the bitterness tingeing her eyes, pulling the corners of her mouth into a permanent frown. She couldn't even think of the last time she had met someone and didn't immediately feel she had to protect herself from that person. Her first response to anyone was sarcasm and bitterness, anything to keep them from getting too close. Even with her friends, it had taken the better part of a year for them to break through her walls.

How had John done it so easily? Why had he even wanted to? God, looking at herself, she couldn't see any reason why he should. She could see nothing in herself that another might find appealing.

Good Lord, she had to get out of here, out of this room. She spun on her heel and stalked to the kitchen. "I haven't eaten anything yet," she muttered. "Who can think on an empty stomach?"

"No, you don't." John moved in front of her, halting her progress. She tried to sidestep around him, but he didn't let her. "No running, kitten," he said quietly, his eyes full of understanding. "You are strong enough to see this through."

"John." Her eyes pleaded for him to understand and let her go.

"You can do this," he reiterated.

"John, he's right," she whispered, fighting tears that she hated to admit were filling her eyes. "I am a horrible friend. A horrible person."

"You know that's not true. You have made mistakes, but you are not beyond redemption. What do you have to do to make things right?"

"I don't know."

"Yes, you do. Just think. What is the opposite of running?"

"What?"

"What is the opposite of running away?" he repeated.

She thought for a moment. "Running back," she finally said.

Something flickered in his eyes and he smiled at her. It was an odd smile, one she hadn't seen on him before, and she didn't know what it meant. "There you go, kitten. There's your answer."

"You think I should go back to Ridgestone?"

John shook his head. "It's not about me. This is still your decision. What do you think you should do?"

"I, um—" She stopped. He said to think about what she *should* do, not what she *wanted* to do. It seemed obvious. Jacob had laid it out well. There were three people in her past she owed explanations to. She should see to that.

Louisa looked at John, gazing into his familiar, comfortably dark eyes, trying to see what he was thinking. He wasn't giving anything away, just letting her decide.

She took a deep breath. "I should return to Ridgestone. Jacob is right. I need to talk to my friends."

Oh good Lord, what was that pain in her chest?

He nodded, pressing his lips together. "Then that is what you will do."

The pain swelled, making it difficult to breathe. She bowed her head and wiped at her eyes, dashing away the tears that had dared to escape.

# CHAPTER NINETEEN

Jacob entered the pub, rubbing his hands against the cold. "Right then, Louisa, the coach is loaded. We are ready to go."

Louisa smiled at her nieces and closed the storybook. "Well, I am sorry to have to leave before discovering if Ethelbert ever managed to get the mud out of his ears. We shall solve the mystery when I visit you at Riverwood." Her eyes met her brother's and they shared a smile.

The girls hugged her and Victoria promised them she would include their letters to her in her own. More hugs were shared, awkward ones with Matthew and Victoria. She was grateful neither of them lingered in the embraces. When they disappeared up the stairs, Louisa turned to look at John standing behind the bar, wiping glasses and setting them on the shelves. He was making an effort to not look at her, instead very intent on his task.

She didn't know what to make of him. Two nights ago he was declaring his love to her on a frozen road and now he didn't speak to her. She had hoped they would have had a chance to discuss what had occurred yesterday, but he had spent the remainder of the day being busy with the inn and boxing mill. She had even waited up for him but had fallen asleep before he arrived in their room. Waking up in the morning, she had found his side of the bed cold and flat; he hadn't come at all.

She didn't know what hurt more: his avoidance of her or his refusal to sleep with her. It sat in her chest, a tight heavy ball.

How had this happened? What did he mean by his behavior? To say one thing and then behave another way? He had said that it had been her decision, that he would not stop loving her, and then ignored her. Was this how he loved her with his love? If this was a taste of how things were to be with him, then perhaps she was better off returning to Ridgestone and not coming back.

Well, she was not about to leave while he continued to play at ignoring her. Louisa pressed her lips together, lifted her chin and marched over to the bar.

John glanced at her when she stopped, then turned his attention back to the glasses.

Louisa spoke. "The coach is packed. I am ready to go."

He took a deep breath and continued cleaning the glasses, but didn't respond.

"Ridgestone is two days away."

The rag continued circling the rim of the glass, a slow rotation.

"I think that glass is clean enough," she offered.

He placed it on the shelf and picked up another one, the rag barely missing a beat.

"Are you not going to say anything to me?"

He shrugged, inordinately obsessed with the glass in his hand. "What would you like me to say?"

"Good-bye? Safe travels?"

"Good-bye, then. Safe travels."

The cold ball of hurt grew, weighing heavily in her chest. He still didn't look at her, the rag in his hand warranting more attention than she. She supposed she should not have expected more, even from the man who had treated her like no other and then claimed to love her. She should have known that it had all been too good to be true. In the end, she was just another female a man had wanted for his own purposes.

"Louisa, the horses are getting cold." She glanced over her shoulder at Jacob's words, seeing him hold her cloak for her.

Nodding, she turned back to John. "Good-bye, then." She spun on her heel and marched her way over to the door, weaving through the tables until she reached Jacob, who helped her with her cloak. Without glancing back at the bar, she stepped out into the cold, white morning.

It wasn't snowing, but the sun was shining brightly off the ground, hurting her eyes. It was the resulting sting that made her eyes water, she told herself, nothing more. Certainly not a big callous galoot. Stephen and Nathan were waiting by the coach while Timothy and Alan were holding the horses' heads. She said a quick farewell to the boys, not wishing to prolong the moment, before Stephen helped her in.

Not that she needed the help, but men did enjoy feeling useful.

Louisa settled herself against the squabs on the far side so she wouldn't have a view of the inn as they left. She was leaving behind nearly four months of effort, four months of hard work. She had taken pride in what she had accomplished with John and now it was wiped away in less than two days. All because her past had finally caught up to her.

The men climbed in beside her, slamming the door shut. As they sat, the coach lurched into motion, the horses' hooves muffled against the snow. Stephen offered her another blanket but she refused with a shake of her head and a small smile. He really was a nice man, treating Bonnie and his wards well.

She swallowed. "Bonnie had her child?" Her voice wavered. Yesterday had been too hectic for conversation with the Ridgestone men.

Stephen smiled broadly. "Yes, a girl. We named her Elizabeth, after my mother."

"Congratulations. I am sure she is beautiful."

"You will see soon enough. We will be staying at Ridgestone until after the Christmas season. The boys are less certain of her worth, as she cannot play ball with them just yet."

Louisa gave him what she hoped passed for a smile and looked out the window. They were heading down the same road she had tried to take the other night. The trees and fields passed by more quickly than they had when she was walking. And on the cart.

John's words came back to her. *The only way to change is to stop running.* She wasn't running. If she was, she was running toward something, rather than away from it. That was also known as returning, which was a new concept for her. For the first time in six years, she was doing the right thing and she knew it.

It was what he had encouraged her to do. This whole thing was his fault. He had pushed and pushed for her to make a decision about what to do, and so she had. And how did he react? He ignored her, avoided her, acted as though he had nothing to do with what was happening. She wouldn't even be in this coach if it wasn't for him. If she had had her way, she would have stayed at the Beefy Buzzard, where her life once more had purpose. That is, if he hadn't caught her on the road and brought her back.

*What is the opposite of running away?* More words echoed in her head. Running back had been her answer. That had been the right answer, hadn't it? What else could she have said?

Stay. *Stay.* That was the opposite of running away. It wasn't running at all, not even back to something. That alternative hadn't occurred to her last night. Was it even a viable one?

Images flashed through her mind of what her life would be like if she stayed at the inn. Days filled with Maisie and the boys, helping out in the kitchen, sitting in the office having tea as she worked with the books. Seeing the inn expand into a successful, reputable business, one that attracted prestigious guests and became a popular stopping point between Bath and London. They may be on an alternate route, but that made little difference. With the right exposure, they could become a lure for the travelers to leave the Bath Road, even if just for the night.

And her nights. Nights serving in the pub, bantering with the customers, watching John laugh and talk with them. He had always been good with the customers; it was the management part he struggled with. Watching him had always brought a warm feeling in her chest, and once they started their affair, a sense of anticipation for the coming encounter. He did wonderful things to her body with his hands and mouth, things she had never experienced with either of her footmen.

Early mornings were her favorite with him, though. Waking up wrapped around his large frame, warm from the blankets and sleeping next to him. Sometimes he would wake her, his hands skimming along her back, touching her gently, reverently. Despite his size and physical strength, he had always been gentle with her, always made her feel comfortable.

Made her feel loved. Looking back, she knew that to be true. It had made her feel . . . odd. Safe. She had trusted that safety, thought his declaration of love solidified it, but his behavior since yesterday morning showed her how foolish she had been.

She opened her eyes, not seeing the passing scenery. She would never have those days, nights, or mornings again. After what he put her through, she could not imagine becoming that intimate with anyone ever again. *We make ourselves vulnerable to each other, kitten.* She had not wanted that, had never wanted to be vulnerable to anyone, had tried to avoid it, but he had managed to wrest it from her anyway.

Damn him, damn him, damn the man. He had done this to her, he had made her vulnerable and made her love him. Yes, she admitted it, she had fallen in love with the big fucking galoot. The cold ball of hurt began to coalesce in her chest and started to burn, pushing hot anger through her veins. She may not know much about love, but she definitely knew that it was not like this. You didn't tell someone you loved them and then push them away like he had.

Louisa turned to face the men, interrupting their conversation without a thought. "Turn the coach around."

"What?" Jacob said.

"I forgot something. We need to go back."

"Louisa—"

"Turn the fucking coach around!"

Silence reigned as they all stared at her. Without moving his eyes from her, Nathan Grant raised his cane and knocked on the roof, giving instructions to the driver.

The hot anger coursed through her, making her tense. The coach couldn't go fast enough for her, and her fury grew with each turn of the wheels. John Taylor had a lot to answer for and she was going to make sure he did.

When the coach turned into the yard, it was still rolling to a stop when she opened the door and climbed out. She hit the ground running and stormed into the inn, throwing the door open.

All heads turned and stared. She didn't care. Louisa honed in on the giant behind the bar, pulling a pint of ale for a patron. He looked up and his eyes widened. He stared at her, the ale overflowing. With a curse, he released the tap and placed the pint on the bar, wiping his hands on his apron. "Louisa?" His voice carried in the silence. "What are you doing here?"

Her eyes narrowed as she stalked toward him and hissed, "You have some nerve. To say you love me and then treat me like a veritable stranger? What? What did I do? The very thing you told me to do. I made a decision. You said that it was my choice and to make a decision and that you would love me no matter what."

He looked at her, his face hard.

Louisa continued. "I suppose I am better off knowing that you are not a man of your word, John Taylor. For shame on you to punish me for doing what you told me to do. Do you like to kick small dogs as well? How dare you.

"You can't do this. You can't tell me to be strong, can't tell me it's my decision and then treat me like a leper when you disagree with me. You said you would be here for me, you big galoot, and you abandoned me when I needed you the most."

He shook his head. "I didn't go anywhere. I'm still here."

"Bollocks that." There was a rumble in the pub and she looked at everyone. "Yes, I said bollocks. And somehow the world is still rotating." She turned back to John. "You ignored me. You avoided me. I did what you told me to do, made a decision, and just because you didn't like what I decided, you separated yourself from me, which one could argue is worse than actually leaving the premises, because I knew where you were. I could see you yet you didn't want anything to do with me."

"Yea gods, Louisa," he interrupted hotly. "You didn't choose me. Give a man time to lick his wounds. You are the one who is leaving me."

"It wasn't forever. I never said it was forever."

"You never say anything. Wait, I'm wrong. You always say how you want to have control over your life, want to be treated as the sentient being you are, and how you don't want to marry me."

"You know why I don't and it has nothing to do with you."

He continued as if she hadn't spoken. "This is me giving you what you want. You made a decision and even though I didn't like it, I didn't try to stop you. You are a sentient being and I am doing my goddamned best to respect that. I sure as hell don't like it, it's eating me alive to let you go, so forgive me if I couldn't bloody well watch the woman I love as she walked away."

She pushed at his chest. "You don't get to say things like that. I never wanted this before I met you and you don't get to take it away now that I do."

"Why did you even come back, Louisa? You have made it clear that we are nothing more than an illicit affair, just two adults satisfying their needs."

"Damn you, John Taylor, damn you. You did this to me. You made me vulnerable, you made me want you. I came back because I fucking well love you, you big galoot."

He blinked. And blinked. Her shout lingered in the now silent pub. Louisa folded her arms across her chest, pressed her lips together and lifted her chin.

He placed his hands on his hips and took a deep breath. "You don't sound too happy about that." His voice was quiet, calmer now.

She shrugged, a small smile tugging at her mouth at having her words used against her. She refused to let that smile show. "I am not too happy about much right now. But I certainly intended to tell you that way."

A small laugh escaped him. "Perhaps in the future we can do this without the cursing."

Louisa smiled back. "Let's not set our expectations too high."

He glanced around the pub. She followed his eyes, seeing them rest on Jacob, Stephen and Nathan standing at the door, watching with differing expressions of interest. "It's not forever?" he asked quietly.

She shook her head. "I will come back. Or—"

He looked at her questioningly when she hesitated. "Or?"

The words came out in a rush. "Or you could come with me? Meet my friends?"

John's brows raised and he cocked his head. "Meet your friends?"

"Well, you already met them." She gestured to the men at the door. "You may as well meet the ones that make them bearable."

He rubbed his head and nodded slowly. "Packard can watch the inn for a week or so. He knows how things work."

"So you will come?"

"On one condition."

Her face darkened but she nodded. "Which is?"

John's arm snaked around her waist and pulled her against him. He seized her mouth in a deep kiss, his lips moving on hers. Louisa let out a startled sound, but wrapped her arms around his neck, her hands gripping his head. Their tongues didn't hesitate to meet, teasing and playing with each other. He bent her over his arm, trying to get closer to her.

John pulled away when the hoots and hollers from the tables penetrated their haze. He ended the kiss slowly, landing little pecks around her mouth. When he straightened, taking her with him, her arms slid down to his shoulders and she let out a deep sigh. When she opened her eyes, he gave her a big grin.

"Was that your condition?" she asked. "Because I'm not quite sure if I met it."

"No, that was just for fun," he replied. "My condition is that you give me lots of your sweet talk."

"Sweet talk?"

He grinned at her. "The kind of stuff that makes me shiver."

She rolled her eyes. "You are being ridiculous."

"I know. Because I am a?"

"A big galoot."

"That's the magic I was looking for." He kissed her again, savoring her lips against his. "Come help me pack?"

"It will be faster if you do it yourself."

"Who wants to be fast?" He looked over at the Ridgestone men. "Change of plans, mates. We're going to leave tomorrow."

Jacob grinned. "So long as you give us the good stuff again."

"Done." He bent and scooped Louisa up in his arms. "We've some business to take care of in the back."

"Put me down, you big galoot! Let me go!"

"When you put it like that"—he chuckled and carried her away to more hoots and cheers—"not on your life."

## CHAPTER TWENTY

*Darrowgate, 1830*

Louisa let out a slow sigh and snuggled her back into the large chest behind her, savoring his warmth. Her nose had chilled overnight, contrasting with the rest of her. Although his embrace remained loose, she knew John was awake from the nuzzling of her neck. She angled her head to give him more access.

"Happy Christmas, kitten," he murmured against her night rail. His hand began to make slow circles over her stomach.

"Mm, happy Christmas. What time is it?"

"I haven't checked yet, but the sun is up. Recently, I think."

"We have some time yet, then." She burrowed in deeper under the covers and his body, dragging the coverlet up over her nose to warm it up. "Has the tweeny not been to light the fire? It is freezing."

He chuckled. "It is December." The bed shifted as he moved, throwing the covers off himself and rising before tucking them back around her. "I'll take care of it."

Louisa turned her head to indulge in a moment of shameless ogling of her husband's bottom. She watched appreciatively as his muscles bunched and clenched. Seven years hadn't lessened his attractiveness to her in the slightest.

The Governess Club School had long since disbanded, it being too difficult for Claire and Sara to manage on their own. Once it had closed its doors, Sara and Nathan had moved to Cloverdale, selling Windent Hall to Bonnie and Stephen, giving them a contingency plan for when Henry Darrow achieved his majority and assumed responsibility for the viscountcy. Ridgestone was now a family estate, housing Claire and Jacob and their three children, Melanie, Rachel and William.

This year they had all agreed to meet at Darrowgate for the holidays, giving Henry a chance to practice playing host. Bonnie of course was acting as hostess while the young man grew accustomed to the role. There had been some endearingly awkward moments when Henry was unsure of what to do or say or how to direct the servants, but they had all been weathered; the boy would have some fun stories to share with his schoolmates when he returned to Eton after the break.

"Good Lord, your hands are freezing," Louisa protested when John climbed back into bed and wrapped his arms around her.

He kissed her shoulder. "You can warm me up. I have a present for you." He nudged her bottom with his growing erection.

"A present is supposed to be something special and new," she retorted. She gasped when his cold hand fondled her breast. She grabbed his hand and pulled it away, tucking it under her side to warm it up. "While that is certainly special, it is hardly new; you've been giving me that present time and again."

John chuckled. "It is an everlasting gift."

"I'm not sure we have that much time, you big galoot. There will be knocks on our door soon."

"Hm." He kissed his way down her arm as he freed his hand and tugged open her nightshirt. His hand disappeared inside and this time her gasp was one of pleasure. "Allow me this prelude. Your real present can be tonight."

She allowed him to lift her nightshirt off her. "Tonight? What plans do you have for tonight?" She rolled over to face him, her hands running over his shoulders and down his chest to grasp his now full arousal.

"Well, I am going to do a lot of this." He kissed her deeply, their tongues meeting without hesitation in a kiss bred from familiarity and passion. "A lot of this." He ran his nose around her nipple before taking it into his mouth. "A lot of this." He cupped her mound and his fingers delved into her wet heat. "And so much more."

Louisa gripped his biceps as her climax shuddered through her body. "Johnny," she sighed. "I do fucking well love you."

He kissed her chin, her nose, her mouth. "I can tell you are sincere by your crude language."

She smiled as he rolled on top of her. "Is there any other way to say it? Sheath, Johnny."

He reached to the nightstand and put one on. With another deep kiss, he slid into her, filling her with ease and love. "What do you think about a daughter?" he asked as he thrust slowly.

"I think they are fine for Claire and Bonnie." She arched her back, meeting his thrusts.

"Not Sara?"

She clutched his shoulders as her arousal grew again. "Don't be cruel. Mm, do that again."

John repeated that thrust several times, making her gasp and wrap her legs around him. "I think we should talk about it."

"Talk about what?" She was focused on what he was doing to her body.

"A daughter."

"You just don't want to wear a sheath."

He buried his face in her neck. "Can you blame me?"

"Yes. This conversation is distracting," she complained. She pulled his head up to kiss him before digging her fingers into his bottom, encouraging his attentions. He picked up his pace and soon they were lying still, their breathing returning to normal, foreheads pressed together.

John gave her a slow, soft kiss as he pulled out of her and removed the sheath. He rolled off the bed and walked to the washstand. Sounds of splashing filled the room as he cleaned himself up. He dried himself and brought the cloth over to the bed. "This will be cold," he said, pressing it between her legs.

Louisa grimaced but remained still under his ministrations. When he was finished, she sat up and found her nightshirt, slipping it over her head. "Where's the letter from Matthew?" A package from Victoria had arrived at the Beefy Buzzard before they left for Darrowgate and there was one from Matthew labeled with instructions to not read until Christmas Day.

"In the nightstand," John answered. He pulled on a pair of trousers. "Can we talk about this?"

She broke the seal and opened the letter, glancing at him. "We made our decision years ago, John. We agreed."

"We renegotiate our inn contract every year. Why not this?"

"Good Lord!" Her attention was on the letter.

"What is it?" John sat on the bed beside her.

"Matthew. He's managed to buy Willowcrest from the new Lord Darleigh and he's gifting it to us."

"What?" John took the letter from her and scanned it. "Yea gods," he whispered.

"He—" The sound of quick footsteps outside their room and rapid knocking interrupted her. She squeezed John's forearm and rose from the bed. "Good timing, Johnny. Here they are."

The door swung open and Joe and Jack scampered into the room. "Mama! Papa! It's Christmas!"

Louisa bent down and scooped up three-year-old Jack, who was at her knee with outstretched arms. She kissed his cheek. "Happy Christmas, boys."

"What did you get us this year?" five-year-old Joe demanded of his father. "I hope it's a training dummy. That would be brilliant."

John ruffled his hair. "You shall have to be patient."

"We all came down from the nursery together," Joe informed them. "We all thought you were taking too long to come and get us, so we decided to come get you."

Louisa glanced at their governess, standing at the door. Miss Morris smiled apologetically. "They are very excited today, Mrs. Taylor."

"With good reason. Let us get dressed and we'll come down. Miss Morris will take you to the kitchen while you wait for a quick scone before dressing for church." At their protests, she remained firm, giving them a stern look. "Church before presents and breakfast; you will celebrate the reason for Christmas before getting greedy." She set Jack down and they went to their governess, joining the other children in the corridor.

Louisa closed the door and John came up behind her, folding his arms around her stomach, and kissed her shoulder. "A daughter would be nice."

She leaned back into him. "We agreed after Jack. Two children was enough."

"But—"

She moved out of his embrace. "We will discuss this later. We must get ready."

Chaos ensued, gifts abounded. After attending services, Bonnie and Stephen saw to their family, consisting of Henry and Arthur Darrow, Elizabeth, Duncan, Andrew and Charlotte; Claire and Jacob with Melanie, Rachel and William; Louisa and John with Joe and Jack; and Sara and Nathan, the former watching the chaos with naked longing. All the children had grown up as cousins, making it a raucous holiday.

It wasn't until darkness had fallen and the children had been put to bed that the adults had a chance to sit and talk among themselves. They gathered in the drawing room after dinner for tea and drinks for the men, Henry pouring the drinks.

John handed Louisa a Scotch. "Is it just me or has Christmas gotten more tiring?" she asked the room.

Claire smiled. "It is the children, I am sure. They add energy to any situation."

Jacob chimed in. "I am convinced they suck it out of their parents and feed off it, like vampires."

Bonnie sipped her tea. "I am impressed mine waited until after eight to knock on our door this morning. The extra sleep helped during the day."

Louisa looked at her husband to see him gazing at her with a knowing half smile. He wiggled his eyebrows, reminding her of his impending gift. She smiled back and gave him a discreet salute with her tumbler.

"I, um, we have some news to share," Sara said, glancing at Nathan, who stood by the fire with John. Stephen and Jacob were sitting in nearby chairs. Nathan smiled encouragingly at her.

Her friends all looked at her, waiting.

"You all know that Nathan and I have not been successful in starting a family." Her eyes watered and her smile wavered. Louisa reached over and patted her hand. Sara took a deep breath and continued. "Well, we have been in contact with an orphanage in Hampshire and will be visiting there on our way home. We will be adopting a young child."

Rounds of congratulations filled the room; the men shook Nathan's hand. "That is a large responsibility," John said to Nathan.

He didn't break his gaze from Sara. "It is important to her and I love her enough for it to be important to me. She was feeling the lack more than I and refused to believe I did not think less of her." He glanced at John before returning his gaze to Sara. "Foolish woman."

John sipped his brandy, looking at his own wife. "They can be. Yet we love them anyway."

Sara spoke once the excitement had died down. "That is not all." Her gaze was locked on her husband. "Just before we left to come here, I was feeling unusual enough for Nathan to send for the doctor. He confirmed that I am with child." She beamed through her tears. "There will be one more of us shortly after Christmas and another by the summer."

This time hugs were called for. Bonnie whispered to Henry, who then called loudly for champagne. John clapped Nathan on the back along with the other gentlemen. He grinned at them. "It certainly was an enjoyable process," he murmured, making them laugh.

"There is no feeling like being a father," Stephen said.

"I look forward to joining your ranks."

Jacob elbowed him and leaned in. "Just so you know, it will be the most memorable time of your marriage." He shook his head ruefully. "Each time Claire was with child—well, there were times I wished she was carrying all the time." John and Stephen nodded in agreement.

Nathan cast his wife a concerned look. "The doctor said it would be fine, but I have no wish to harm Sara or the babe."

"Trust me," Jacob said, clapping him on the back. "We've all been there. You won't be able to keep her off you." They all chuckled discreetly.

Footmen were handing out the champagne Henry was pouring. Once everyone had a glass, he cleared his throat and his face reddened. "Um, I suppose a toast is called for. So, uh, to Uncle Nathan and Aunt Sara."

"Stephen?" Bonnie prodded.

"Try this, Henry." Her husband whispered something in his ward's ear.

Henry nodded. "Uncle Nathan and Aunt Sara, family is—well, it is—I mean—" His voice cracked.

Claire stood up and interrupted, smiling at him sympathetically. "Family is a precious thing. All these years, you have never been alone, but part of a larger whole, part of our family. Now you have the distinct blessing—and sometimes the curse"—there were chuckles in the room—"of bringing two more into our family. We will welcome both of these children with open arms and celebrate them with you as you have celebrated ours with us. To Sara and Nathan." She lifted her glass and the others followed suit.

Later, as John escorted Louisa up to their room, she held closely on to his arm, ensuring her breasts brushed against him. "You know, I've been thinking."

"About what?"

"Everything that happened today. If we accept Willowcrest from Matthew, we could sell the inn."

"Sell the inn," he said slowly.

"It has become highly profitable and popular. More and more people are leaving the Bath Road to stay with us. It would fetch a very pretty penny and we could send the boys to a good school."

"We could send them to a good school without selling. Or we could sell Willowcrest. Do you want to live in a place with such a disturbing history for you?"

She was silent for several moments. "With Matthew only having daughters, Joe is still his heir. It would be helpful if he were to attend school with his future peers and not be known as the son of innkeepers. Isn't it wonderful about Sara and Nathan?"

He accepted the change in subject. "Indeed."

"I hope she has an uneventful pregnancy. It would destroy her if something were to happen for her to lose the baby."

"Let's not wish any misfortune on her."

"I wasn't. I am proud of her, however, of opting to visit the orphanage."

John opened the door to their room and led her in. "I agree. A loving home such as theirs will be better than an orphanage."

Louisa turned to him, stepping naturally into his embrace. "What if we were to do that?"

"What?"

"You want a daughter. I don't want to carry another child. Even if I wanted to, there is no guarantee it would be a girl; you were convinced Jack was one. If we were to visit the orphanage with them, we could find a little girl in need of one of those loving homes you mentioned."

John looked at her for a long moment. "You know that even with sheaths there is a risk of pregnancy."

"Yes, but I would prefer if we don't try. I really don't want to carry another one, John." Her eyes begged him to understand. "It was so difficult last time. I can't—I love our sons and I know I would be able to love another one, should that happen, but I just can't do it again, not willingly."

"I know." He drew her in closer for a hug, pushing away the memory of her near death. "I don't want to lose you," he whispered into her hair. They hadn't told any of their friends what had happened.

"And I have no plans of leaving you. If we go to the orphanage, we both get what we want."

He rubbed her back before undoing her laces. "You know if there were a way to make love to you without there being any risk, I would take it. Just don't ever tell me to stop touching you."

She smiled at him and undid his waistcoat to pull his shirt out of his trousers. "Why would I punish myself like that? I have been looking forward to my promised present all day."

Her dress slithered to the floor. "I like the idea of the orphanage," he said. "We should talk to Nathan and Sara first, though. I don't want to step on their toes."

"Good idea. Now give me my present, you big galoot."

What to know how the Governess Club started?
Continue reading . . .

# THE GOVERNESS CLUB: CLAIRE

"Can any of you honestly say she hasn't thought about it?"

Silence reigned; teacups hovered between saucer and mouth. Eyes flitted away with guilt—or secret shame, unwilling to admit that it had indeed crossed their minds.

"You're not being fair," one chided softly.

"But who genuinely wants this for the rest of their lives?"

"There's nothing wrong with being a governess," another chimed in.

"Of course not. Not if one disregards the fact that for women of our station it signifies a lowering of one's situation. We were not born to be in service."

"It's not quite service, per se . . ."

"How is it anything else? We are being paid to render a service. Our lives are theirs to dictate. I cannot even count the number of times I have been called upon to even out the numbers at a dinner party. And they think they are bestowing some great honor upon me when they know full well I have attended more illustrious tables than theirs."

"Now you're just being aggressive."

"And I dislike being termed 'one whom another pays for a service,'" said another. "It makes me feel dirty, like a . . ."

"Say it, dear. A *whore*. We are being paid for a service, which in essence is exactly what a whore is paid for."

"I believe my half day is nearly up. It is a long walk back, and the children will be expecting me back for their evening meal. I have no wish to be caught in the rain." A small redhead pulled on her gloves and left the room.

"Louisa, what is the matter with you? You know very well your logic is flawed. The whole of the working class are paid for services; it is only a minority who have a negative stigma attached to them, and that is based on the service they render, not simply the fact that they are getting paid."

Louisa sighed and sipped her tea. "I didn't mean to offend anyone."

Claire patted her arm. "We know. And Sara knows that, I'm sure."

Bonnie spoke up. "What caused this rant, Louisa? You are not usually so ferocious in your opinions."

Staring into her tea, Louisa said, "The Waldrons had a house party last week. One of my brother's friends was a guest."

"Oh dear."

"When he first saw me, he seemed genuinely delighted. And he was. I welcomed his compliments and platitudes because it reminded me of how my life had been before . . . well, before. But when his attentions became more marked and aggressive, I knew the truth. All he said was . . . he said . . . that surely I must expect this as part of my duties."

"Did you—I mean did he—"

"One thing I can thank my brother for is teaching me how to defend myself against unwanted male attention." A small smile accompanied Louisa's words. Twin sighs of relief escaped her two friends, and she raised her eyes to theirs, beseeching their understanding. "There must be more to life for us than this. We were raised to expect better."

"But how?" asked Bonnie. "None of us earn enough money to live independently for the duration of our lives, and our marriage prospects have dwindled more quickly than our social statuses."

"It's not like we have regular exposure to the kind of gentlemen who would elevate us back up anyway, even if they could," Claire joined in. "The gentlemen we work for are already married, and their friends see us as nothing more than sport, if they see us at all. We can no longer trust gentlemen of the titled class."

"But who says we need a man or marriage to escape our positions? And who says that *independent* means *isolated?*" Louisa asked.

"I don't think I quite follow," Bonnie said.

Louisa turned to Claire. "Have you made any progress on Ridgestone?"

Claire blinked. "No, but my father's—*my* solicitor remains optimistic."

"And each of us has been saving our wages, correct? Even Sara, I'm sure." At the confirming nods, Louisa became more adamant. "We could do it."

"Do what?"

"We could pool our resources and live independently, yet not isolated, and without marriage. Say we continue saving our money for three more years, five at most. That would give Claire ample time to see if regaining Ridgestone is possible and for us to save nest eggs capable of supporting us, albeit not in the style we were raised, but still comfortably. If Ridgestone is a possibility, then we already have a place to live. If not, then with all four of us contributing, we could afford a place large enough for the four of us."

**An Excerpt from**

## THE GOVERNESS CLUB: BONNIE

Bonnie looked down at the blond boy walking next to her and pasted on a confident smile. "I am sure next time we will have more success."

Henry glanced at her, but did not smile or share her enthusiasm. "It's too late in the year, I think. It's a poor time to fish." He shifted the two poles he carried to the other shoulder. "And the worms are difficult to find. You said that they burrow deeper into the ground the colder it gets."

"That is true," Bonnie conceded. "But I do not think it is so cold that they will be hibernating just yet. They will be deeper, yes, but earthworms do not fully enter hibernation until it is almost freezing."

"I remember," Henry replied.

"Besides, it will simply mean that we have to dig a bit deeper," Bonnie said with forced cheerfulness. "How about that, Arthur? Would you like to dig deeper holes in the garden?" She gave the three-year-old's hand a squeeze. He just looked at her with solemn brown eyes.

"Mother does not like us ruining her garden," Henry said

quietly. "Father said it's best to dig at night when she can't see us. The deeper holes would not please my mother."

Bonnie closed her eyes and bit back a sigh. "My lord, I do not think your mother would begrudge you worms for fishing."

Henry said, "Still, I would rather not."

The trio crested the hill and Darrowgate came into view. The house, granted with the viscountcy by King Henry VII, was in the tribute shape of an *H*. As they drew closer, the large red stone building imposed itself on the landscape, a testament to the legacy of the Darrows.

Bonnie led the boys through the garden; Henry kept his stoic eyes on the house and Arthur removed his thumb from his mouth long enough to trail his fingers on the flowers in late bloom. By the time they had climbed the four small steps to the terrace, the thumb was firmly back in place.

"Burdis," Henry called the butler as they entered the main hall from the rear. "Please inform Mrs. Dabbs that there will be no fish complementing dinner tonight." He handed the poles to the portly man.

"Of course, my lord. Better luck next time. Hodges," Burdis turned his steady gaze to Bonnie. "There is a gentleman waiting in the drawing room. His name is Montgomery."

Bonnie was curious. "For me?"

"He asked for the viscount." Burdis lowered his voice. "He does not seem aware of the recent change. They were friends."

"Oh." Bonnie was startled. She took a deep breath and looked down at Henry. "Shall we greet this visitor, my lord?"

Henry regarded her with solemn eyes. "You don't need to address me like that. I am still Henry."

Bonnie knelt down to his level. "You know well enough that you are the viscount. It is proper. You had best get used to it."

"As the viscount, I insist you address me as you always have, as Henry." He looked at Burdis. "And for the other servants to call you Miss Hodges."

The butler inclined his head in acknowledgment. Bonnie gave Henry a weak smile and smoothed his coat lapels. "Mr. Montgomery is waiting." At Henry's nod, they moved to the drawing room, Arthur's hand in hers, his older brother with shoulders squared and chin raised.

Mr. Montgomery looked up at their entrance, his hands stretched toward the fire, warming his fingers. Seeing them, he turned and moved across the room, his eyes sharp as he looked them over. He stopped in front of Henry.

"Henry," he said, his voice infused with a Scottish burr. "You have grown. Do you remember me?"

Henry didn't answer. Glancing down at him, Bonnie could see his throat working as though he was trying to force a sound out of his mouth. She rested a hand on his shoulder and felt his paralysis.

The man looked to the other boy. "Arthur, is it?" The younger boy buried his head in Bonnie's skirts.

It was Bonnie's turn to fall under the man's regard. His green eyes gazed at her unblinking. "You are?" he prompted.

Automatically, Bonnie cast her eyes down and dipped a small curtsey. "Hodges, sir, the governess."

"Did the boys want to see me, then? They heard their uncle had arrived?"

Bonnie was confused. "I was unaware they had any uncles."

He waved her off. "I will see them later. I am awaiting the viscount."

Henry drew a deep breath as though he were about to speak, but nothing came out.

Bonnie kept her voice steady and quiet. "Henry is the viscount, sir."

Mr. Montgomery furrowed his brow. "I know very well who the viscount is, Miss Hodges. I am friends with their father."

Now Henry had moved to stand against her skirts, although he didn't clutch her legs as Arthur did. "I regret to inform you that both the viscount and his wife recently perished in a coaching accident. Henry is the viscount."

His eyes narrowed. "Impossible."

"I assure you, I speak true."

An Excerpt from

# THE GOVERNESS CLUB: SARA

"Well," Mr. Pomeroy said as he sat beside Sara in his gig and picked up the reins. "I can honestly say that not many visits have gone worse than that. Indeed, I believe we may have set a new precedent."

Sara gave him a sympathetic smile and held onto the side as the gig lurched into motion, enjoying how the movement made her side press into his momentarily. "I don't think it was that bad."

"Oh no," he said, "I assure you, this will become material at rectories all over England of how not to conduct visits."

Sara shook her head. "You cannot be so hard on yourself. Mrs. Simpson was simply not in a good visiting mood. I doubt anyone would be, with an absent husband and three sick children, not to mention the other two who need constant attention."

The vicar returned her smile, finally. "I am sure she appreciated you finishing up her laundry and putting a loaf of bread in the oven."

"And you taking the two out for a walk," Sara returned. "All she needed was a few moments of quiet to herself."

He sighed. "I will return in a day or two to check on her and see if she needs any more help. And I will let Dr. Moore know of the illness. Perhaps he can do something for the children."

"That is a good idea. I don't know if I am able to accompany you then, but I can send along a basket."

"Oh, I wasn't suggesting you join me, Miss Collins," Mr. Pomeroy said, looking at her with earnest brown eyes. "I believe I now have a good grasp on the needy families in the parish."

Sara's stomach dropped. Was he implying that her help was no longer needed? Dear heavens, if she didn't accompany him on these visits, how could she prove to him that she would be a useful wife for a vicar? She swallowed and forced herself to speak. "That is good."

Oh bother, that was more of a squeak than her voice. Mr. Pomeroy looked at her with concern in his eyes. "Are you unwell?"

Sara shook her head, unwilling to try to speak again.

His concern did not abate. "I would never forgive myself if you were to take sick after visiting Mrs. Simpson with me." He reined in the horse and turned to face her, taking her hands in his.

"I am fine," Sara assured him, though her voice was still little more than a squeak. His hands warmed hers, sending slow frissons of comfort up her wrists. She took a shaky breath and enjoyed the sensation.

"Have I distressed you in any way? I wish I had some water or lemonade to offer you. Your voice is still strange." He rubbed her hands between his, his eyes filled with concern and anxiety.

Looking into his chocolate eyes, so full of emotion, all on her behalf, filled Sara with a sense of peace and security. He was a good man, a kind man, and would make her a fine husband. Her anxiety eased and her throat cleared, allowing her to speak normally. "Truly, I am well."

Relief reflected in his eyes. "Thank God."

She gave him a weak smile. "I am sorry for concerning you."

Mr. Pomeroy looked at her, his face serious and intent. "The health and well-being of all my parishioners are my concern, Miss Collins. I would not be able to forgive myself if you were harmed while helping me with my work."

"I—"

"I should not have put you into a situation where you were at risk. We are fortunate that nothing serious occurred. We must be more cautious in the future."

Sara bent her head and looked at her hands, still being held in his. She ran her thumb over his, marveling at how soft and large they were.

His concern warmed her heart and she smiled to herself. Louisa was wrong; he did care for her. How could he express such worry over her well-being if he did not have some affection for her? She needed him to know, however, that she was up to the task of being a vicar's wife.

Sara raised her eyes and met his gaze. "I am sorry for causing you concern, Mr. Pomeroy. But I assure you, in my experience of helping my father, I have seen and been exposed to much worse than the colds of Mrs. Simpson's children."

Mr. Pomeroy's eyes held a rueful quality as the anxiety left them. He smiled at her. "I suppose that is true. I keep forgetting that you have more experience at this than I do."

They shared a smile for a long moment. It was the horse nickering that broke them apart. Mr. Pomeroy suddenly seemed to realize he was still holding her hands and dropped them, an embarrassed look coming over his face. He picked up the reins again and once more set the gig in motion.

"Are we returning to Ridgestone?" Sara asked after several moments of quiet.

He pursed his lips. "There is one more visit I was planning on making and it is directly on the way to Ridgestone. Would you mind terribly if you accompanied me? I can return you home if you would prefer."

She smiled. "Of course not. Whom would we be visiting?"

"The new owner of Windent Hall. He arrived just the other day and I wish to welcome him to the village."

"Oh." A new person in the neighborhood. The usual nervous ants started walking around her throat, making her feel queasy. She took a breath to regain some sort of control. She was a grown woman, for heaven's sake. It was far past time to be so affected by the thought of meeting someone new.

*Besides,* she thought, looking at the vicar, *the last person I met was Mr. Pomeroy and look how well that has turned out.* She cleared her throat. "Do you know what his name is?"

"Mr. Nathan Grant, recently from London."

Mr. Grant. A new neighbor. She could do this. Mr. Pomeroy was here to help her.

Sara nodded. Yes, she could do this.

## ABOUT THE AUTHOR

Ellie Macdonald has held several jobs beginning with the letter *t*: taxi driver, telemarketer and, most recently, teacher. She is thankful her interests have shifted to writing instead of taxidermy or tornado chasing. Having traveled to five different continents, she has swum with elephants, scuba dived in coral mazes, visited a leper colony and climbed waterfalls and windmills, but her favorite place remains Regency England. She currently lives in Canada. The Governess Club series is her first published work.

Discover great authors, exclusive offers, and more at hc.com.

Give in to your impulses . . .
Read on for a sneak peek at six brand-new
e-book original tales of romance
from Avon Impulse.
Available now wherever e-books are sold.

**BEAUTY AND THE BRIT**
*By Lizbeth Selvig*

**THE GOVERNESS CLUB: SARA**
*By Ellie Macdonald*

**CAUGHT IN THE ACT**
BOOK TWO: INDEPENDENCE FALLS
*By Sara Jane Stone*

**SINFUL REWARDS 1**
A BILLIONAIRES AND BIKERS NOVELLA
*By Cynthia Sax*

**WHEN THE RANCHER
CAME TO TOWN**
A VALENTINE VALLEY NOVELLA
*By Emma Cane*

**LEARNING THE ROPES**
*By T. J. Kline*

An Excerpt from

# BEAUTY AND THE BRIT
*by Lizbeth Selvig*

Tough and self-reliant Rio Montoya has looked
after her two siblings for most of their lives. But
when a gang leader makes threats against her
sister Bonnie, even Rio isn't prepared for the
storm that could destroy her family. Rio seeks
refuge for them all at a peaceful horse farm in
the small town of Kennison Falls, Minnesota,
but her budding romance with the stable's
owner, handsome British ex-pat David Pitts-
Matherson, feels as dangerous as her past.

"**D**id I ever tell you how much I hate British arrogance?" Chase grinned and captured the ball, dribbled it to the free-throw line, turned, and sank the shot. "Nothin' but net."

"Did I ever tell you how much I hate Americans showing off?"

"Yup. You have."

David laughed again and clapped Chase on the arm. Not quite a year before, Chase had married David's good friend and colleague Jill Carpenter, and this was the second time David had overnighted with Chase at Crossroads Youth and Community Center in Minneapolis. He was grateful for the camaraderie, and for the free lodging on his supply runs to the city, but mostly for the distraction from life at the stable back home in Kennison Falls. Here there were no bills staring up at him from his desk, no finances to finagle, no colicky horses. Here he could forget he was one disaster away from . . . well, disaster.

It also boggled his mind that he and Chase had an entire converted middle school to themselves.

"All right, play to thirty," Chase said, tossing him the ball. "Oughta take me no more'n three minutes to hang your limey ass out to dry."

"Bring it on, Nancy-boy."

A loud buzzer halted the game before it started.

"Isn't that the front door?" David asked.

"Yeah." Deep lines formed between Chase's brows.

The center had officially closed an hour before at nine o'clock. Members with I.D. pass cards could enter until eleven—but only did so for emergencies. David followed Chase toward the gymnasium doors. Voices echoed down the hallway.

"Stop pulling, Rio, you're worse than Hector. He's not going to follow us in here."

"It's Bonnie and Rio Montoya." Surprise colored Chase's voice. "Rio's one of the really good ones. Sane. Hardworking. I can't imagine why she's here."

*Rio?* David searched his memory but could only recall ever hearing the name in the Duran Duran song.

"Don't be an idiot." A second voice, filled with firm, angry notes, rang out clearly as David neared the source. "Of course they're following us. They may not come inside, but they'll be waiting, and you cannot handle either of them no matter how much you think you can. Dr. Preston's on duty tonight. He might be able to run interference."

"They won't listen to him. To them he's just a pretty face. Let me talk to Heco. You never gave me the chance."

"And I won't, even if I have to lock you in juvie for a year."

"God, Rio, you just don't get it."

"You're right, Bonnie Marie. I don't. What in God's name possessed you to meet Hector Black after curfew? Do you know what almost went down in that parking lot? Do you know who that other dude *was?*"

Chase hustled through the doorway. "Rio? Bonnie? Something happen?"

David followed five feet behind him. The hallway outside the gym glowed with harsh fluorescent lighting. Chase had the attention of both girls, but when David moved into view, one of them turned. A force field slammed him out of nowhere—a force field made up of amber-red hair and blazing blue eyes.

Frozen to the spot, he stared and she stared back. Her hair shone the color of new pennies on fire, and her complexion, more olive and exotic than a typical pale redhead's, captivated him. Her lips, parted and uncertain, were pinup-girl full. Her body, beneath a worn-to-softness plaid flannel shirt, was molded into the kind of feminine curves that got a shallow-thinking man in trouble. David normally prided himself on having left such loutishness behind in his university days, but he was rapidly reverting.

"Rio? You all right?" Chase called, and she broke the staring contest first.

David blinked.

"Fine," she said. "I'm sorry to come in so late. I needed a safe place for this one."

An Excerpt from

# THE GOVERNESS CLUB: SARA
### by Ellie Macdonald

Sweet Sara Collins is one of the founding members
of the Governess Club. But she has a secret:
She doesn't love teaching. She'd much prefer to
be a vicar's wife and help the local community.
Nathan Grant is the embodiment of everything
that frightens her. When Sara decides it's time
to take a chance and experience *all* that life has
to offer, Nathan is the first person she thinks of.
Will Sara's walk on the wild side ruin her chances
at a simple, happy life? Or has she just opened the
door to a once-in-a-lifetime chance at passion?

Mr. Pomeroy helped her down from the gig, and Sara took a long look at Windent Hall. Curtains covering the windows shielded the interior from a visitor's view, lending the building a cold and unwelcoming front. Rotted trees and dead grass lined the driveway, and cracks were visible along the red brickwork. Piles of crumbled mortar littered the edge of the manor house, and even the front portico was listing to the side, on the verge of toppling over.

The place reeked of neglect, which was to be expected after thirty years of vacancy. What Sara hadn't expected was the blanket of loneliness that shrouded the house, adding to the chilly ambiance. She couldn't help feeling that it had been calling out to be noticed, only to be ignored that much longer.

She couldn't suppress the shiver that ran down her body.

Sara turned to Mr. Pomeroy as he offered his arm. "Are you certain we should be here? We are uninvited."

He led her gingerly up the front steps. "Even so, I feel it is my duty to welcome him to the community. One can see that taking on this place is a task of great proportions. He needs to know that he is welcomed here and be informed of the local tradesmen and laborers available."

His logic was sound. But she couldn't keep from wincing

when the door protested his banging with a loud crack down the middle. Mr. Pomeroy and Sara shared a glance. He grimaced apologetically.

The door creaked open, only to stop partway. A muffled curse was heard from the other side, and eight fingers appeared in the opening. Grunting started as whoever was on the far side started to pull. Mr. Pomeroy shrugged and added his efforts in pushing. With a loud squeal, the door inched open until Sara and the vicar were able to pass through.

They stepped into a dark foyer, dustcovers over everything, including a large chandelier and all the wall sconces. The man who had opened the door was walking away down a corridor on one side of the main staircase. "I don't get paid enuff fer this," they could hear him muttering. He pushed open a door and pointed into the room. "Youse wait in there." He disappeared farther down the corridor.

Sara stared. Mr. Pomeroy stared. They looked at each other. With another shrug, Mr. Pomeroy started down the corridor, and she had little choice but to follow.

It was a parlor, as far as Sara could tell, underneath all the dust. The pale green walls were faded and damaged, giving the impression of sickness. No paintings adorned them, and none of the other small pieces one expected in a room such as this were evident. The furniture that was not hidden by dustcovers was torn and did not appear strong enough to hold any weight whatsoever. She sat on the sofa gingerly, hoping it would not give out underneath her.

"Perhaps we should not have come today," she whispered to Mr. Pomeroy. "It does not appear Mr. Grant is prepared to receive visitors of any sort."

The vicar acknowledged her point with an incline of his head. "We are here now, however. We will not stay long, simply offer our welcome and depart."

They had been waiting in the sparse room for nearly twenty-five minutes before she heard a tapping out in the corridor. It drew closer, and Sara turned her head to the door, wondering what was causing the sound. A gold tip struck the floor at the threshold, and Sara's eyes followed a black shaft upward to a matching gold top shaped into the form of a wolf's head. The head was loosely grasped by lean fingers, confident of their ability to control the cane.

Her eyes continued to rise, taking in the brown coat, striped waistcoat, and snowy white cravat before reaching the gentleman's face. Her eyes widened in recognition, and her breath caught in her throat when she realized that the man was none other than the stranded traveler from a few days prior.

Up close and stationary, his icy blue eyes were even paler, and at this moment, the bloodshot orbs exuded barely concealed disdain that made her even more aware of their lack of an invitation to visit. She barely registered the ants in her throat, for she was too riveted by his face.

An Excerpt from

# CAUGHT IN THE ACT
## Book Two: Independence Falls
*by Sara Jane Stone*

For Liam Trulane, failure is not an option. He is determined to win a place in Katie Summers' life before she leaves Independence Falls for good. First, he needs to make amends for the last time they got down and dirty. But falling for his rivals' little sister could cost him everything in the second installment of a hot new series from contemporary romance writer Sara Jane Stone.

"What are you going to do with it?" Katie asked, drawing him back to the present and the piece of land that proved he was walking down the path marked success. The equity stake in Moore Timber his best friend had offered Liam in exchange for help running the company was one more milestone on that road—and one he had yet to prove he deserved.

"Thinking about building a home here someday," Liam said.

"A house? I would have thought you'd want to forget about this place. About us. After the way you ended it." Katie raised her hand to her mouth as if she couldn't believe she'd said those words out loud.

Liam stopped beside her, losing his grip on the goat's lead and allowing the animal to graze. "I messed up, Katie. I think we both know that. But I panicked when I realized how young you were, and how—"

"I was eighteen," she snapped.

"By a few weeks. You were so innocent. And I felt all kinds of guilt for not realizing it sooner."

"Not anymore," she said, her voice firm. Defiant. "I'm not innocent anymore."

"No." Liam knew every line, every angle of her face. There

were days he woke up dreaming about the soft feel of her skin. But it was the way Katie had looked at him after he'd gone too far, taken too much, that haunted his nightmares. In that moment, her green eyes had shone with hope and love.

Back then, when he was fresh out of college, returning home to build the life he'd dreamed about, that one look had sent him running scared. He wasn't ready for the weight of her emotions.

And he sure as hell wasn't ready now. Eric had given Liam one job since handing over part of the company—buy Summers Family Trucking. Liam couldn't let his best friend, now his business partner, down. Whatever lingering feelings he had for Katie needed to wait on the sidelines until after Liam finished negotiating with her brothers. There was too much at stake—including his vision of a secure future—to blow this deal over the girl who haunted his fantasies.

He drew the goat away from the overgrown grass and started toward the wooded area on the other side of the clearing. "We should go. Get you home before too late."

But Katie didn't follow. She marched down to the fir trees. "I'm twenty-five, Liam. I don't have a curfew. My brothers don't sit around waiting for me to come home."

"I know."

Brody, Chad, and Josh were waiting for him. Liam had been on his way to see her brothers when he'd spotted her car on the side of the road. They'd reluctantly agreed to an informal meeting to discuss selling to Moore Timber.

She spun to face him, hands on her hips. "I think you wanted to take a walk down memory lane."

"Katie—"

"Back then, you never held back." She closed the gap between them, the toes of her sandal-clad feet touching his boots. "So tell me, Liam, what are we doing here?"

He fought the urge to reach for her. He had no right. Not to mention bringing her here had confirmed one thing: After seven years, Katie Summers still held his mistakes against him.

She raised one hand, pressing her index finger to his chest. Damn, he wished he'd kept his leather jacket on. Her touch ignited years of flat-out need. No, he hadn't lived like a saint for seven years, but no one else turned him on like Katie Summers.

An Excerpt from

# SINFUL REWARDS 1
## A Billionaires and Bikers Novella
*by Cynthia Sax*

Belinda "Bee" Carter is a good girl; at least, that's
what she tells herself. And a good girl deserves
a nice guy—just like the gorgeous and moody
billionaire Nicolas Rainer. Or so she thinks,
until she takes a look through her telescope
and sees a naked, tattooed man on the balcony
across the courtyard. He has been watching
her, and that makes him all the more enticing.
But when a mysterious and anonymous text
message dares her to do something bad, she
must decide if she is really the good girl she has
always claimed to be, or if she's willing to risk
everything for her secret fantasy of being watched.

An Avon Red Novella

I'd told Cyndi I'd never use it, that it was an instrument purchased by perverts to spy on their neighbors. She'd laughed and called me a prude, not knowing that I was one of those perverts, that I secretly yearned to watch and be watched, to care and be cared for.

If I'm cautious, and I'm always cautious, she'll never realize I used her telescope this morning. I swing the tube toward the bench and adjust the knob, bringing the mysterious object into focus.

It's a phone. Nicolas's phone. I bounce on the balls of my feet. This is a sign, another declaration from fate that we belong together. I'll return Nicolas's much-needed device to him. As a thank you, he'll invite me to dinner. We'll talk. He'll realize how perfect I am for him, fall in love with me, marry me.

Cyndi will find a fiancé also—everyone loves her—and we'll have a double wedding, as sisters of the heart often do. It'll be the first wedding my family has had in generations.

Everyone will watch us as we walk down the aisle. I'll wear a strapless white Vera Wang mermaid gown with organza and lace details, crystal and pearl embroidery accents, the bodice fitted, and the skirt hemmed for my shorter height. My hair will be swept up. My shoes—

Voices murmur outside the condo's door, the sound piercing my delightful daydream. I swing the telescope upward, not wanting to be caught using it. The snippets of conversation drift away.

I don't relax. If the telescope isn't positioned in the same way as it was last night, Cyndi will realize I've been using it. She'll tease me about being a fellow pervert, sharing the story, embellished for dramatic effect, with her stern, serious dad—or, worse, with Angel, that snobby friend of hers.

I'll die. It'll be worse than being the butt of jokes in high school because that ridicule was about my clothes and this will center on the part of my soul I've always kept hidden. It'll also be the truth, and I won't be able to deny it. I am a pervert.

I have to return the telescope to its original position. This is the only acceptable solution. I tap the metal tube.

Last night, my man-crazy roommate was giggling over the new guy in three-eleven north. The previous occupant was a gray-haired, bowtie-wearing tax auditor, his luxurious accommodations supplied by Nicolas. The most exciting thing he ever did was drink his tea on the balcony.

According to Cyndi, the new occupant is a delicious piece of man candy—tattooed, buff, and head-to-toe lickable. He was completing armcurls outside, and she enthusiastically counted his reps, oohing and aahing over his bulging biceps, calling to me to take a look.

I resisted that temptation, focusing on making macaroni and cheese for the two of us, the recipe snagged from the diner my mom works in. After we scarfed down dinner, Cyndi licking her plate clean, she left for the club and hasn't returned.

Three-eleven north is the mirror condo to ours. I

straighten the telescope. That position looks about right, but then, the imitation UGGs I bought in my second year of college looked about right also. The first time I wore the boots in the rain, the sheepskin fell apart, leaving me barefoot in Economics 201.

Unwilling to risk Cyndi's friendship on "about right," I gaze through the eyepiece. The view consists of rippling golden planes, almost like . . .

Tanned skin pulled over defined abs.

I blink. It can't be. I take another look. A perfect pearl of perspiration clings to a puckered scar. The drop elongates more and more, stretching, snapping. It trickles downward, navigating the swells and valleys of a man's honed torso.

No. I straighten. This is wrong. I shouldn't watch our sexy neighbor as he stands on his balcony. If anyone catches me . . .

**Parts 1, 2, and 3 available now!**

An Excerpt from

# WHEN THE RANCHER CAME TO TOWN
## A Valentine Valley Novella
### by *Emma Cane*

Welcome to Valentine Valley! Emma Cane
returns to the amazing and romantic town for
the latest installment in her sparkling series.
When an ex-rodeo star falls in love with an
agoraphobic B&B owner, he must pull out
all the stops to get her out of her shell.

With the pie in the oven, Amanda set the timer on her phone, changed into old clothes suitable for gardening, smeared on sunscreen, and headed outside. The grounds of the B&B took just as much work as the inside. She'd hired a landscaper for some of the major stuff like lawn and tree care, but the flowers, shrubs, and design work were all hers. She felt at peace in her garden, with the high bushes that formed walls on either side. The terraced lawn sloped down amidst rock gardens to Silver Creek, where she kept kayaks, canoes, and paddleboards for her guests. She had little hidden walkways between tall shrubs, where unusual fountains greeted visitors as a reward for their curiosity. She'd strung lights between the trees, and at night, her garden was like her own private fairy world.

One she had to share with guests, of course.

As she headed across the deck that was partially covered by an arbor, she glanced toward the hot tub beneath the gazebo—and did a double take. Mason Lopez sat alone on the edge of the tub, his jeans rolled up to his knees, his feet immersed. Though he was staring at the bubbling water, he seemed to be looking inward.

She must have made a sound, because he suddenly turned

his head. For a moment, she was pinned by his gaze, aware of him as a man in a way she hadn't felt about anyone in a long time.

She shook it off and said, "Sorry to disturb you." She was about to leave him in peace, but found herself saying instead, "Is everything all right?"

He smiled, white teeth gleaming out of the shadows of the gazebo, but it was a tired smile that quickly died.

"Sure, everything's fine. My meeting just didn't go as expected."

She felt frozen, unable to simply leave him when he'd said something so personal. "I bet you'll be able to work it out."

A corner of his mouth quirked upward. "I'm glad you're sure of that."

"You're not?" Where had that come from? And then she walked toward him, when she should have been giving him his privacy. But he looked so alone.

"Will you join me?" he asked.

She was surprised to hear a thread of hope in his voice. As a person who *enjoyed* being alone, this felt foreign to her, but the need to help a guest overruled that. She sat down cross-legged beside him. They didn't talk at first, and she watched him rub his shoulder.

He noticed her stare and gave a chagrinned smile. "I injured it years ago. It still occasionally aches."

"I imagine the hard work of ranching contributes to that."

"Yeah, it does, but it's worth it. I love working the land that's been in my family for almost seventy-five years. But we've been going through a tough time, and it's been pretty obvious we need a championship bull to invigorate our breeding program. I thought if I met with some of the ranchers here, we could find some investment partners."

"That was what your meeting today was about?"

"Yeah. But the Sweetheart Ranch is a large operation, and it's all they want to handle right now."

"We have other ranches around here."

He glanced at her and grinned. "Yeah, I have more meetings tomorrow."

"I'm sure you'll be successful." She looked away from him, the magnetism of his smile making her feel overheated though she was sitting in the shade. Or maybe it was the proximity of the hot tub, she told herself.

An Excerpt from

# LEARNING THE ROPES
*by T. J. Kline*

From author T. J. Kline comes the stunning
follow-up to *Rodeo Queen*. When former
rodeo queen Alicia falls for perpetual playboy
Chris, she must find a way to tame him.

An Excerpt from

# LEARNING THE ROPES

### by T.J. Kline

Alicia Kanani slapped the reins against her horse's rump as he stretched out, practically flying between the barrels down the length of the rodeo arena, dirt clods rising behind them as the paint gelding ate up the ground with his long stride. She glanced at the clock as she pulled him up, circling to slow him to a jog as a cowboy opened the back gate, allowing her to exit. 14.45. It was only good enough for second place right now. If only she'd been able to cut the first barrel closer, it might have taken another tenth of a second off her time.

She walked her favorite gelding, Beast, back to the trailer and hooked his halter around his neck before loosening his cinch. She heard the twitter of female laughter before she actually recognized the pair of women behind her trailer and cringed. Delilah had been a thorn in her side ever since high school, when Alicia had first arrived in West Hills. There'd never been a lack of competition between them, but it seemed, years later, only one of them had matured at all.

"Look, Dallas, there's Miss Runner-Up." Delilah jerked her chin at Alicia's trailer. "Came in second again, huh?" She flipped her long blonde waves over her shoulder. "I guess you can't win them all . . . oh, wait." She giggled. "You don't seem to win any, do you? That would be me." The pair laughed as if it were the funniest joke ever.

"Isn't it hard to ride a broom *and* a horse at the same time, Delilah?" Alicia tipped her head to the side innocently as Delilah glared at her and stormed away, pulling Dallas with her.

Alicia snidely imitated Delilah's laugh to her horse as she pulled the saddle from his back and put it into the trailer. "She thinks she's so funny. 'You haven't won. I have,' " she mimicked in a nasally voice. "Witch," she muttered as she rubbed the curry comb over Beast's neck and back.

"I sure hope you don't kiss your mother with that mouth."

Alicia spun to see Chris Thomas, her best friend Sydney's brother, walking toward her trailer. She'd rodeoed with Chris and Sydney for years, until Chris had gone pro with his team roping partner. For the last few years, they'd all been pursuing the same goal, the National Finals Rodeo, in their respective events. So far their paths hadn't crossed since Sydney's wedding nearly two years before. She'd suspected she might see him here since they were so close to home and this rodeo boasted a huge purse for team ropers.

"Chris!" She hurried over and gave him a bear hug. "Did you rope already?"

"Tonight during the slack." Most of the team ropers would be competing tonight before the barbecue and dance. "I see Delilah's still giving you a hard time."

She shrugged and smirked. "She's still mad I beat her out for rodeo queen when Sydney gave up the title."

"That was a long time ago. You'd think she'd let it go." Chris stuffed his hands into his pockets and leaned against the side of her trailer, patting Beast's neck. "Maybe you should put Nair in her shampoo like she did to you."

Alicia cringed at the memory. "It was a good thing I smelled it before I put it on my head. That could've been traumatizing, but I got her back."

"That's right. Didn't you put liniment in her lip gloss?" She smiled at the reminder of the prank, and Chris laughed. They'd had some good times together in the past. She wondered how they'd managed to drift apart over the past few years. She missed his laugh and the way he always seemed to bring the playful side of her personality to the surface.

"So, how'd you do?"

"Second—so far," she clarified. "Again."

He chuckled and crossed his arms over his chest. His biceps bulged against the material of his Western shirt, and she couldn't help but notice how much he'd filled out since she'd last seen him. And in all the right places. "Second's nothing to complain about."

"It's nothing to brag about either," she pointed out, tearing her eyes away from his broad chest. She finished brushing down the horse, feeling slightly uncomfortable with the way he continued to silently watch her, as if he wanted to say something but wasn't sure how to bring it up. Finally she turned and faced him. "What?"